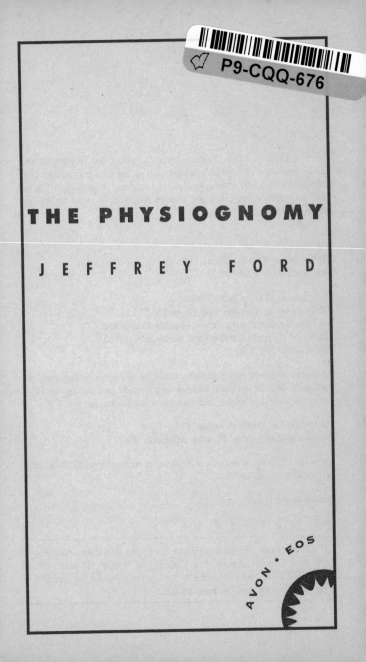

THE PHYSIOGNOMY

JEFFREY FORD

AVON · EOS

AVON BOOKS, INC.
1350 Avenue of the Americas
New York, New York 10019

Copyright © 1997 by Jeffrey Ford
Published by arrangement with the author
Visit our website at http://www.AvonBooks.com/Eos
Library of Congress Catalog Card Number: 97-11961
ISBN: 0-380-79332-6

First Avon Eos Printing: August 1998
First Avon Books Trade Printing: September 1997

AVON EOS TRADEMARK REG. U.S. PAT. OFF. AND IN OTHER COUNTRIES, MARCA REGISTRADA, HECHO EN U.S.A.

Printed in the U.S.A.

WCD   10 9 8 7 6 5 4 3 2 1

"COMPACT, RICHLY TEXTURED, ENTHRALLING . . . SERIOUSLY, LOGICALLY, STUNNINGLY SURREAL."

—*Kirkus* (★Starred Review★)

Not every fool and his brother could achieve the status of Physiognomist, First Class in less than fifteen years. Time and again I had conducted hairsplitting physiognomical investigations. Who was it who had discovered the identity of the Latrobian werewolf in a six-year-old girl when that beast had wrought havoc among the towns just beyond the circular wall? Who had fingered Colonel Rasuka as a potential revolutionary and headed off a coup against the Master years before the would-be perpetrator even knew himself what he was capable of? Many had said I was the best, and I wasn't going to damage that estimation, no matter how trivial the case, no matter how remote the location of the crime.

Obviously, this was a job for one of those first year graduates who can't help wounding himself with his own instruments. The religious ramifications of the affair elicited a distant aching in my hindquarters. I remembered the time I had pleaded with the Master to do away with all religion. Its practice had died out in the City. Out in the territories, though, lifeless icons still held sway. His answer was "Let them have their hogwash."

"It is a corruption of nature," I countered.

"I don't give a fig," he said. "I'm a corruption of nature. Religion is about fear, and miracles are monsters." He reached over and, with graceful sleight of hand, pulled a goose egg from behind my ear. When he cracked it on the edge of his desk, a cricket jumped forth. "Do you understand?" he asked.

—From *The Physiognomy*

For
Lynn, Jackson and Derek:
my guides to the earthly paradise

I left the Well-Built City at precisely 4:00 in the afternoon of an autumn day. The sky was dark, and the wind was blowing when the coach pulled up in front of my quarters. The horses reared against a particularly fierce gale and my papers—describing the case that had been assigned to me no more than an hour earlier by the Master, Drachton Below, himself—nearly flew out of my hands. The driver held open the door for me. He was a porcine fellow with rotten teeth, and I could tell from one look at his thick brow, his deep-set eyes that he had propensities for daydreaming and masturbation. "To the territory," he yelled over the wind, spitting out his words across the lapels of my topcoat. I nodded once and got in.

A few minutes later we were speeding through the streets of the city toward the main gate. When the passersby saw my coach, they gave me that curious one-finger salute, a greeting which had recently sprung up from the heart of the populace. I thought of waving back, but I was too preoccupied with trying to read the clues of their physiognomies.

After all my years of sweeping open the calipers to find the "soul," skin deep, even a glimpse at a face could explode my wonder. A nose to me was an epic, a lip, a play, an ear, a many-volumed history of mankind's fall.

An eye was a life in itself, and my eyes did the thinking as I rode into the longest night, the dim-witted driver never letting up on the horses, through mountain passes, over rocky terrain where the road had disappeared. With the aid of the Master's latest invention, a chemical light that glowed bright orange, I read through the particulars of the official manuscript. I was headed for Anamasobia, a mining town of the northern territory, the last outpost of the realm.

I reread the case so many times that the words died from abuse. I polished my instruments till I could see myself in their points. I stared out at moonlit lakes and gnarled forests, at herds of strange animals startled into flight by the coach. And as the Master's light began to dim, I prepared an injection of sheer beauty and stuck it in my arm.

I began to glow as the light failed, and an image from the manuscript presented itself to my eye's-mind— a white fruit said to have grown in the Earthly Paradise, purported to have all manner of supernatural powers. It had sat under glass on the altar of the church in Anamasobia for years, never spoiling but always at the perfect moment of ripeness.

Years before, the local miners who worked the spire veins beneath Mount Gronus had broken through a wall into a large natural chamber with a pool and found it there in the withered hand of a mummified ancient. The story of its discovery had piqued the interest of the Well-Built City for a time, but most considered the tale primitive lunacy concocted by idiots.

When the Master had handed me the assignment, he laughed uproariously and reminded me of the disparaging remarks concerning his facial features I had whispered into my pillow three years earlier. I had stared, dumbfounded by his omniscience, while he injected himself in the neck with a syringe of sheer beauty. As the plunger pushed the violet liquid into his bulging vein, a smile began to cross his lips. Laconically, he pulled the needle out and said, "I don't read, I listen."

I bit the white fruit and something flew out of it, flapping around the interior of the coach and tangling itself in my hair. Then it was gone and the Master, Drachton Below, was sitting across from me, smiling. "To the territory," he said and offered me a cigarette. He was dressed in black with a woman's black scarf tied around his head, and those portions of his physiognomy that had, years earlier, revealed to me his malicious hubris were accentuated by rouge and eyeliner. Eventually he broke apart like a puzzle that put me to sleep.

I dreamed the coach stopped on a barren windswept plateau with a shadowy vista of distant mountains in the moonlight. The temperature had dropped considerably, and, as I burst out of my compartment, demanding to know the reason for the delay, my words came as steam. The absolute clarity and multitude of stars silenced me. I watched the driver walk a few yards away from the coach and begin drawing a circle around himself with the toe of his boot. He then stood in the middle of it and mumbled toward the mountains. As I approached him, he unzipped his pants and began urinating.

"What nonsense is this?" I asked.

He looked over his shoulder at me and said, "Nature calls, your honor."

"No," I said, "the circle and the words."

"That's just a little something," he said.

"Explain," I demanded.

He finished his business and, pulling up his zipper, turned to face me. "Look," he said, "I don't think you know where we are."

In that instant, something about his garish earlobes made me think that perhaps the Master had set the whole excursion up to have me done away with for my whispered indiscretions.

"What do you mean?" I asked.

He walked toward me with his hand raised, and I felt myself begin to cringe, but then he brought it down softly on my shoulder. "If it will make you feel any better, you can kick me," he said. He bent over in front of me, flipping his long coattails up in the back so as to present a clearer target.

I kicked the seat facing me and came awake in the coach. As I opened my eyes, I could already sense we had stopped moving and that morning had finally come. Outside the window to my left I saw a man standing, waiting, and behind him a primitive town built entirely of wood. Looming over the town was what I took to be Mount Gronus, inexhaustible source of blue spire, the mineral that fueled the furnaces and engines of the Well-Built City.

Before gathering my things together, I studied the stranger. Cranium derivative of the equine, eyes set wide, massive jaw—a perfectly good-hearted and ineffectual political functionary. I deemed him trustworthy and prepared to meet him. As I opened the door, he ceased his whistling and walked forward to greet me.

"Welcome to Anamasobia," he said, holding out a gloved hand. His obesity was canceled by an insistent chin, his overbite by the generosity of jowls. I clasped his hand and he said, "Mayor Bataldo."

"Physiognomist Cley," I told him.

"A great honor," he said.

"You are having some trouble?" I inquired.

"Your, honor," he said as if on the verge of tears, "there is a thief in Anamasobia." He took my valise and we walked together down the hardened dirt path that was the only street in town.

The mayor gave me a tour as we walked, pointing out buildings and expounding on their beauty and utility. He taxed my civility with colorful tidbits of local history. I saw the town hall, the bank, the tavern, all constructed from a pale gray wood full of splinters and roofed with slate. Some of them, like the theater, were quite large with the crudest attempts at ornamentation. Faces, beasts, lightning bolts, crosses had been carved into some of the boards. On the southern wall of the bank, people had carved their names. This tickled the mayor to his very foundation.

"I can't believe you live here," I said to him, mustering a shred of sympathy.

"Heaven knows, we are animals, your honor," he said, slowly shaking his head, "but we can certainly mine blue spire."

"Yes, very well," I said, "but once, at an exhibition at the Hall of Science in the Well-Built City, I saw a monkey write the words 'I am not a monkey' five hundred times on a sheet of parchment with a quill. Each line was rendered with the most magnificent penmanship."

"A miracle," he said.

I was led to a sorry looking four-story dwelling in the center of town called the Hotel de Skree. "I have reserved the entire fourth floor for you," said the mayor.

I held my tongue.

"The service is magnificent," he said. "The stewed cremat is splendid and all drinks are complimentary."

"Cremat," I said through tight lips, but it went no further, because coming toward us on the left side of the street was an old blue man. Bataldo saw me notice the staggering wretch and waved to him. The old man lifted his hand but never looked up. His skin was the color of a cloudless sky. "What manner of atrocity is this?" I asked.

"The old miners have lived so long in the spire dust that it becomes them. Finally they harden all the way through. If the family of the man is poor, they sell him as spire rock to the realm for half what a pure sample of his weight would bring. If the family is well-off, they register him as a 'hardened hero,' and he stands in perpetuity somewhere in town as a monument to personal courage and a lesson to the young.''

"Barbaric," I said.

"Most of them never get that old," said the mayor, "cave-ins, natural poison gasses, falling in the dark, madness. . . . Mr. Beaton, there," he said, pointing after the blue man, "he'll be found next week somewhere, heavy as a gravestone and set in his ways.''

The mayor showed me into the lobby of the hotel and informed the management that I had arrived. The usual amenities followed. The old couple who presided over the shabby elegance of the de Skree, a Mr. and Mrs. Mantakis, were, each in his own way, textbook examples of physiognomical blunders. Nature had gone awry in the development of the old man's skull, leaving it too thin to house real intelligence and nearly as long as my forearm. I realized, as he kissed my ring, that I could not expect much from him. Not in the habit of beating dogs, so to speak, I showed him a smile and gave an approving nod. The missus, on the other hand, exhibited ferretlike tendencies in her pointed face and sharp teeth, and I knew I would have to check my change after every monetary transaction that passed between us. The hotel itself, with its tattered carpets and fractured chandelier, spelled out a gray, languorous rage.

"Any special requests, your honor?" said Mr. Mantakis.

"An ice-cold bath at dawn," I told him. "And I must have complete silence in which to meditate upon my findings.''

"We hope your stay will be—" the old woman began, but I cut her off with a wave of my hand and demanded to be taken to my rooms. As Mr. Mantakis took my valise and led me toward the stairway, the mayor announced that he would send someone for me at four. "A gathering to stand as an official welcome for you, sir," he called after me.

"As you wish," I said and mounted the rickety stairs.

My lodgings were fairly spacious—two large rooms, one to serve as my sleeping quarters and one as an office with a writing desk, a lab table, and a divan. The floors creaked, the autumn breeze of the northern territory leaked through the poorly caulked windows, and the wallpaper of vertical green stripes and an indefinite species of pink flower gave rise to thoughts of carnival.

In my bedroom I was startled to find one of the hardened heroes the mayor had told me about. An old man dressed in miner's overalls stood slightly bent in the corner, supporting a long oval mirror.

"My brother, Arden," said Mantakis as he put my valise down next to the bed. "I didn't have the heart to send him to the city as fuel."

As the old man was about to leave, I asked him, "What do you know of this fruit of the Earthly Paradise?"

"Arden was there when they found it about ten years ago," he said in his slow-witted drawl. "It was pure white and looked like a ripe pear you want to sink your teeth into." As he said this, he showed me his crooked yellow teeth. "Father Garland said it should not be eaten. It would make you immortal, and that flows against the will of God."

"And you subscribe to this twaddle?" I asked.

"Sir?" he said, unsure of my question.

"You believe in it?"

"I believe whatever you believe, your honor," he said and then backed out of the room.

2

I studied my own image in the mirror held by the petrified Arden and considered my approach to the case. It was true that the Master had banished me to the territory as a punishment, but that was not an invitation to perform shoddily. If I were to shirk my duties, he would immediately know and have me either executed or sent to a work camp.

Not every fool and his brother could achieve the status of Physiognomist, First Class in less than fifteen years. Time and again I had conducted hairsplitting physiognomical investigations. Who was it who had discovered the identity of the Latrobian werewolf in a six-year-old girl when that beast had wrought havoc among the towns just beyond the circular wall? Who had fingered Colonel Rasuka as a potential revolutionary and headed off a coup against the Master years before the would-be perpetrator even knew himself what he was capable of? Many, including Drachton Below, had said I was the best, and I wasn't going to damage that estimation, no matter how trivial the case, no matter how remote the location of the crime.

Obviously, this was a job for one of those first year graduates who can't help wounding himself with his own instruments. The religious ramifications of the affair elicited a distinct aching in my hindquarters. I remembered the time I had pleaded with the Master to do away with

all religion. Its practice had died out in the City, replaced
by a devotion to Below that seemed born of the people's
desire to participate in his own unique form of omniscience. Out in the territories, though, lifeless icons still
held sway. His answer was "Let them have their
hogwash."

"It is a corruption of nature," I countered.

"I don't give a fig," he said. "I'm a corruption of
nature. Religion is about fear, and miracles are monsters."
He reached over and, with graceful sleight of hand, pulled
a goose egg from behind my ear. When he cracked it on
the edge of his desk, a cricket jumped forth. "Do you
understand?" he asked. That was when I noticed his con-
tinuous eyebrow and the small tufts of primate hair adorn-
ing each of his knuckles.

The sheer beauty was coursing through me, trans-
forming the ineffable into images, susurrations, aromas. In
the mirror, behind my reflection, I saw a garden of white
roses, hedgerow and morning glory vine, that drop by drop
melted into a view of the Well-Built City. The chrome
spires, the crystal domes, the towers, the battlements all
shone in the sunlight of a more hospitable region of the
mind. This also began to swirl and eventually settled out
again into the drab surroundings of my room at the Hotel
de Skree.

I thought for a moment that the drug had played one
of its time tricks on me, compressing the usual two hour
hallucination into mere minutes, but that was not the case,
for standing behind me, looking over my shoulder into
the mirror, was Professor Flock, my old mentor from the
Academy of Physiognomy.

The professor was looking rather spry, considering he
had passed away ten years earlier, and he wore an affable
expression, considering it was my own prosecution that
had sent him to the most severe work camp—the sulphur
mines at the southern extremity of the realm.

"Professor," I said, not turning around but addressing

him through the glass in front of me, "a pleasure, as always."

Dressed in white, as was his habit back at the academy, he moved closer to me and put his hand on my shoulder. I felt its weight as if it were real. "Cley," he said, "you sent me to my death, and now you call me back?"

"I am sorry," I said, "but the Master could not tolerate your teaching of tolerance."

He nodded and smiled. "It was foolishness. I have come to thank you for eradicating my crackpot notions from the great society."

"You hold no grudge?" I asked.

"Of course not," he said. "I deserved to be baked like a slab of ham and strangled on fumes of sulphur."

"Very well then," I said. "How should I proceed with this case?"

"The Twelfth Maneuver," was his reply. "Anamasobia is a closed system. Merely read every subject in town, review your findings, and look for the one whose features reveal an inclination toward larceny and a religiopsychotic reliance on the miraculous."

"How will the latter be revealed?" I inquired.

"As a blemish, a birthmark, a wart, a mole with an inordinately long black hair growing from it."

"As I suspected," I said.

"And Cley," he said as he began to vanish, "full body exams. Leave no stone unturned, no dark crevice unexamined."

"Naturally," I said.

I lay down on my bed and stared across the room at the illusion of Arden slowly moving, the mirror becoming a waterfall in his hands. Off in the muffled distance, the Mantakises were emitting screams of either lust or violence, and I recalled my own last romantic encounter.

One night, a few months earlier, after working on the Grulig case, a ghastly homicide in which the Minister of Finance had had his head separated from his body, I de-

cided to stop at the Top of the City for refreshment. I
rode the crystal enclosed elevator up the sixty floors to
the roof, where, beneath a crystal dome, there was a bar
with tables and chairs, a woman playing a harp, a twilight
view of what seemed like the entire world.

I walked up to a fetching young thing seated by herself
at a window table and told her I would buy her a drink.
I cannot remember her name or her features, but I recall
a certain aroma, not perfume, more like a ripe melon. She
told me about her parents and some problem they were
having, about her childhood, and then, when I could no
longer tolerate entertaining the inconsequential, I offered
her fifty belows to take a coach with me to the park.

While riding along I mixed her a cocktail, and when
she wasn't looking, poured in a good measure of sheer
beauty. The general public was not permitted the drug, so
I had an idea it might create an interesting effect. After
finishing the drink, she soon began screaming at whatever
it was she saw before her, so I put her on my lap to
comfort her. Eventually it became clear that she was having a conversation with her dead brother while, all the
time, I was busy soothing the flesh.

As she lay on the marble slab of an old war monument,
beneath giant swaying oaks, her skirts pulled up, her legs
pointing the way to the Dog Star, I inserted my instrument
of pleasure into the index finger of my leather glove so
as not to come in contact with her inferior chemistry. It
was over in an instant, a technique I had worked diligently
to perfect. "I love you," I said and left her there. In the
following weeks I wondered how often she had thought
of me. With a warm feeling of melancholy, I drifted off
to sleep as the hideous wallpaper undulated and the cold
wind of the territory rattled the panes.

I was awakened at four by the voice of Mrs. Mantakis.
"What is it?" I called. "Mr. Beaton is here to escort you
to the mayor's house." I got quickly out of bed and began
to freshen up. I changed my shirt, combed my hair, and

licked my teeth. It was only as I was putting on my topcoat that I caught the name Beaton. By the time I reached the lobby, I remembered him, and there he was, hunched over, blue, threatening to fall. As he saw me approach, he shuffled forward and, slowly enough so that I might have drunk a cup of tea, handed me a letter from the mayor. When he mumbled, a few grains of blue dust fell from his open mouth and drifted to the carpet.

Your honor, read the letter, *since you expressed such interest in Beaton's condition this morning, I thought you might like an opportunity to study him up close. Should he stiffen irreparably on your journey, simply continue on the road he takes you to and you will arrive at my house. Yours, Bataldo.* But by the time I had finished reading, it appeared Beaton had already traded his human status for that of mineral. There had been no sound from him at all, no last grunt or cry, no whispered crackle of flesh giving way to stone. He stood staring up at me with a look of insipid expectation, his hand forward, the fingers parted only the width of the letter. I reached out and touched his face. It was as smooth as blue marble, even the wrinkles and the beard. When I drew my hand away, his eyes suddenly shifted to stare into mine and then froze solid. The unexpected movement momentarily frightened me. "Perhaps you will heat my apartment this winter," I said to him as an epitaph. Then I called for Mantakis.

The missus came in, and I asked her how to get to the mayor's house. In less than two minutes she told me five different ways to get there, none of which I truly committed to memory. But there was still plenty of light before sundown, and I had a general sense as to where I was going. "Do something with Beaton, there," I said. "He seems to have taken a stand."

She took one look at the blue miner, shook her head, and told me, "It is said that when he was born, they dropped him on his head." I hurried out the door of the de Skree as she rattled on.

The street was empty as I headed north to find a certain alley between the general store and the tavern that had been mentioned in all five sets of directions. The sun was on the decline and a strong wind blew down on me. As I walked along through the shadows of the buildings, I wondered if the mayor was playing a joke on me or if he was truly trying to satisfy my well-known scientific curiosity. I had seen nothing in his face that would lead me to believe he had the courage to make light of me, so I dismissed the idea of a slight and turned my attention to finding my way. The cold air was invigorating and it drove off the last few tentacles of the beauty.

I had not gone far when I heard someone approaching from behind. "Your honor, your honor," I heard over the wind.

Before turning I thought that they might have sent someone to lead me, but instead it was a young woman carrying a baby. She wore a shawl over her head, but from what I could see of her she appeared quite attractive. I greeted her.

"Your honor," she said, "I was hoping you would look at my son and tell me what to expect from him in the future." She held the baby up in front of me so that I was eye to eye with a squashed little face. One glance told the story all too plainly. In the lout's features I read a brief novel of debauchery and dissolution unto death.

"Brilliant?" she asked as my eyes probed the child's form.

"Somewhat less," I said, "but not exactly an idiot."

"Is there any hope, your honor?" she asked after I had told her full well my conclusion.

"Madam," I said with exasperation, "have you ever heard of a mule whose excrement is gold coin?"

"No," she said.

"Nor have I. Good day," I told her and again turned north.

When I entered the long alleyway that ran between the

general store and the tavern, the sun was resting at a point just beyond late afternoon, but as I exited the alley, I stepped out into dusk and felt the great beast of night begin to murmur. There, standing next to a bush, was one of the hardened heroes, holding a hand-painted sign that read THIS WAY, YOUR HONOR. An arrow beneath the words pointed the way up a path that twisted ahead into a darkening wood.

The wind ran through me, quickening my pace. I cursed the moronic statue with its blue-toothed smile and pop eyes, and then a large black bird suddenly swooped low out of nowhere and shit on the arm of my topcoat. I screamed after it and followed its flight upward toward the snowcap of Gronus, where it was obvious some wild storm was raging. The stain sickened me with its aroma of pineapple, but it was too cold to take the coat off.

As I passed beneath the boundary of the treetops into the shadows of the wood, I remembered Beaton's eyes, how they had shifted and froze, and then I realized that night had come. The branches were barren, and I trod through piles of yellow leaves that littered the path. Stars shone clearly beyond the skeletal canopy above, but none of them seemed to be where I expected. I made a mental note to repay the mayor's kindness when it was his turn to step before the calipers. "There's always the possibility of surgery," I said aloud to comfort myself. I walked on slowly, sticking to the path as best I could and hoping at every turn that I would see the lights of a house.

Rationale was what was needed to keep my mind clear. I was not much for the unknown. Ever since childhood, the dark had been one of my greatest challenges. There was no face to it, no signs to interpret, no clues to decipher in an attempt to discern a friend or foe. The physiognomy of the night was a great blankness that scorned my instruments and harbored the potential for true evil. I can't tell you how many of my colleagues had this same problem and were prone to sleeping with a light on.

I attempted to concentrate upon the case, what I could expect and how long it would take to diligently read the features of the entire town. It was precisely here, stumbling through the woods, that I had a brainstorm, one of the rare ones that came without an injection. "If these fools believe in the potency of this stolen fruit to cause miracles," I thought aloud, "perhaps what I need to be on the lookout for is someone whose character has changed drastically since the crime was committed." Be assured, I was not affording the fruit any strange powers—that was all drivel to me—but if one did believe that it would make him a genius or bestow the power of flight or cause him to become immortal, would he not then comport himself differently? As I had told my students at the academy each semester of my tenure there: "The physiognomist is more than his chrome instruments. The acute and reasoning mind is the mother of all tools; let her suckle you to insight."

As this grand thought played itself out, I rounded a bend and came in view of the mayor's residence. Two hundred yards up what appeared to be a steep incline, I saw the glow of candlelight shining through a battery of windows lining the front of the house. I was about to begin the climb, when I heard something approaching on the path behind me. The noise started small and far away, but grew exponentially with each heartbeat. I thought absolutely nothing in the few moments before it burst from the darkness like a monster clawing free of a nightmare and stopped only inches from me, hooves pawing the air.

What had materialized was a coach and four, being driven by the porcine mystic who had brought me from the Well-Built City. He sat grinning in the light from the lamp that hung beside him. "The Master has sent me to escort you," he said. I had a million imprecations to shower upon him, but his mention of the Master stopped me cold. I nodded once and got in.

3

"Where is Beaton?" the mayor asked me. "I wanted to send him to town for some ice." The guests, dressed in their pathetic finery, broke out in fits of laughter. If I'd only had my scalpel, I'd have cut them all to ribbons, but as it was, I smiled and gave a slight bow. In a mirror on the other side of the room I watched the mayor put his arm around my shoulders.

"Let me show you my house," he said. He smelled strongly of alcohol, and I gracefully slid him off me.

"As you wish," I said, and followed him through the crowds of guests, drinking, smoking, jabbering like a room full of monkeys. Out of the corner of my eye, I caught sight of Mrs. Mantakis and wondered how she had beaten me to the party. One drunken fool stopped me and said, "I see you have been talking to the mayor," and pointed to the bird excrement on my topcoat. The mayor laughed uncontrollably and patted the fellow on the back. Amid this sea of gabbling wretchedness was intertwined a discordant music played by old men on strange instruments made from pieces of trees. "Absence," the drink of the evening, a clear liquid with a bluish tinge, was brewed by the miners. The hors d'oeuvres were chived cremat— something like grass on a dog turd on a biscuit as hard as a dinner plate.

16

We stopped to greet the mayor's wife, who pleaded with me to get her husband a position in the City. "He's upright," she said. "He's an upright man."

"I'm sure he is, madam," I told her, "but the Well-Built City is not looking for a mayor."

"He can do anything," she said and tried to give him a kiss.

"Get back to the kitchen," he told her. "The cremat is running low."

Before leaving, she kissed my ring with all the passion she had intended for him. I wiped it on my trouser leg as we continued through the crowd, the mayor shouting at me over the noise of the party. I couldn't make out a word of it.

We finally left the main room, stepping out into a long hallway. Bataldo waved over his shoulder for me to follow him. He showed me up one flight of stairs, and when I reached the landing, he pushed back a set of doors that led to his library. Three of the walls were lined with books and the third held a sliding glass partition that opened onto a balcony. Once inside, he moved to a small table that held a bottle of absence and two glasses. I stared at some of the titles on the shelves and before long found four of my twenty or more published treatises. I was sure he hadn't read *Miscreants and Morons—A Philosophical Solution*, since he had not yet committed suicide.

"You've read my work?" I asked as he handed me a drink.

"Very interesting," he said.

"What did it tell you?" I asked.

"Well . . ." he said and fell silent.

"Did it tell you I don't care to be toyed with by an ape such as you?" I asked.

"What do you mean, your honor?"

I threw my glass of absence in his eyes, and, when he cried out and began rubbing them, I drove my fist into his throat. He reeled backward, wheezing noises escaping his mouth, and eventually fell onto the floor where he writhed to catch his breath. I hurried over to him. "Help me," he whispered, and I kicked him in the side of the head, drawing blood. Before he could plead again, I stuck the heel of my boot into his gaping mouth.

"I should kill you for sending Beaton," I said.

He tried to nod.

"Take one more liberty with me, and I will relay to the Master that this entire town is in need of extermination."

He tried to nod again.

I left him there on the floor, opened the door to the balcony, and stepped outside, hoping the breeze would dry my perspiration. I abhorred violence, but I was called to use it occasionally. In this case, as a symbolic gesture to slap the town awake after a long dream of ignorance.

A few minutes passed before the mayor came staggering out to join me. His head was bleeding and there was vomit on his shirt front. He had a glass of absence which he sipped in between groans. When I looked over at him he leaned back against the railing and raised his glass to me. "A first-rate beating," he said and smiled.

"Unfortunately, it was what the moment called for," I told him.

"But if you look out here, your honor, you will see something," he said, pointing into the dark.

"I can't see a thing," I said.

"We are now at the northern border of the town. Out there, a few yards away, is the beginning of a vast, unexplored forest that may go on forever. It is believed that the Earthly Paradise lies somewhere deep in its heart." He took a handkerchief from his vest pocket and laid it against the cut on his head.

"What does this have to do with me?" I asked.

"One year we sent an expedition of seasoned miners in an attempt to discover the celestial garden, and all perished but one. He barely made it back alive and when he wandered into town two years later, dazed and broken, he told stories about demons in the Beyond. 'With horns and wings and ridged backs, like in a child's catechism,' he said. They had also encountered a fire-breathing cat, a black reptilian hound with tusks, and herds of a type of reindeer whose antlers grow together into nests where a bright red bird usually took up residence.''

"I'm not beyond another painful encounter. Get to the point," I said.

"The point is, you must understand the people of Anamasobia. There is a certain sense of humor here born from living in the shadow of the ungodly. For the past few years, the demons have been spotted on the northern border of town. One of them flew out of a fog one night and snatched up Father Garland's dog. You see, in the face of this threat, we must continue, so we laugh as often as possible." He nodded to me when he finished as if that would help me to understand.

"Get cleaned up," I told him, "and meet me downstairs. I will address the townspeople."

"Very good, your honor," he said and then spun quickly around. "Did you hear that?" he asked.

"What?" I said.

"Out there, in the bushes," he said.

"The demons?" I asked.

He pointed at me and started to laugh. "There, I had you," he said. "You have to admit it."

I punched him as hard as I could in the left eye, chafing my knuckles. While he leaned over, swimming through the pain, I told him I would leave my topcoat in his library and that he should have it cleaned for me by the time the party was over. Then I left and returned to the purgatory beneath me.

The mayor's wife handed me a chived cremat as I ordered her to set up folding chairs for the guests. "Right away," she said and was already overseeing the operation when I turned to look. The aroma of the hors d'oeuvres was penetrating, and instinctively I tossed it off the plate I held. It rolled onto the carpet. For some time I was taken with watching the unwitting guests come within a hairsbreadth of stepping on it—a metaphor for their search for meaning. Finally, a woman ran it through with a slender high heel and carried it off into the crowd.

"We are ready for you," said the mayor's wife, awakening me from my reverie.

I had a method I employed when speaking to large groups of the dim, a way of making them focus on my message. I began by doing some quick readings of faces in the crowd and making predictions. No one could resist its appeal. "You, over there," I said, pointing as I strode back and forth in front of the assembled guests, "you will live in poverty for your entire life. You, the woman with the flowers in her hat, should you really be cheating on your husband? Dead within the year. A child on the way. Worthless as the day is long. A mockery of nature. I see a marriage to a man who will beat you." I bowed to thundering applause.

"Ladies and gentlemen of Anamasobia," I began as silence returned, "just as Mr. Beaton was transformed from flesh to spire rock this afternoon, you too have been changed. You are no longer citizens; you are no longer mothers or fathers, sisters, brothers, et cetera. You are now suspects in my case. Until I leave, that is all you are. I will be calculating each of your physiognomical designs in order to flush out a criminal. Most of you, I should think, are aware of my credentials. You will disrobe for me. I am a man of science. I probe gently with an educated touch. If I am forced to delve into the topography of your private areas, I will do so wearing a leather glove. My instruments are so sharp that even if they do happen to nick you, you will not discover the cut for hours. Remember, move swiftly. Pose for me in utter silence. Don't ask me to tell you my assessment. I guarantee, you won't want to know it."

My oration was smooth and cleanly, and I could see that the women, though failing to understand, were taken by my innate command of the human language. The men nodded and scratched their heads. They knew enough to know I was their superior. It was a job well done. I moved through the crowd so they could get a better look at me. The beating I had given the mayor gave me newfound energy and I conversed roundly. They asked me what books they should read, how to raise their children, the best way to make money, how many times a day did I bathe. I told them everything.

Someone had lowered the lights to a faint glow, and I had had a glass or two of absence when from out of the crowd stepped a physiognomy that my eyes slid over without a scratch. She walked up to me and said, "May I ask you a question about Greta Sykes?" Stunned by her beauty, I nodded, not realizing what she was asking. "How could you have been sure that she was the werewolf simply by an insufficient nostril-to-forehead measurement when the elegance of her jawline canceled out all upper facial anomalies?"

I stared at her features for a minute, then stared away for another. "My dear," I finally said, "you've forgotten about the Reiling factor, after the great Muldabar Reiling, that states that a pitched gait, such as Greta Sykes had, reinstates the importance of the upper facial features even after they have been canceled by elegance."

She stared away for a minute, and in that time I eyed her hair, her eyes, her figure, her long fingers.

"Did you see her in her wolf form?" she asked, as I skimmed over the red and yellow paisley of her dress.

"Did I see her? I beat her on the head with my umbrella when she went for my ankle once. In her wolfen form, she was hairy and—no lie—a veritable saliva factory. Her teeth were like daggers, her nails as long as knitting needles. All this from a seemingly innocent child.''

"Were you frightened?" she asked.

"Please," I said and then someone turned the lights out all together so that the room was pitch-black. I reeled from the sudden attack of my old enemy night, and thought for a moment I would fall, but then I heard the voice of the mayor.

"For your honor's pleasure, we have tonight the rare fire bat found only in the veins of Mount Gronus.''

I heard a box being opened. Then the mayor cried out, "Shit, it bit me," just before the sound of flapping leather wings was heard overhead. It circled toward me from out of the dark, a phosphorescent flying rat, and I jabbed at it with my glass. It gained altitude and then flew in circles above the guests. Every time it made a complete loop, a round of applause went up.

I said to the person I felt standing next to me, "This is Physiognomist Cley. Get word to the mayor that I have had as much of the bat as my patience will tolerate.''

A few minutes later, I heard Bataldo scream, "Bring up the lights.'' The minute the lamps were lit the bat went crazy, smashing into things and diving down to snatch at women's jewelry. The mayor had, standing next to him, a particularly limited looking fellow with a bald head and a faraway grin. "Call it back," the mayor said. The man of limitations stuck his pinkie fingers in his mouth and blew nothing but air. The bat continued on its destructive course. The man blew. The mayor called for a shotgun. A chandelier, a wounded valet, and two windows later, the fire bat of Mount Gronus fell dead atop a platter of chived cremat. It remained there for the rest of the evening while the guests danced the quadrille.

"Find me that girl," I told the mayor as I was leaving. "Send her to me. I need an assistant.''

"You are talking about Arla Beaton.''

"Beaton . . .''

"His granddaughter. Beaton was the one who returned from the expedition to the Earthly Paradise," he said as he helped me on with my topcoat.

"And what did he find when he finally reached Paradise?" I asked as the scent of pineapple rose up to greet me.

"He never said."

4

The tub was cast iron, crouching atop lion paws, and it sat on a screened porch at the back of the Hotel de Skree where I boldly disrobed in the first rays of a dim morning. Thick hedges bordered the grounds, and the wind scattered yellow leaves across the lawn. Stepping into the ancient vat, my feet and ankles and calves went almost instantly numb. As my hindquarters submerged, a fist of ice grabbed me by the brain stem and tugged. I held my peace and sank into it. These were harsh gray waters, and the beauty was no match for them.

While I soaked, my teeth chattered and I contemplated the expedition to the Earthly Paradise—miners, carrying pickaxes and wearing lantern hats, wandering off into an uncharted wilderness, searching for salvation. All that now remained of that exquisite folly was a blue statue standing in the lobby of the hotel. I then went on to think of the mayor and the infernal fire bat before I realized it was imperative that I read Beaton. In my eye's-mind I saw him holding out a message to me he had come all the way from paradise to deliver.

I called loudly for Mantakis, who eventually appeared on the porch, wearing an apron and carrying a feather duster. He displayed a long face and was as tiresome as could be with his sighs and labored step.

24

"Snap out of it, Mantakis," I commanded.

"Your honor," he said.

"What's your problem, man?"

"I missed the party last night," he said.

"You missed nothing," I replied. "The mayor loosed a dangerous animal on his people and there was nothing to eat but turds."

"The missus said you were quite eloquent in your oration," he said.

"How would the missus know?" I asked, soaping my left armpit.

"The missus—" he began, but could I really have let him go on?

"Mantakis," I said, "I want you to send Beaton up to my study."

"Begging your pardon," he said, "but I think the family wants him."

"The family can have what is left of him when I am through," I said.

"As you wish," he said and lightly dusted the air in front of him.

"Mantakis," I said as he was about to leave the porch.

"Your honor?" he asked, looking back over his shoulder.

"You missed the party quite some time ago," I said.

He nodded in agreement as if I had told him the sky was blue.

I heard them lugging Beaton up the steps to the study as I dried off in my room and prepared an injection. The voices of the two workmen who wrestled with the stone echoed up the stairway and through my door. Their curses became a boys' choir as the beauty put her arms around me and began to slowly breathe. I dressed amid waves of an inland sea, my eyes twin lighthouse beacons casting visions on reality. Professor Flock made an appearance to help me with my tie, and then the fire bat circled and swooped for five minutes while I hid beneath the bed.

Down on the floor there in the dark, up to my nose in dust, I heard the Master whisper in my ear. I felt his breath and the presence of his body nearby. "Now answer the door," he said. "There is no bat."

As I slid out from beneath the bed, I heard a knocking at my door. I hurried to my feet and dusted myself off. "Who is it?" I called.

"Miss Beaton, is here to see you," shouted Mrs. Mantakis.

"Bring her to my study," I said. "I'll be in shortly."

I went to the mirror and tried to compose myself. I studied my features, a mock physiognomical exam, in an attempt to win back my reason. I was doing quite well, when out of the corner of my eye I saw Arden's blue lips begin to move. They remained stone, yet they moved like flesh. A strained voice struggled like a mole burrowing up through a landslide to call faintly for help.

I closed the door behind me and went across the hall to the study. She was there, sitting next to my desk. When I entered, she stood and bowed slightly. "Your honor," she said.

"Be seated," I told her.

As she sat, I watched her body bend.

"Where did you learn the Physiognomy?" I asked her.

"From books," she said.

"My books?" I asked.

"Some," she said.

"How old were you when you began your studies?"

"I began in earnest three years ago when I was fifteen," she said.

"Why?"

After a lengthy pause, she explained: "Two of the miners of Anamasobia had developed a grudge against each other. No one knew exactly what the cause was. Things got so bad between them that they decided to settle things by having a pickax duel in the stand of willows on the western side of town. The willows were at their peak and their tendrils hung almost to the ground. The two men entered from different sides, wielding axes, and two days later someone went in and discovered that they had killed each other. Simultaneous head wounds. The senseless horror of the event upset the town. In response, Father Garland told us one of his parables about a man born with two heads, only one mouth, and a shared eye, but this did little to explain the tragedy for me. The Physiognomy, on the other hand, has a way of dismantling the terrible mystery of humanity.''

I reviewed my findings on her breasts. ''And what do you see when you look in the mirror?'' I asked.

''A species striving for perfection,'' she said.

''I love an optimist,'' I told her. She smiled at me, and I was forced to turn away. To my surprise, facing me was her grandfather, newly nestled in the corner of the room. The sight of him nearly made me jump, but I controlled the impulse. ''What do you think of your grandfather, that ill-figured boulder there?''

''Nothing,'' she said.

I turned to look at her, and she was staring peacefully at the old blue man. ''I may have to do some chiseling during my analysis,'' I told her.

''I'd be honored to help in excavating that head,'' she said.

''What might we find?'' I asked.

''The journey to paradise,'' she said. ''It's there. He told it to me when I was a young child. Sometimes a moment of the story will come back to me all in a flash and then, a minute later, I will have forgotten it. It's there, encased in spire rock.''

''I suppose we will find a white fruit at the center of his brain,'' I said.

''Or a cavern,'' she said.

I acquiesced with a smile and quickly asked, ''Who is the thief?''

She uncrossed her legs, and I pulled up a chair. Leaning forward, as if in the strictest confidence, she whispered, "Everyone thinks Morgan took it and fed it to his daughter, Alice."

"Why?" I asked, leaning close enough to smell her perfume.

"The child is different now," she said, pursing her lips, her eyelids descending.

"Does she fly?" I asked.

"People say she now has all the right answers."

I took out a cigarette and lit it as a means of changing the subject. "Have you recently been in contact with any members of the opposite sex?" I asked, staring directly into her eyes.

"Never, your honor," she said.

"Do you have any aversion to the naked human form?" I asked.

"None at all," she said, and for a moment I thought she smiled.

"Does the sight of blood or suffering bother you?"
She shook her head.

"Are either of your parents dim-witted?"

"To some extent, but they are simple, kind people."

"You must do whatever I say," I told her.

"I fully understand," she said, moving her head suddenly so that her hair flipped back over her shoulder.

I couldn't help myself and leaned over to measure the distance from her top lip to the center of her forehead with my thumb and forefinger. Even without the chrome exactitude of my instruments, I knew she was a Star Five—an appellation reserved for those whose features reside at the pinnacle of the physiognomical hierarchy. It sickened and excited me to know that if not for the fact that she was female, she would have been my equal.

When I pulled my hand away, she said, "Star Five."

"Prove it," I said.

"I will," she said.

We left the hotel, and as we proceeded up the street toward the church, I asked her to recall for me the essence of the renowned Barlow case. She hurried along beside me, her hair twisting in the wind, as she recited from memory exact facial measurements I had made myself ten years earlier on an obscure doctor who had flatly denied having written subversive poetry.

To be candid, Arla Beaton reminded me of my first love, and I knew she would mean nothing but trouble for me. Involving a woman in the official business of the realm was strictly forbidden, but how could I ignore her? In the work I had done all my life, she was for me, in the concise elegance of her features, my earthly paradise. As she driveled on about the case in question, quoting me, quoting Barlow's rotten poetry, I temporarily lost my head and allowed myself to remember.

When I was a young man studying at the academy, we had a series of classes in the human form. These were early classes in "the Process" (a term used to describe the eight-year curriculum of the physiognomist), and they were extremely difficult so as to weed out those who were not worthy.

I had an advantage over many of my classmates, because I refused friendships and eschewed social life. In the evenings, when the others were out visiting the cafés of the City, I took my notebooks and returned to the academy. Every night I descended to the bowels of the enormous old building to the Physiognomy labs. The human form lab was a small room with just enough space inside for a table and chair. When you sat down, you faced a window with a curtain drawn across it. Simply by speaking, you could command the curtain to open. As it did, a stark white, well-lit room behind it appeared. The academy saw to it that a subject for study was in that room twenty-four hours a day. These were naked forms, and by speaking you could order them to bend and pose for you. I often wondered how much these human puppets were paid or if they were paid at all. They were usually of inferior physiognomical design—who else would do such work?—yet this made them all the more interesting as subjects.

I saw my first Zero there—a person devoid of any craniometric, facial, or bodily merit. This fellow was a real favorite with the students. He was often there late at night, I supposed, because he was so dim there was nothing else he could have been doing. Reading him, though, was like staring into infinity, seeing nature with her pants down, so to speak—both unsettling and sublime. I went one night expecting to find old Dickson there, as blank and crooked as a half-melted snowman, but when the curtain drew back at my command, I found something completely different.

She had the most exquisite body I had ever seen. All perfection and her nipples were like the points of straight pins. I had her twist and turn and jump, get down on all fours and lie on her back. Still, I could not find the slightest blemish. Her face was smooth and radiant, her eyes the deepest green, her lips full, and her hair a cascade of auburn that moved like a divine sea creature swirling in a tidal pool. That first night I stayed with her till dawn, and my commands for crude motor movement slowly gave way to whispered pleas for the wink of an eye or the flexing of a pinkie.

I should have been dead tired that next day, but instead I was filled with a strange excitement, a smoldering in my solar plexus. I could not concentrate on my studies, all the time wondering how I might meet her and have a chance to converse instead of merely command. I returned the next two nights, and to my delight she was there behind the window. On the third night, I told the curtain to open, and the sight of Dickson, drooling, brought an audible groan from me that in turn made that idiot simulate silent laughter. Right there, I devised a plan to discover who she was.

The following morning, I bribed the old fellow who oversaw the operation of the labs. "Just a name," I said to him and slipped fifty belows into his jacket pocket. He said nothing but kept the money and walked away. What I had requested was clearly against the law, and I waited for two days, wondering if I would be turned in. On the night of the second day, the authorities showed up at my apartment. Four men in long black coats, one holding back a huge mastiff with a chain thick enough to haul an anchor. "Come with us," the leader demanded, and they hustled me outside and into a carriage that swept me across town to the academy. During the ride I had given myself up to being sent to the sulphur mines or, at best, executed on the spot.

I was shaking and my mouth was incredibly dry as the four silent agents and the dog ushered me down into the basement where the labs were located. We entered a hallway I had never seen before and from that hallway entered a large stone chamber with metal doors fitted into the walls.

The agent who had spoken to me at my apartment said, "The Master, Drachton Below, has taken a special interest in your progress and has decided to grant your request." He then walked over to one of the doors, pulled on its metal latch, and slid out a table holding the body of my love. "You requested her name?" said the agent. "She is number two forty-three."

"But she's dead," I said, tears coming to my eyes.

"Of course she's dead," he said. "They are all dead. This one was a suicide, distraught over the indictment of her parents in court by Physiognomist Reiling. Her body has been hollowed out and preserved and then fitted with special gear work and the grafted neurons of dogs—all of the Master's invention."

He leaned over and touched her behind the head, turning her on. She opened her eyes and sat up. "Sing," he said to her and she began to grunt pitifully. The other agents laughed. "Now go home and don't speak a word of this to anyone," he said. As I hurried toward the door of the chamber, I looked back and saw the men gathered round her, removing their black coats. The dog, free of its leash, was madly running in circles.

5

The architecture of the church at Anamasobia elicited two initial reactions in me, neither of which I allowed myself to act on. The first was to laugh uproariously at the absurdity of its conception; the second, to light a match and burn it to the ground. Composed of that horrid gray wood, the structure had been built to resemble the outline of Mount Gronus. Had Arla not been with me to explain, I would have thought it just an enormous pile of splintered lumber that came, somehow, to a point. As on the summit of the true mountain, there were representative crevices, cliffs, and sheer drops. None of the steps that led to its crooked doors was the same width or height; there was no symmetry to the placement of the windows, which were paper-thin slices of spire rock engraved with holy scenes. Set atop its highest peak was what appeared to be a miner's axe forged from gold.

"Who is responsible for this mess?" I inquired.

"It was entirely conceived of by Father Garland the first year he appeared in Anamasobia. He swore God had controlled the hand that drew the plans for it," Arla said.

I took her slender hand, pretending to help her up the steps, but before we reached the door, it was I who stumbled and momentarily leaned against her. She surprised me with her strength, and the smile she gave in helping me drained all of mine.

"You must be more careful," I told her before pulling back the taller of the two doors.

"Thank you," she said, and we entered into the darkness.

The bad joke that was the exterior of the building was drawn out to nauseating proportions within, for to enter the church was to enter an underground cavern. There were splintered wooden stalactites and stalagmites affixed to the ceiling and floor. Shadowy constricting pathways led off from the entrance to the right and left of us into utter blackness, while directly in front was a rope bridge that traversed a miniature ravine. Across the bridge and through the sharp outcroppings, like the partially open mouth of a giant, I could make out a large cavern lit only by candlelight.

"Isn't it incredible?" asked Arla as she led the way across the bridge.

"Incredibly insipid," I said, feeling the surrounding darkness like a weight against my eyes. "Church as high adventure."

"The workers and their families feel at home here," she told me.

"Undoubtedly," I answered and nervously began inching my way out above the abyss.

In the altar chamber the pews were hewn from spire rock, and lining the walls were occasional statues that I slowly realized were more of the blue, hardened heroes. Large white candles flickered here and there, dripping wax and infusing the scene with a dim shifting light that was like the last few moments before nightfall. The altar itself was also a large flat boulder, and behind it hung an immense portrait of God as a miner.

"When Father Garland gives his sermons do they represent the release of methane gas?" I asked.

She did not seem to understand that I was joking and answered in earnest, "Well, he does refer to sin as a cave-in of the soul."

As she went off down a dark corridor to search for Garland, I stood alone, staring at God. According to the portrait, the Almighty's physiognomy suggested he might be well suited for digging holes and little else. To start with, his face was dotted with all manner of fleshy wens. There were hairs protruding from the ears, and the eyes looked in two directions. I could not see his general physiognomy as being influenced by the animal kingdom, but there were certain breeds of dogs and an entire line of simians he might have influenced. He held an axe in one hand and a shovel in the other, and he flew upright, long blue hair streaming behind, through a narrow underground tunnel. He came at the viewer out of the dark with an expression that suggested there had been a recent cave-in in his overalls. Obviously, this was a scene from the Creation.

This was not my introduction to the odd religious practices of the territories. I had read of the existence of a church, out in the western reaches of the realm, built of corn husks. Their deity, Belius, takes the form of a man with a bull's head. These strange Gods scrupulously watch the miserable lives of the outlanders and sit in judgment over them. The illusory guiding the ignorant to some appointed heaven beyond life where their clothes fit and their spouses don't drool. On the other hand, in the City, there was Below, a man, and the Physiognomy, an exacting science, a combination of reality and objectivity capable of rendering a perfect justice.

I heard Arla and Garland approaching down the corridor behind the altar and was about to look away from the portrait when it struck me I had seen that face somewhere before. My mind raced to think, but already Arla was introducing me to the father. Making sure the thought was filed away for later, I turned and found before me an exceedingly small man with white hair. He held out a doll-size hand with tiny fingernails sharpened to points.

He showed us to his study, a small cave at the back of

the church, and offered us a liquid derivation of cremat. We kindly settled for a glass of something he said he had brewed himself—an amber-colored liquid that smelled like lilac and tasted like dirt. I couldn't stop drinking it.

Garland's voice had a strange whistling sound behind it that was most irritating. Combining this with his freakish little face and his aphorisms—"When two become one, then three becomes none and zero is the beginning"—he was hopelessly less than adequate. Arla, on the other hand, stared at him with a certain reverence that bordered on the unseemly. I could see I would be forced to shatter her perception of this pretentious runt.

"Tell me, Father," I said, after we were settled in and he had said a short prayer, "why you should not be my primary suspect."

He nodded as though it were a fair question. "I already know the way to paradise," he said.

"What about the fruit?" I asked.

"Plump and sweating sugar every minute. I touched it, and it felt like flesh. Did I ever think of biting it? Even having only heard of it, did you not already think of biting it? Everyone here wanted it. But as long as we left it alone, the power of that combined desire kept us on the path of righteousness. Now we are heading for a blizzard of sin."

"Did anyone show a particular interest in it?"

"One or two," he said.

"Who took it?" I asked.

He slowly shook his head. "For all I know demons swept down one night from out of the wilderness and crept into the altar chamber while I was sleeping."

"I've heard a lot of talk recently about an Earthly Paradise. Can you tell me exactly what that is?"

Garland pinched his nose with the fingers of his left hand and then sank into a pose of deep thought. Arla leaned forward in her seat, waiting for him to speak.

"The Earthly Paradise, your honor, is the one small

spot in this enormous world where nature has made no mistakes. It is God's last best work before he was buried alive. It is a place that accommodates all sin and all glory and turns them drop by drop into eternity."

"God was buried alive?" I asked.

"Every day we dig closer to him," he said.

"What will happen when we get there?"

"We will have reached the beginning."

"Of what?" I asked.

"The beginning of the end." He sighed when he was through and looked over to smile at Arla. She smiled back and he said, "Tell your mother thank you for that whipped tadberry pie."

"Yes, Father," she said.

"I hear from the mayor that your dog was recently taken by a demon," I said.

He nodded sadly. "Poor Gustavus, probably rent to pieces by a pack of the filthy creatures."

"Can you describe it?" I asked.

"It was as Arla's grandfather said, like the way you always supposed a demon would look. It left a strange smell behind as I saw it flapping away."

"Did it have sharp nails?" I asked.

"What do you mean?"

"What do you think I mean?"

"I think you are equating me with the demon in some way because of my nails," he said, never losing his composure. "I keep them sharpened in order to pull out splinters like the one now lodged in my heart."

"I've got a pair of chrome tweezers you can use," I said. Then I turned to Arla and asked her to leave the room. "The father and I have personal business we must discuss."

When she was gone, I told Garland I would need his church in which to perform my investigations of the townspeople.

"You mean they will disrobe in my church?" he said, standing.

"That is the procedure," I said. "You will be on hand to keep the crowd orderly and silent."

"Impossible," he said and took a step toward me, thrusting out those two little hands as if he intended to use them.

"Easy, Father," I said. "I'd hate to have to enlighten you."

Then he grimaced, and I noticed his front teeth had also been sharpened. He was turning red in the face and shaking slightly. I put my hand in my coat pocket and around the handle of my scalpel.

"Grace is God's lantern." He grunted, and instantly he began to relax. He stood very calmly for a few moments.

I nodded. "You can see this is better," I said.

"Come with me, your honor. I have something here that will interest you," he said. He walked over to the wall behind his desk and gave it a gentle push. A door swung back behind which I could see a flight of stairs leading down. He stepped through and then began to descend. "Come, your honor," he called back weakly.

My first thought was that he meant to ambush me in some dark alleyway underground, but I followed, one hand on the railing and one in my pocket on the scalpel. I had decided that with the first pass of the instrument, I would take an eye, after which I would finish him with my boot. As I continued down the long stairway, the prospect of a challenge began to appeal to me.

I found Father Garland kneeling in a marble room, well lit by torches lining the walls. Before him sat a huge wooden chair, holding what looked like an enormous and badly abused cigar. But as I drew closer, I made out the distinct features of a long, thin man, with a long, thin head. His skin, though leatherized by time, had remained completely intact. It even appeared that there were eyeballs still behind the closed lids. There were webs between his fingers and one was pierced by a thin silver ring.

"What have we here," I asked, "the God of cremat?"

Garland rose and stood next to me. "This is the one they found in the mine with the fruit," he said. "Sometimes I think he is not dead at all but just waiting to return to paradise."

"How old is it?" I asked.

He shook his head. "I don't know, but even you must agree there is something unusual here."

"It isn't the unusual I doubt," I said.

"What then?" asked Garland. "The fruit, the Traveler—they are miracles, surely you can see."

"All I see is a dried-out cadaver with the craniometry of a vase, and all I hear coming from your mouth is superstitious twaddle. What am I supposed to gather from this?" I asked.

"I will turn my church over to you tomorrow, but tonight I would like you to do something for me."

"Perhaps," I said.

"I want you to read the Traveler's face."

I looked up to see if it would be worth it, and I noticed a few tantalizing features. The long forehead was misshapen but gracefully so. "It might be interesting," I said.

Garland offered his paw to me and I shook it.

Outside, I found Arla sitting on the bottom step of the church. She was staring out across the huge field that separated the end of town from the beginning of the wilderness. The wind was blowing the long grass, and dark clouds were gathering over the distant trees.

"The snow is coming," she said without turning around.

That afternoon, I had Mantakis take a message to Bataldo stating that the populace should assemble outside the church the next morning at ten. Then Arla went to my study to make the preliminary readings on her grandfather's face while I took the beauty to bed. As I lay there waiting for the warmth to begin to creep, I thought two things. The first was that perhaps someone had taken Garland's dog so the church would be unguarded at night while the father slept. The second was that the physiognomy of the child the woman had begged me to read in the street the previous day seemed utterly familiar to me. Then Professor Flock appeared with a brief report from the sulphur mines. "Hot as can be," he said, puffing and grunting. Sweat dripped from his reddened face. From behind him, I heard shouting and the cracking of whips. "And my god, the smell, the very elimination of excrement." He moaned before disappearing. Soon after, I sank into an hallucination involving Arla and the demons that quickly burned the beauty's wick. When I awoke, two hours later, three inches of snow lay on the main street of Anamasobia and more was being driven down on fierce winds from Gronus.

6

 Snow, almost nonexistent back in the Well-Built City, was an inconvenient little miracle I could have lived without, but as I changed my shirt and freshened up, I felt invigorated by the thought that I would soon get a chance to do some real work. When I was ready, I grabbed my bag of instruments and my topcoat and went next door to the study to inform Arla that we were to return to the church. On my way across the landing, I called down to Mrs. Mantakis to bring us up some tea. She offered to also prepare dinner, but I declined, since a full stomach was likely to put me in too generous a mood.

I found Arla at my study desk, writing in a notebook of her own. She sat rigidly upright, but her hand moved furiously across the paper. In the minute I stood silently and watched her, she had filled an entire page and gone on to the next.

"Tea is coming," I said finally to alert her I was there.

"One minute," she said and continued writing.

I was slightly put out by her failure to officially acknowledge my presence, but there was something about the controlled desperation with which she wrote that prevented me from interrupting her. She was still writing when Mrs. Mantakis brought the tea.

She entered with a look in her eye that suggested she

did not approve of my young female guest. "Did your honor enjoy the mayor's party?" she asked while setting the silver tray down on the table before me. She wore the most ridiculous bonnet and a white apron with ruffles and angel appliqués.

"Quite a gala," I said.

"Just after you left, they barbecued the fire bat and there was enough for everyone to have a little piece. You know, they say it makes you see better at night."

"Before or after you vomit?" I asked.

"Oh, your honor, its taste is quite special, like a spicy rabbit, or have you ever had curried pigeon?"

"You're through," I told her and pointed to the door.

She scurried out with her hands folded and her head bowed.

"A regrettable woman," I said to Arla as I lifted my teacup.

"I'm coming," she said.

Finally, she came and sat with me. The top button of her blouse had unfastened and her eyes were tired and beautiful. As she poured herself a cup of tea, I asked her if she would like to assist me in performing a reading that night.

I saw great promise in her when she did not ask who the subject was but simply replied, "Yes, your honor." She showed no sign of excitement or fear. She barely even blushed. When she sipped her tea she nodded vacantly at a spot an inch away from my eyes. It had taken me years to learn that technique.

"Now then, what did your grandfather reveal?" I asked, breaking her spell on me.

"He's a classic sub-four with traces of the avian," she said.

"Did you notice anything unusual, as I did, about the eye-crease-to-jaw measurements?" I asked.

"That was the most interesting part," she said. "It's only a hairsbreadth off the Grandeur Quotient."

"Yes, so close, yet so far."

"Holistically, he's a three," she said.

"Come, come, there is no place for nepotism in Physiognomy. I'll retire my calipers if he is any more than a two point seven. Anything else?" I asked.

"No," she said, "but as I rubbed my hands across his face, I had a memory of him telling me a piece of that story he had referred to as the 'Impossible Journey to the Earthly Paradise.' It is just a fragment, but I remembered it vividly. I wrote it down in my notebook."

"Give me a few particulars," I said.

She set down her tea and leaned back. "The miners had come to an abandoned city in the wilderness and stayed there for three nights after having done battle with a pack of demons. Grandfather had killed two of the creatures, one with his long knife and the other with his pistol. He had pulled their horns out with a pair of pliers in order to keep them as souvenirs.

"The city was near an inland sea and composed of huge mounds of earth riddled with tunnels. On the first night they stayed there, they witnessed strange red lights in the sky. On the second night one of the men reported seeing the ghost of a woman, wearing a veil, walking through the crude streets. On the third night, Mayor Bataldo's uncle, Joseph, was killed in his sleep by something that left a hundred pairs of puncture wounds. Whatever it was that had killed him followed them out into the wilderness for many days till they crossed a river and lost it."

The night was frigid and the snow blew relentlessly against us as we made our way toward the church of Anamasobia. A flock of urchins was working on a snowman out in front of the mayor's office. If I didn't know any better I would have thought it was meant as an effigy of myself. Had Arla not been beside me and had I not been on an errand of official business, I'd have put my boot through it. "No matter," I thought, being in a good mood, "their congenital ignorance is sufficient punishment."

A few moments later, Arla called over the wind, "Did you see those boys were building a likeness of the Traveler? It has become a childhood tradition ever since he was discovered."

"Children," I said, "a race of bizarre deviants."

Then she said something and actually laughed aloud, but her words were swallowed by the wind.

I never thought I would be pleased to enter that Temple of the Off-Kilter, but not to have the snow driving into my face made the church almost acceptable. As Arla closed the big misshapen door behind us, I stood for a moment, listening to the immediate silence and behind it the wind howling as if at a great distance. Her hair was wet and the smell of it seemed to fill the dark foyer. My hand involuntarily came up to touch her face, but luckily she had already begun to move toward the bridge. We crossed over, myself a little unsteadily, reeling with her wet-forest scent. I'd have given a thousand belows to have been reading her that night instead of Garland's six-and-a-half-foot dried-dung manikin.

The father was there, waiting for us, and somehow he had moved the Traveler to the flattened boulder that was the altar.

"Your honor," he said and bowed, his disposition apparently having lightened since that afternoon.

I waved halfheartedly to acknowledge him.

"Arla, my dear," he said, and she went over to him and kissed him on the forehead. As she did, I noticed him rest his pointy little hand lightly on her hip.

"How did you get him in here?" I asked, wanting to shorten their coziness.

"The Traveler is light," he said, "almost as if he were made of paper or dried corn stalks. Of course, I had to drag his feet, but I barely lost my breath bringing him up the stairs."

The thought of Garland losing his breath seemed a near impossibility.

I stepped up to the altar and rested my bag of instruments down next to the subject's head. Arla followed and helped me off with my topcoat. As she removed her own, I began laying the tools out in the order in which I would need them.

"Can I be of assistance?" Garland eagerly asked.

"Yes," I said, not looking up from my work, "you can leave us now."

"I thought I might watch. I'm keenly interested," he said.

"You may go," I told him without raising my voice.

He sulked over to the corridor that led to his office, but before he finally left, he offered an aphoristic blessing: "May God be everywhere you are about to look and absent where you already have."

"Thank you, Father," Arla said.

I turned to look at him and quietly laughed in his face before he disappeared down the corridor.

"Hand me that cranial radius," I said to her, pointing to the first instrument, a chrome hoop with representative screws at the four points of the compass; and, with this, we began.

In order to perform the reading, I had to overcome my initial revulsion at touching the brown shiny beetle-back skin of the Traveler. One of the first things we learned at the academy was that dark pigmentation of the flesh is a sure sign of diminished intelligence and moral fiber. In addition, the consistency of it, like a thin yet slightly pliant eggshell, put a fear in me that my sharp instruments might leave a crack in the subject's head. I put on my leather gloves and then set to work with the radius.

The slender nature of the cranium made Mantakis's thin head seem almost robust, but at the same time there was something so concise and elegant about this expression of Nature that the computations, when I figured them in my workbook—a tiny leather-bound volume in which I recorded all my findings in secret code with a needle dipped in ink—at once pointed to both a severe paucity of rational thought and a certain sublime divinity. The numbers seemed to be playing tricks on me, but I let them stand since I had never read anything before quite like the Traveler. *Is he human?* I wrote at the bottom of the page.

"Pass me the nasal gauge," I said to Arla, who stood close by me, rapt with interest. Now I could see that to have invited her along on this venture might have been a mistake. I did not want her to sense my uncertainty in the face of the Traveler. What could be worse than a pupil discovering a lack of confidence in her mentor?

"He is most peculiar looking up close," she said. "Nothing physically would suggest anything but the weakest link to humanity, yet there is something more there."

"Please," I said, "we must let the numbers do the thinking." I fear she took this as a reprimand and was from then on completely silent.

The bridge of the nose began almost at the hairline, and instead of flanging at the nostrils tapered to a sharp point with two small slits, like the puncture wounds of a penknife on either side. "Madness," I muttered, but, again, I put down precisely what I found. Instead of the math solidly confirming my suspicions that he represented a species of prehistoric protohuman, the measurement was in direct ratio to that of a Star Five, my own and Arla's illustrious physiognomical evaluation.

The hair itself was long, black, and braided, and appeared as healthy as Arla's beautiful tresses. There was a point where the braiding ended, but the hair had continued to grow a full six inches. From the look of it, I was forced to wonder if it was still not growing beyond death, slowly reaching outward through the centuries. I removed my glove and tentatively ran my fingers through it. Soft as silk, and I could almost feel life in it. I wiped my hand on my trousers and quickly put the glove back on.

I continued, calling for Arla to pass the various instruments—the Hadris lip vise, the ocular standard, the earlobe cartilage meter, etc. I took my time, working slowly and carefully, recording, as always, precisely what I found, yet all the time a feeling of frustration was mounting in my intestines. The representative mathematics of this strange head was acting more like magic, conjuring something utterly superior to even my own features. When all I had left to apply was the calipers, my specialty, I stepped back from the altar and motioned to Arla that we would take a break.

I turned away from the Traveler and lit a cigarette in order to calm my nerves. Sweat trickled down from my brow, and my shirt was damp. Arla said not a word but gave me an inquiring look, as if I should relate to her my findings so far.

"It is too early to make any determination," I said.

She nodded and glanced past me at that long face. From the cast of her gaze, I knew what it was she was looking at—the same eye-crease-to-jawline measurement we had earlier discussed about her grandfather. I didn't need the calipers to know that I would find a measurement there well within the bounds of the Grandeur Quotient.

"Your honor," she said, "I think he is moving."

I spun around, and she brushed past me. She put her hand out and laid it on his chest. "I feel it," she said, "the slightest movement."

I reached over and withdrew her hand with my own. "Now, now," I said, "at times we can doubt what we see, but I'm afraid there is no doubting Death, especially since it has had residence in this fellow for a thousand years or more."

"But I felt it move," she said. There was a look of fear in her eyes, and I could not let go of her.

"Garland probably upset the internal structure of the thing when he moved it. You must feel the breaking of brittle bones turned to salt or the rearrangement of petrified organs. That is all.''

"Yes, your honor," she said, but still stepped back with a look of horror on her face.

How could I have told her that all of my calculations to this juncture pointed to an individual of great awareness and subtle nuance? How could I admit that this freak of nature, with his insect skin and webbed fingers, was, as far as I could tell, the very pinnacle of human evolution? "Where does this put me?" I wondered. I wanted desperately to change my findings. It would have been easy, and I knew, for all involved, it would have been better, but the magic that had infected my computations had put a hex on me that tied me to the bitter truth.

I spread the calipers wide and once again approached the subject. For the first time since beginning, I saw the face devoid of geometric and numeralogical inference. Instead of angles and radii, I saw that he wore a sly, close-lipped smile, and that from the shape and position of his lidded eyes, he had been a man of great wisdom and humor. Then I looked up to see the candles flickering all around the dim cavern that was the church. The Master's voice ran through my head. "Cley," he said, "you are buried alive." I began to feel trapped and claustrophobic. I forced myself to hide my fear and placed one tip of the instrument at the direct center of his forehead . and the other at the end of his long chin where grew a small pointed beard. I tried to take the reading, and then instantly realized I had no idea what I was doing. The Physiognomy, with its granite foundation in the history of culture, suddenly dissolved like a sugar cube in water. I stood between my love and that slab of living Death and felt Garland's blizzard of sin sweeping over me.

"Aha," I said, a bit too theatrically, "here is what I was looking for."

"What is it?" Arla asked.

"Well, if you take into consideration the meager nostril

slits and divide them into the center forehead to center chin measurement, as I have just done, this activates the Flock vector, which in turn conclusively proves our subject is little more than an animal with an upright stance.''

"The Flock vector?" said Arla. "I'm unaware of it."

As was I, but I created a history for it and talked at great length about the brilliance of my professor.

A look of disappointment crept across her face, and I was unsure if it was for me or for her own desire to be witness to a grand discovery. At that point, though, all I wanted was the beauty and to sleep for a very long time.

As I put away my instruments, Arla asked if I would like her to get Garland. I brought my finger to my lips and waved for her to follow me. She looked surprised, but she helped me on with my topcoat and then put on her own. I took one more glance at the Traveler before fleeing. His expression seemed somewhat different now. The mouth was slightly open, as if satiated after having devoured the Physiognomy right out of me.

I couldn't, for the life of me, recall the most basic theories, and the geometery of things had all become circles. The sudden nature of the loss made me dizzy, leaving me sick to my stomach. I no longer had an angle on the world, an anchor in myself. Arla helped me across the swaying bridge, through the doors, and down the steps. When she did not let go of me out amid the swirling snow, I knew she knew there was something wrong.

After a few deep breaths I insisted she unhand me and then, by force of will, trod along in my normal, determined gait. My eyes, devoid of the ability to measure, saw no meaning. Everything was just inexplicably there and brimming with uncertainty. "Structure determines existence in the physical world," I said to myself. At least I had remembered this much, but the meaning of it melted down to the base of my spine and froze.

I left her in the street outside the Hotel de Skree. "Tomorrow, ten sharp," I said. "Don't be late."

7

Up in my room, I pushed a vial and a half of the beauty into my favorite vein. I was perilously skimming the edge of overdose, but I needed strong medicine to tolerate my fear. I could feel the violet liquid almost immediately begin to perk in my head and chest, but before she had me fully in her grasp, I went over to my valise and took out the derringer I carried as insurance against hostile subjects. Placing a chair, back to the wall, I sat with my feet pulled up and listened hard for a lurking danger I could not put my finger on.

Cursed Anamasobia had become the hell of physiognomists, and I prayed to everything—Gronus, Arla, the Well-Built City—that my amnesia was not permanent. If it were, my life would be lost, and I knew I would eventually have to turn the derringer on myself.

"The Flock vector, I like it," said the professor who now stood before me, laughing. He was dressed all in white and as young as on the first day of class I had had with him.

"That damn Traveler has erased everything," I said, unable to see the humor.

"Perhaps you'll be joining me soon," he said.

"Be gone!" I yelled. He evaporated instantly, but the sound of his mirth lingered like the smoke of an extinguished cigarette.

In the wind outside, I heard low voices, passing on gossip. The lights flickered. The Mantakises were either groaning or singing, and the floor began to move like water. I bobbed in the tide, trying to think of numbers and rules, but all I was capable of seeing in my eye's-mind was a parade of meaningless faces. The harder I thought, the faster they sped by, disappearing into the wall above the bed. During my career, I had read each of them, each revealing to my instruments and well-trained eye a certain measure of guilt, but now they might as well have been lumps of cremat for all the meaning they bestowed. I couldn't find the sum, and, when I tried to divide, my brain went haywire, emitting showers of green sparks. If I even attempted to think of the mathematical formula for figuring surface-to-depth ratios, I would immediately picture Mayor Bataldo, leaning on his balcony, saying, "A first-rate beating," and smiling like a classic moron.

I was, though, able to read a message of doom written on my own countenance as it peered back at me from Arden's mirror across the room. My hands shook from the beauty chills, those tremors of the nervous system that occasionally rack the long-time user, and the paranoia was exquisite. For a moment, I thought I saw the face of a demon at the window, staring in through the falling snow. To calm myself, I got up, grabbed my instrument bag off the dresser, and brought it to the bed. Still holding the derringer in my left hand, I opened the bag with my right and took the chrome instruments out one by one. I laid them on the bed in a straight line and then stood and stared. The sight of each of them brought back to me the damnable face of the Traveler. I was reaching for the calipers when I heard someone begin climbing the stairs to my room, one heavy step at a time.

Even as I spun to face the door, bringing the derringer up for better aim, the question struck me, Why do they call this man-thing the Traveler? It seemed to me he hadn't gone anywhere for centuries. But like an enormous dry cornstalk rattling in the autumn wind, I saw him in my eye's-mind now coming to me, wearily mounting the stairs, his very skin creaking, his exhalations, heaves of dust. I wondered if he was using the banister. "Mantakis," I yelled at the top of my voice, yet only the slightest murmur escaped me.

The sound of steps ceased at the landing and I cocked the trigger. I had never fired the gun before, and I wondered if it was, in fact, loaded. Three methodical raps sounded upon my door and in the silence that followed I detected the faint wheeze of labored breathing. "Come in," I said.

The door opened, and it was a good thing I did not give in to the urge to pull the trigger, because standing before me was the pig-faced driver of the coach and four. The miserable wretch stared, glassy-eyed, as if he were walking in his sleep.

"The Master requested that I fetch you," he said without the slightest trace of his misbegotten humor.

"Drachton Below is here?" I asked, unable to hide my astonishment.

"You must accompany me," he said.

"Very well," I mumbled. I put on my overcoat and gathered up my instruments. Hastily I put them in the bag and snapped it shut. When the driver turned to begin his descent, I slipped the derringer into the pocket of my coat. Shaking like a leaf, my mind swimming through rough seas of beauty, I staggered toward the door. I knew that whatever came of this, it would be no good.

The driver took each step at the same dense pace with which he had ascended. When I reached the landing outside the Mantakis's bedroom door, I heard Mrs. Mantakis gibbering on and on about something, and the very sound of her voice drained the energy out of me. I leaned, exhausted, against the wall for a moment and closed my eyes.

"Your honor," said the driver.

I instantly awoke and somehow we had gotten outside the hotel. The moon was bright, and I was startled that the weather had turned warm and the snow seemed to have all melted.

"But how could this be?" I asked.

"The Master is waiting," he said, holding open the door of the coach.

I nodded once and got in.

As we drove down the main street of town, I wondered where he could be taking me. I had a million questions, but soon I realized that the whole episode must be the result of the beauty, working its magic on me. "It's not real," I said to myself. When we passed the church and headed across the field to the boundary of the wilderness, I leaned back in my seat and closed my eyes. I hoped that if I could fall asleep and wake up, I would be back in my room at the Hotel de Skree, or better yet, back in the Well-Built City.

I must have fallen asleep, because I was awakened by the jolt of the carriage coming to an abrupt stop. "Persistent hallucination," I whispered. Looking out the window was like looking into a pool of ink. I could not make out the merest glimmer of light. Suddenly, the door of the coach swung open and there was the driver, holding a lit torch in his hand. The flame from it blew and sputtered in the warm wind, and the way it lit his inadequate face made him appear now more sinister than stupid.

"Where in Harrow's hindquarters are we, my good man?" I asked, stepping out into the night. I slid my left hand into the pocket of my overcoat and put my fingers around the derringer. My right hand followed suit with the opposite pocket and found the handle of my scalpel.

"The entrance to the mines of Mount Gronus," he responded. "Follow me, your honor."

We walked a few paces up a dirt path to the timber-lined opening of the main shaft. "Are you quite certain the Master is here?" I asked.

He said nothing but plunged into the deeper darkness and forged unhurriedly ahead. I scrabbled to keep up with him, the whole time my mind turning over the possible questions the Master would ask me. "No matter how bad it gets," I told myself, "if you know what is good for you, you won't mention Arla."

We walked for a long time through pitch black. It is true, he had the torch, but what could it light? For every few yards of night it burned away, there were oceans more that would flood in. This darkness everywhere had me constantly on the verge of screaming. I have no idea how I was able to continue, but continue I did. We seemed to be traveling down to the heart of nothing when all of a sudden, we turned to the right and stepped into a small cavern that was lit as brightly as day by some luminescent source I could not detect. Sitting in a high-backed chair situated in front of a garden of waist-high stalagmites, legs demurely crossed, smoking a long thin cigarette, was Drachton Below. Curled up at his feet with its back to me was a very large doglike creature covered with long silver hair.

"Cley, good to see you," he said and blew a stem-thin trail of smoke from his lips. He wore burgundy silk pants and a lime green jacket. The pale skin of his hairless chest almost reflected the brilliant light that was everywhere.

"Master," I said, bowing slightly.

"And how is the investigation going?" he asked, inspecting the back of his right hand.

"Splendidly," I said.

"Really . . ." he replied.

"But are you real?" I asked. "I recently took the beauty, and I am in a jillywix as to the corporeality of this meeting."

"What do you mean by *real*?" he said and laughed.

"Are you here?"

"Not only am I here, but, look, I've brought along an old friend of yours." With this, he nudged the creature lying at his feet with the sole of his sandal. "Up," he commanded. It growled slightly, kicked its back legs spasmodically once, and then began to rise. I was astonished when it did not come to rest on four legs, but continued till it was standing on two like a dog convinced it is human.

"Wait . . ." I said, because something about it began to appear familiar to me. Then it turned and I saw the lupine face of Greta Sykes, the Latrobian werewolf. "Not this," I said, taking in her form. She was larger than when I had first tracked her down, and there were two rows of metal bolts that pierced both scalp and skull at the crown of her head. Her incisors and claws still appeared as sharp, but now beneath the thick coat I could detect the human breasts of a young woman. Trapped in her eyes was a look of great suffering and sorrow.

"Your little werewolf. I've done some work on her, messed around with the brain and added some new pain centers. She doesn't change into a little girl anymore; now she is an effective agent."

"Your genius astounds me," I stammered.

"Down," he told her, and she lowered herself to the floor, curling up at his feet once again. "Cley, your genius had better astound me at the completion of this case. I want that white fruit."

"I am about to enact the Twelfth Maneuver," I said.

He laughed at me. "Whatever," he said, waving his hand. "If you fail, I will have Miss Sykes here perform the Last Maneuver on you and the rest of that tedious town."

"As you wish, Master," I said.

"And what is this I hear about a certain young lady who is serving as your assistant?"

"Just a secretary, sir. There are a lot of bodies to read down there. I need someone to help me keep track."

"You're a sly one, Cley," he said. "I don't care what you do with her. I want the fruit. The Well-Built City needs me to live forever."

"But of course," I said.

"Now," he said, turning his profile to me and placing the much-diminished cigarette in his mouth, "take that surrogate penis out of your coat pocket and let's see some of the old scientific exactitude."

"Am I to shoot?" I asked.

"No, you are to stand there till the end of time. I'm not giving medals for stupid questions this week. You'd better get to it," he said speaking out of the smiling side of his mouth.

I pulled out the gun and raised my arm to aim. The derringer swerved and dipped at the behest of the beauty, my fear, and the increasingly pungent odor of Greta Sykes. "What if I were to miss," I thought as I closed one eye for clearer vision. That thought exploded in my mind a moment before the gun went off, its report ricocheting off the blue walls of the cavern.

I came awake suddenly, sitting straight up. Across the room from me there was a neat hole in the center of Arden's mirror and a sleet storm of shattered glass on the floor in front of it. I shook my head in an attempt to clear it. The bright day outside my window revealed an end to the snowstorm. I threw the derringer on the floor and took out a cigarette. There was the sound of rustling a floor below, and then I heard Mantakis hurrying up the stairs. His pounding at the door thickened my headache and spiked my eyes.

"Your honor," he called, "did I hear a gun go off?"

"A little experiment, Mantakis," I said.

"An experiment?" he asked.

"To see if you were awake," I said.

"I am," he said.

"What is the time?"

"Your honor, it is nine-fifty."

"Draw me a bath and bring me a steaming bowl of that excrement that passes for sustenance here."

"The wife has made a cremat goulash that is a testament to her abilities," he said.

"My very fear, Mantakis."

I almost lost consciousness while adrift in the acrimonious waters of my bath. With the freezing temperature, the blowing snow, and the fact that I felt as if I really had traveled to Mount Gronus through the night, my mind reeled and my consciousness began to constrict in the manner of my other apertures. Just as I was going under, Mantakis appeared and swept a steeping bowl of goulash under my nose, which had the miraculous effect of smelling salts. I actually thanked him for that whiff of death and then ordered him to take it, and himself, away.

I sat, frozen, and searched every inch of my mind for the lost Physiognomy. I couldn't turn up a single digit, not even a fraction of a chin. "What do you do when the surface gives way and you fall in?" I said to the snowdrifts beyond the screen. Then the Master came to my thoughts, carried by a chilly gust of wind, and for a moment I wondered if perhaps he had not truly contacted me by somehow swimming through the beauty and into last night's hallucination. The memory of Greta Sykes standing before me led me to believe the entire incident was nothing more than a nightmare concocted from my own worst fears, but the Master was rich in magic, a primitive phenomenon I had no knowledge of. For all their grotesque weirdness these thoughts did not concern me as much as the prospect of facing the faces of Anamasobia emptyheaded.

8

Mayor Bataldo was standing in a small snow-drift waiting for me outside the hotel. He was dressed in a long black coat, and atop his bulbous head was a ridiculous black hat with a broad brim. Seeing me, he flashed a grin so full of whimsy that I wanted, right then, to give him another beating.

"Beautiful day, your honor," he said.

"Contain yourself, Mayor, my patience is a brittle thing today," I told him.

"The people of Anamasobia await you at the church," he said, his smile fading but never quite completely gone.

We started down the street, snow crunching beneath our boots, the town as still and silent as a graveyard. As we walked, the mayor reeled off the details of his preparations.

"I have assigned you a bodyguard, the most vicious of the miners, a fellow named Calloo. He will protect you in the event one of the citizens protests the protocol. Father Garland has set a screen up on the altar so that those who must disrobe will have some privacy. By the way, the father is beside himself with the idea of both nudity and science infiltrating his church on the same day."

"Keep him away from me," I said. "Whatever status he has in this town due to his religious station means nothing to me. I'll have him whipped like a mongrel if he interferes."

"Arla has suggested that you would like to see Morgan and his daughter, Alice, first, since they have generated some suspicion in the town."

"Very well," I said.

"Look, there are your specimens," said Bataldo, pointing ahead of us.

We were close enough to the church for me to appraise the haphazard line of oafish reprobates. When they noticed us approaching, they grew silent, and it did me some good to see a suggestion of nervousness and perhaps a tinge of fear come into nearly all the faces. Some of the bigger and more brutal looking of the miners showed no emotion at all. How could I really frighten them after their having spent such a large portion of their lives in darkness with the possibility of a cave-in or the invisible danger of poison gas always lurking? At least they did not openly show their contempt.

I was about to head for the door of the church when the mayor took my arm and stopped me. "A moment, your honor," he said. Then he turned to the crowd and, waving his arms in the air, called out down the line, "All right, as we practiced. Ready, one, two, three . . ."

The townspeople broke into a raggedly coordinated chorus of, "Good morning, your honor," yelling like a pack of schoolchildren greeting their teacher.

It took me by surprise, and all I could think to do was give a half bow in acknowledgment. This brought peals of laughter from them. Bataldo was beside himself with glee. My anger surged in me, and for a moment I almost lost sight of the situation. Had I actually taken out the loaded derringer and shot the mayor as I so wanted to at that moment, it might have jeopardized the entire case. Instead, I took a breath, turned away, and made for the entrance to the church. It did not help that I tripped on the first of those crooked steps, for that brought forth another torrent of hilarity at my expense.

I realized I was sweating profusely as I made my way

over the unsteady bridge just inside the doors of the church. With the Physiognomy nowhere in sight, I knew my only recourse was to pretend. In short, to put on a mask of competency, behind which I could hide my emptiness. The shadowy nature of the church was a blessing that would aid me. My greatest problem would be Arla, who now came toward me beaming with beauty and an uncanny knowledge of that which had once defined my importance.

"Are you ready to do some work?" I asked sternly as I handed her my bag of instruments.

"I was up all night rereading my texts," she said. "I hope I will be of service."

She wore a plain gray dress and had her hair pulled back in what I took to be an attempt to appear more professional by appearing less feminine. Still, with all the problems circling in my head like a coven of crows, I was instantly overcome by her presence. I touched her shoulder lightly and for a moment was transported to the Earthly Paradise. Then I saw Father Garland appear from behind the wooden screen he had erected on the altar, and heaven turned instantly to hell.

He came toward me like the strident possum that he was, his sharpened teeth gleaming in the torchlight. Pushing his way in between Arla and me, he said, "The mayor has warned me not to interfere with your proceedings, and I have agreed to suffer this humiliation for the good of the town, but you, you will pay in the hereafter. There is a certain chamber in the mine of the afterlife set aside for the sacrilegious where the torments surpass the living pain of loneliness and loss of love."

"Yes," I said, "but does it surpass one unbearable moment of having to listen to you?"

"I noticed you did not stay to discuss your findings on the Traveler with me last night," he said, smiling sharply. "It was our deal, I recall, that you would apprise me of your results."

"Prehuman," said Arla, coming to my defense.

"That is correct," I said, "a creature preserved from before the ascendancy of man. Interesting for its novelty as a museum piece but physiognomically empty of revelation."

"I will pray for you," said Garland. He turned and walked to the first row of stone pews, kneeled down, and clasped his hands.

"Spare me," I said and accompanied Arla to the altar. Waiting for us there was the fellow the mayor had assigned to accost unruly subjects. It seemed Bataldo had gotten the right man for the job, because Calloo, as he was called, was the size of the full-grown bear I had once seen in a traveling circus outside the walls of the Well-Built City. He had a thick black beard and hair nearly as long as Arla's. I did not need the Physiognomy to see that his hands, his head, in short, every part of him was an affront to the common sense of nature. In addition to his strength and size, he exhibited few outward signs of human intelligence. When I gave him his orders, he relayed to me that he understood by means of grunts and nods. I sent him off to fetch the first of the subjects and then set out my instruments on the stone altar just as I had the night before.

If the eight-year-old girl, Alice, whom everyone suspected of having been fed the fruit by her father, had all the right answers, what I wanted to know was who was asking the questions. I sat before her naked form, making believe I was jotting down notes in my tiny book with the straight pin and ink. Along with the loss of my knowledge went this notation system, which now seemed to me an extravagance of the minuscule I could no longer grasp the genius of. Arla was doing a cranial reading as I questioned the girl.

"Alice," I said, "did you eat the white fruit?"

"Eat the white fruit," she said, staring at me with an expression that made Calloo look like a savant.

"Alice," I said, "have you changed recently in your thinking?"

"Stinking," she said.

I shook my head in exasperation.

"Have you seen the fruit?" I asked.

"Clean the suit," she said.

"Am I missing something here?" I asked Arla.

She shook her head and came over to whisper to me that the girl was a retrograde two on the intelligence scale and that the measurements showed her to be pure of heart.

"Next," I yelled.

It turned out that her father was no less brilliant than she. He had an inordinately large penis, which obviously revealed the curse of his ignorance. Arla showed great diligence in measuring this organ, but I cut her off in the middle of her work, saying, "There's nothing there. Next!"

With our lead suspects cleared by Arla's computations and my necessarily more intuitive approach, we began to go to work on the rest of the town. So far, my plan to make it seem as if I was using this opportunity to mentor my assistant had worked well. "And what did you find?" I would ask her with each instrument she applied. She handled the chrome tools with great adeptness, calling out numbers for me to record in my book. I was, of course, going to allow her to catch the thief for me. Occasionally, her confidence would falter, and she would look to me with a question in her eyes. Then I would say, "Go on, continue. I am watching. I will let you know when you have made an error." With these words of encouragement, she would smile, as if thanking me for my generosity, and I began to think that the whole affair might work out better than I had imagined.

They filed in one by one, a never-ending nightmare of the repulsive and displeasing. With my new blindness, picking a thief out of this populace was like trying to identify a scoundrel in a room full of lawyers. Their nakedness was very unsettling. All that flesh and their blatant sex staring me in the face made my stomach queasy. When Arla ordered the mayor's wife to bend over, I lit a cigarette, hoping the smoke would obscure from me her dilapidated mysteries.

Then, on our twentieth subject, a man named Frod Geeble, the owner of the tavern, Arla stopped in her application of the calibrated navel standard and· said to me, "You'd better double-check me here."

I gave her a nervous look, and she squinted as if for an instant she saw through to my unknowing. Quickly, I put down my notebook and approached the subject. She held out the instrument to me; although I could recall the name of it, I had no idea how it worked. Instead of accepting the standard from her, I bent over and put my left eye up to the fat man's navel, looking in as if peering through the end of a telescope. Unable to think of what else to do, I stuck my index finger into the flesh ditch. Frod Geeble belched.

"Interesting," I said.

"What number do you come out with?" she asked.

"That was my question for you," I said.

"I feel uncertain after having discerned evidence of depravity in the abundance of eyebrow hair," she said.

"Forget your uncertainty," I said.

"But I read last night, in your work *The Blemished Corpulence and Other Physiognomical Theories* that the physiognomist should never operate out of uncertainty."

In order to circumvent her discovery of me, I stood up and looked Frod Geeble in the eyes, asking myself, Could this man have stolen the sacred fruit? It struck me then that this was the only method of judging another human being that the uninitiated had. The slovenly nature of such a method of discovery made me shudder at the utter darkness so many lived in. Still, I had a feeling he hadn't done it.

"He has brown eyes," I said. "This negates your concern."

"Very well," she said. "He is innocent."

"Free drinks at the tavern for your honor," said Frod Geeble as he dressed.

Calloo was on his way out to fetch the next subject when I called him back. "Bring me the mayor this time," I said.

The hulking miner broke into a broad grin at this suggestion and, for the first time, spoke intelligibly. "Pleasure, your honor."

I had to smile myself.

The mayor held his hands cupped over his privates as he stepped forward for inspection. Arla showed no timidity but went at him with all of my devices just as she had the others. When she was done calling out her findings to me, and I had gone through the charade of jotting them down with the pin, I asked her to step aside. She moved back. The mayor, though no physiognomist himself, took one look at me and very astutely read the malicious intent in my gaze. The folds of loose flesh on his chest and stomach as well as his bottom lip began to quiver.

"I know," he said, giving a nervous laugh, "you have never seen such a resplendent specimen."

"On the contrary," I said, "very piglike."

"I am not a thief," he said, losing his sense of humor.

"Undoubtedly, but I do see a small character flaw that I may be able to adjust," I said. I got up and went over to where my coat hung on the back of a chair and retrieved the scalpel from its pocket. With the instrument in hand, I walked up in front of the mayor, waving the blade inches from his eyes. "I detect an asinine sense of humor that may be your undoing if we cannot correct it early enough."

"Perhaps I can simply work at being more serious," he spluttered.

"Now, now, Mayor, this won't hurt a bit. I'm just trying

to see where to make the appropriate cut. Perhaps lower down, near the seat of your intelligence," I said, and stepped back in order to run the dull side of the blade across his testicles.

"Arla, please," he said over my shoulder.

Then I remembered that she was there, watching. I wanted badly to vent the entirety of my frustration on him, but the stronger urge to not let Arla see my anger stole my initial impulse to cut into him like a cake.

After I had dismissed him and he was dressed and gone, Arla said to me, "I saw through you."

"Whatever are you talking about?" I said.

"You were trying to get him to confess," she said.

"I was?"

"You did notice the aberrant nature of his posterior, did you not?" she asked.

"Be specific," I said, as if I were quizzing her on her determination.

"The patch of hair he had growing on his left buttock. I believe it is called the Centaur Quality? Unremitting proof of the potential for thievery."

"Very good," I said. "I have already put him in the suspect category."

We saw half the town by nightfall, and I was as far from resolving the case as when I had started. For all I knew, the Traveler had awakened and stolen the fruit. Arla had come up with a short list of possible criminals, but none of them seemed as if anything miraculous had befallen them. Perhaps they were hoarding the fruit till the case was over. I paid Calloo a few belows for his work and just barely caught myself from thanking him. My near slip came, most likely, from the fact that I was so thankful the day was over. I packed my bag, put on my coat, and watched longingly as Arla let her hair down.

"Meet me at the hotel in an hour," I said to her.

She nodded and left the church. Her abrupt departure made me wonder if she was on to me. I needed to consider if I could safely put my trust in her. But what I needed more than anything was the beauty. I could not remember when I had gone so long without it. My hands were shaking slightly, and I was beginning to feel my skull itch, a sure sign that I was overdue for a violet fix. Garland was still kneeling there praying as I left. I slammed the front door behind me as hard as I could, hoping his wooden Gronus would topple down upon him. Instead, I tripped again on the bottom step and landed facedown in the snow.

9

Mrs. Mantakis was behind the desk at the hotel when I entered, counting belows and chittering furiously to herself like a weasel caught in a leg trap. I wiped the snow off my feet onto the welcome mat and approached her. Even when I was standing before her, she paid no attention to me but went on with her monologue: "If he thinks I'm going to stand out in the cold all day waiting and then be told to come back tomorrow so that he can lay his greedy eyes on my—" I cleared my throat, and she looked up suddenly.

"Your honor," she said, "so good to see you. You must have had a long, hard day. What can I do for you?" She swept the money off the counter and smiled insipidly to cover her rancor.

"Today was wearisome," I said, "but tomorrow will be twice that, seeing as I will have to spend time studying you and your husband."

"Why will that be difficult?" she asked. "My mother used to say I have fine attributes." Her smile turned into a sneer with the wrinkling of her nose, the widening of her nostrils.

"I didn't know your mother was a veterinarian," I said.

She held her tongue, as well she should have, knowing I was tired.

"Send two bottles of wine up to my office. Also, dinner

for two, and it had better not be any form of cremat. I don't care if you have to fry that dim-witted husband of yours. Then get to bed early; there will be a long wait in the snow again tomorrow.''

"As you wish," she said, eyeing my jugular.

"A town of militant morons," I said to myself as I trudged up the flights of stairs to my room. Once inside, I took off my topcoat, slipped off my shoes, and lay on the bed. What I wanted was a moment of rest, but, of course, my mind could not leave the case alone. When I tried to recall some of the subjects we had seen, all I could get a picture of were amorphous blobs of flesh. Arla then came to my eye's-mind, and even in my diminished condition stirred my desire. There was no doubt, I was falling in love with her. This never would have happened had I retained the Physiognomy. I could see now that the loss of reason proceeds in a geometrical progression until unholy chaos pushes every methodical theory from one's mind. What was worse, I was not completely hostile to the sensation it engendered.

There was only one thing that could clear my mind, and I got up and went to my valise for a clean hypodermic. Since Arla was most likely on her way, I only administered a sparing dose, seeing as I did not want her to witness one of my deep stupors. The beauty was all I had left to rely on, and true to her form she came to me splendidly, growing out from the point of entry between the big and second toe of my right foot in spreading tendrils of bliss.

I believed the dose too small to bring hallucinations, although the lamps in the room did emit a very faint music—strings and oboes, if I recall. It was just a fine, light feeling that lifted my spirits and gave me the energy to dress. At least the luckless Mantakis had cleaned up the shards on the carpet and replaced the glass in the mirror his hardened brother would hold for eternity. I made a mental note to commend him at bath time the next morning.

He came to my room a half hour later to let me know that dinner had been served next door and that the Beaton girl had arrived. I quickly dabbed a touch of formaldehyde beneath each ear, an aroma the scientific mind cannot resist, and went next door with a low smoldering of excitement in my bowels.

When I came in the room, I found Arla standing in front of the statue of her grandfather, her palms resting gently on either side of his face.

"Communing with the family tree?" I asked.

"Make that rock," she said and turned to smile at me.

I was pleased to see she appeared to have left the business of the case behind for a while. I was also pleased to see her dressed not so drably as earlier. She wore a dark green dress with yellow flowers on it that hung well above her knee. Her hair was down and, to my beauty-enhanced vision, literally shining. When her eyes met mine, it was all I could do to keep from smiling.

On the small table, Mantakis had laid out two plates of food. I could not believe my eyes when I saw a real caribou steak, vegetables I could recognize, and not the faintest scent of cremat anywhere. Beside the plates were two bottles of wine, one red, the other blue, along with two fine crystal glasses. I sat down before one of the plates and motioned that she should join me.

She took a seat and immediately cut into the steak and began eating. I poured us each a glass of blue wine, hoping she did not realize it was the more potent of the two. Then I leaned back in my chair and said, "You did some very fine work today."

"I told you I would," she said.

I desired a slightly more respectful response and perhaps that she did not chew so loudly, but these were minor annoyances lost amid the deluge of her charm. We ate and exchanged pleasantries, had a good laugh over Morgan and his daughter, Alice, possibly having anything to do with the crime. Just when everything was moving along smoothly and I had gotten her to accept another glass of wine, Professor Flock materialized behind her. I had momentarily forgotten that at least half of my contentment grew from the beauty.

"You didn't think I'd miss this little get-together, did you, Cley?" he asked.

Arla looked up and around at this moment as if she detected the buzzing of a mosquito, but I realized she was merely reacting to my reaction. I couldn't very well yell to my old mentor to be gone in front of her. I focused on her eyes and worked hard to ignore him.

"Quite the little brisket, old boy," he said, "and I'm not talking about dinner, though I may be talking about dessert, eh?" He was dressed in a loincloth and carried a shovel. His face was haggard, and the sweat dripped off him.

Arla took a drink and then said, "I have had more daydreams in which I remember pieces of my grandfather's journey."

"Interesting," I said.

Flock leaned over her and looked down the front of her dress. "I suggest the Twelfth Maneuver," he said, snickering sardonically.

"Yes," she said, "I recall him telling me, surprisingly enough, about a being he met that closely fits the description of Father Garland's Traveler."

"You don't say," I said, watching the professor make lewd movements behind her.

"Yes," she said, "and I remembered him saying that this being told him the name of paradise."

Flock said to me, "Watch, Cley, this is how I died." Then I could see fumes rising around him, and the smell of sulphur permeated the room. Dropping the shovel behind him, he grabbed at his throat with both hands. His face turned red and then quickly to purple, his tongue protruded, his eyes popped wide.

"Wenau," she said.

The professor fell forward over Arla, her head piercing his incorporeal chest, and I leaped to my feet in an attempt to keep him from crushing her. The hallucination faded in a moment, and I was standing before her, leaning over.

"Almost my very reaction," she said.

"Interesting," I said and sat gracefully back down, trying to disguise my agitation.

We finished dinner with no more interruptions from unwanted guests. Arla stood up, taking her wine, and went over to the window. She looked out at the moon, which shone in full view, and asked, "Do you think we have seen the thief yet, or shall we discover him tomorrow?"

"From the information we have so far, I cannot tell. Remember, the Twelfth Maneuver requires that we read all inhabitants."

"Tell me about the Well-Built City," she said.

"It is all crystal and pink coral, spires, and ivy-covered trellises. There is a large park and broad avenues. It is the brainchild of Drachton Below, the Master. The story goes that he had been a pupil of the great genius Scarfinati, who had taught him a memory system by which you construct a palace in your mind and then adorn it and fill it with ideas that have been transformed through a mystic symbology into objects. Hence, when you need to remember something, you simply stroll through the palace in your memory, find the object—a vase, a painting, a stained-glass window—and the idea in question is again revealed to you. Below had been such a curious youth that instead of a simple palace, his knowledge could be housed in nothing less than a city. By the time he appeared in Latrobia, a young man of twenty, he had constructed every inch of the metropolis in his mind. He knew where every brick was to be laid, how every façade was to be ornamented before the work even began. It was said that he whispered something in the ears of the men and women he sought to work for him, and from that moment on, they were like joyous machines, tireless unto death, with no need of instructions. It was built well before I was even born, in so short an amount of time that that in itself is as much a miracle as its actual construction.''

"And did he bring the Physiognomy with him?'' she asked.

"The Physiognomy had been in existence in one form or another dating back to when the first people looked into one another's eyes. But Below, needing some law to govern his creation, codified it and made it a mathematics of judgment concerning humanity.''

"I always hoped to go there someday to study in the great libraries and perhaps even attend one of the universities.''

"You are truly idiosyncratic, my dear. No woman there would ever dream of going to a university; no woman has access to the libraries.''

"And why is that?'' she asked.

"They know full well that they are inferior to men in general, just as certain men are inferior to others. Not only do they know it, it is a law,'' I told her in my softest voice.

"You can't really believe that,'' she said.

"Of course I do,'' I said. "Look, you've read the literature. Women's brains are smaller than men's; it is a scientific fact.''

She turned away from me with a look of disgust.

"Arla,'' I pleaded, "I cannot change nature.'' I could feel her growing cold. She took a step away from me, and I tried to think of something that would bring back her tranquillity. "Women have certain attributes, certain, shall we say, biological possibilities. They have a place in the culture, but . . .''

She seemed to brighten and turned to face me. "Oh, I think I know what you mean,'' she said, smiling.

"You do?'' I asked. My mind reeled, and I felt gravity

drop away. The beauty, the wine now thought for me as I put my arm around her and prepared to kiss her. In the back of my mind, I was wondering where I had left the leather glove I habitually employed in such crucial moments.

Then it came, as unexpected and devastating as the loss of the Physiognomy. She slapped my face and tore away from my grasp.

"Women have their place in the culture," she said, mocking me. "Just remember, it is I who am conducting this investigation. I may be a woman, but I am smart enough to know you have somehow lost your abilities."

"Arla," I said. I had wanted to speak her name sternly, but instead my word came like the cry of a child.

"Don't worry," she said. "I won't tell anyone. I will finish the investigation, because I want you to know, even if it remains a secret, that it was I who solved the case."

I could not believe what I was thinking, but I was actually going to apologize. By Harrow's hindquarters, my world was shredding in every direction. "I'm sorry," I said and the words were like a pound of cremat on my tongue.

"You are sorry," she said. "I will see you tomorrow at ten. This time, don't you be late. Hopefully you will exhibit a more professional demeanor in the morning." With this she grabbed her coat, crossed the room, and was gone.

I was completely immobilized by both her revelation that she had perceived my loss of the Physiognomy and of her opinion of me. This was true humiliation—and worse, true loneliness. Because I felt the greatest need to get away from myself, I went next door, quickly put on my coat, and went after her.

Outside, the darkness of the night frightened me more than usual as the brisk wind, following Arla's lead, also slapped me in the face. I saw her distant figure as she made her way up the empty street. My plan, if you could call it that, was not to confront her—I knew that would be a mistake—but merely to follow her. I could not bear her leaving. Sticking to the deep shadows in front of the buildings, I ran, a skill I hadn't utilized since childhood.

She stopped once and turned around, standing and watching for a moment. I too stopped, hoping she did not see me. Then she took to the alley between the bank and the theater. I moved up to the end of the alleyway and waited until she had traversed its entirety. When she was out of sight, I made my move. In this manner, I tracked her from a distance through a thicket of pines and then across a small meadow, running along on the toes of my boots so that she would not detect the sound of the hardened snow crunching beneath them.

On the other side of the meadow there stood a one-story ramshackle house made of that splintered gray wood everything in Anamasobia was constructed of. I could see a warm light glowing from its one front window. She entered and closed the door behind her. I tiptoed up to the front of it and then, if you can believe this, got down on my hands and knees like a dog and cautiously crawled up beneath the window.

I peered in on a living room furnished with crude chairs made of tree limbs. Sitting in two of them, staring at each other, were an old man and woman. In the light thrown off from the fireplace, I could see that he had the telltale blue tinge that suggested he was well on his way to becoming one of the ghastly hardened heroes. Here was a tableau of utter dullness. Obviously, she had not lied about the mental capacity of her parents. I scowled and crawled around to the side of the house.

I breathed a sigh of relief when I saw there was another window. Making my way up beneath it, I reached into my pocket and took out the derringer. I had resolved to shoot myself if she discovered me. It would have been a humiliation I could not have endured. From inside I could hear someone moving around, and then I heard the most unworldly noise, a strange crying sound. "Perhaps she is repentant for having treated me so shoddily," I thought. This gave me the courage to look.

To my utter astonishment, it was not she who was crying. It was, of all things, a baby. I watched, hypnotized, as she held the bawling runt in one arm and took down the top of her dress, revealing her naked breasts. I could not help it, but I sighed audibly. In spite of the hazardous situation I found myself in, I felt my manhood give a tiny nudge against my trousers.

At that moment, I heard a strange hissing noise behind me and turned quickly to look, adrenaline shooting through my system. I saw nothing at first. The noise came again, and I could make out that it was up high. In the lower branches of a huge tree approximately twenty yards behind me I detected a pair of yellow eyes glaring at me. I did not have time to wonder what it was, because as soon as I saw it, I noticed the huge batlike wings begin to move.

Now I thought nothing, cared for nothing, but stood straight up and began to run. I could hear the demon following above me, could feel the air it sent out from the beating of its wings. I dashed across the meadow, actually running like an athlete, with the monstrosity in close pursuit. Even with my terror to drive me on, I was quickly winded. I tripped and went sprawling in the snow. Hearing it hovering just above me, I turned on my back, raised the derringer, which was still in my hand, and fired. Through the residual smoke of the blast, I caught a vague glimpse of the creature as it quickly ascended. With that momentary, hazy glance, I could tell that old man Beaton had gotten the description right: a hairy, horned devil with cloven feet and a spiked tail—exactly as I remembered from the religious books I had collected as objects of ridicule during my student years.

When it was almost completely out of sight, I could barely make out that it had released something it had been carrying under one arm. "A boulder," I thought and began rolling over in the snow as fast as I could, there being no time to get up and run. The missile hit with a distinct noise, like a large melon squashing against the earth, only a foot or two to my left. When I was certain the demon had departed, I crawled over to it. On inspection, I found it was not a melon but, instead, the head of what I took to be poor Gustavus, Father Garland's missing dog.

I don't recall my walk back to the hotel. I was surprised no one had heard the gunshot and come to investigate. I do remember taking a large dose of the beauty and crawling beneath the covers. Of course, I left the lamps burning, for now the evil night had shown me the face of its minions. Sometime near morning I woke in a cold sweat, filled to brimming with a nauseating anger born of jealousy. "So," I said to my reflection in Arden's mirror, "not only has Arla lied to me, but she has already cheated on me." I spat out the word "impure." By dawn, the only regret I had was that I had apologized to her.

10

My miserable rooms at the Hotel de Skree were a veritable earthly paradise compared to the thought of what I would face at the church that morning. I would have preferred to wrestle a demon than go and meet Arla and pretend at cordiality, while all the time I knew that she knew I had, through the diseased magic of Anamasobia, been transformed into a fraud. "The slut could easily give me away in front of the whole rogue's gallery," I thought. Even if I were to make it through the day's proceedings without trouble, I had given up hope of ever solving the case, which meant that whatever tribulation and torture I would escape in the territory would later be heaped a hundredfold upon me by the Master.

Still, I got up, bathed, dressed as neatly as always, put my instruments in order, donned my coat, and went to work. It was lightly snowing by the time I left the hotel. Standing outside, dressed again in his absurd black hat, was the recurring nightmare of Mayor Bataldo, smiling as broadly as ever. After having run the scalpel over his testicles the day before, I now wondered what it would take to subdue his idiocy. For a moment, I pictured cutting it out of him, a large laughing black mass, like a comedic tumor on the brain.

"Your honor," he said, waving as though we were longtime friends who had not met in months.

I had run out of imprecations and could do no more than nod tersely.

"A splendid selection of our populace awaits your educated opinion," he said and took up walking next to me.

Then it struck me that if I could not shoot him, I might make some use of him. "Why was I never informed that the Beaton girl had a child?" I asked.

"An excellent question," he said and stopped to look bemusedly at the falling snow. "I suppose I never thought it was important."

"How is it she has a child and is not married?" I asked.

"Please your honor," he said with a laugh, "need I really explain to you, a man of science, how it happens?"

"No, you dolt. I mean, what was the situation?"

"Well, I believe she was in love with one of the young miners, a fellow by the name of Canan, who, after creating the situation, as you so delicately put it, was done in by another situation, namely a cave-in," he said.

"They were not married?" I asked.

"You have to understand something about Anamasobia," he said. "The rules of refined society are sometimes bent a little here and there, living as we do in such proximity to the ungodly, as I explained to you a few nights ago. I'm sure they would have eventually taken the vows."

"I see," I said. "Is the child male or female?"

"Male," he replied and we continued on our way toward the church.

"She is a promiscuous young woman," I said.

"Promiscuous in her mind, making love to many ideas, and always has been very rebellious."

"How can you allow such things to go on among your people?" I asked, stopping again.

"In the territory, such qualities are not always a detriment," he said. "She is a fine person, though, sometimes too serious for me."

"And who might I find who would not be?" I said, ending the conversation.

He laughed quietly all the way to the church.

Arla awaited me at the altar. I greeted her with an emotionless hello and she returned the salutation in the same curt manner. I laid out the instruments, and we began at once.

I wondered how life could be any more disappointing when, after sending Calloo for the first subject, he brought back with him Mrs. Mantakis. Not having the stomach to face her in the flesh, I told the old marsupial to leave her clothes on.

"But, your honor," said Arla, "do you not wish to inspect her biological possibilities?"

I lit a cigarette and said, "Very well," with as little reaction as possible. As Arla put her through her paces, having her assume all manner of horrid postures, I sat with my arms folded and stared like a man facing a wall. As she applied the callipers and other instruments, calling out the mathematics of her findings, I did not bother with the charade of the tiny notebook and pin, but simply nodded as if I were committing it all to memory. When Arla measured the earlobes, I believe I heard Mrs. Mantakis growl.

"A thief, for sure," Arla said to me after the old woman had dressed and left the church.

"A thief but not a liar," I thought to myself.

The morning wore on, a steady stream of the bereft, the congenitally damaged, geniuses of stupidity passed before my sight without leaving any impression but one of vague disgust. Arla, for her part, though I could palpably feel her hatred for me, worked methodically, keeping her snide remarks to a minimum.

I knew that eventually I would have to accuse someone of the crime if I wanted a chance to save my own skin. I knew also that the punishment for so serious an offense would be execution—the Master's new and efficient system of justice for any crime more serious than spitting on the sidewalks of the Well-Built City. "Who shall it be?" I asked myself with each subject that passed before me. Then Calloo brought in Father Garland, and I conceived of my plan of revenge against Anamasobia.

Arla was visibly upset by the presence of the little holy man. Her clear skin blushed a deep red as the father appeared before us, dressed for paradise. I took a quick glance to see if his shrunken penis came to a needle's sharpness like his teeth and nails. Imagine my surprise when my sight corroborated my suspicions. He said nothing but moved his hand in a sign of a religious blessing for us. I had so hoped that he would act up so that I could call Calloo and have him squashed. Arla's hands shook as she moved the instruments over his face and body. When she applied the Hadris lip vise, I almost told her to leave it on him as a good deed to all mankind.

After he was dressed and was preparing to leave us, he turned and said to me, "I have committed no crime but that of love."

"The charge is tedium," I said as he left, and I began working out in my mind how I would convince the town that he had stolen the fruit. I knew that a good measure of my scheme would need be lofty rhetoric, a commodity so exotic in Anamasobia it would convince by way of its novelty.

"Next!" I yelled and Calloo made for the door. I thought that I could work out my speech as we went through the next few dozen unfortunates.

But Arla called out, "Wait, Willin," to the giant. "Go wait outside for a moment and we will let you know when we want the next one."

"Do you need a break?" I asked flatly.

She sat down and looked at me as if she were about to cry. Seeing her in this state melted my anger at her somewhat. "She has seen her error," I thought, "and is about to apologize to me for last night."

"Is there something you wanted to tell me?" I asked, speaking like a schoolmaster to a favorite pupil who has done some minor wrong.

"It's him," she said.

"What are you talking about?" I asked, confused by her response.

"Father Garland. He is the one." Tears began to roll down her face.

"Are you sure?" I asked.

"I tell you, it's all there. It's as clear as was your face in my window last night," she said.

I remained silent. My guilt at being found out was canceled by my excitement at the thought that I might survive this nightmare. She then launched into a detailed explanation, using the logic of Physiognomy, which of course meant nothing to me but sounded mightily convincing.

"I wish it weren't so, but I can't deny what I read in his face." She wiped the tears from her eyes. "I hate you and this damn system," she said.

"Good work," I whispered. Then I bellowed for Calloo. When he appeared, I told him to get the mayor and to have him gather the citizens into the church.

The people of Anamasobia began filing into the church, filling the pews and then taking up positions in the shadows along the walls beneath the torches where the gallery of hardened heroes stood. There was a great hubbub of hushed conjecture punctuated occasionally by laughter or a loud proclamation of innocence uttered by those who naturally assumed guilt for everything.

The mayor came up onto the altar and shook my hand. He looked genuinely relieved that we had discovered the thief. "I offer my congratulations to your honor," he said. "I do not understand your methods, but they are obviously amazing."

I gratefully acknowledged his adulation and asked him to place one of his people at the door in case the suspect tried to escape. He motioned to Calloo to come to him, and then he whispered something in the big man's ear. Calloo made his way through the crowd to take up a position at the entrance to the altar chamber.

As Arla took down the screen and began putting my instruments neatly into my bag, I scanned the room in order to find Garland. I knew he must have been at least somewhat suspicious that we had called no one in after him. I found him easily enough, sitting in the front row, glaring up at me. I smiled at him and stared into his eyes for a good long time. When he did not avert his glance, I did, in order to look out at the crowd and call for silence. I clapped my hands as if calling a pet dog and the talking turned to whispers and then to silence.

Now that it was time for me to speak, I paced back and forth gathering my thoughts and turning them into the raw material of oration. The crowd watched my every move, and I felt powerful again for the first time in days. In a dramatic flare, designed to heighten the tension, I turned my back on them and stared up at the droll portrait of the miner god that hung behind the altar and for the past two days had born witness to the entire investigation. The idea came to me that I would start by relating my run-in with the demon, so that they might see me as a man of action as well as a superior intellect.

All the time I was strutting and posing, Arla had continued putting away the chrome tools. I wanted to wait until she was finished and had left the "stage" so that all attention could be focused on the revelation I was about to proclaim. She was almost done but for the callipers. When she went to lift them, they slipped out of her grasp and hit the floor with a sound that ricocheted off the cavernlike walls of the chamber. As she bent over to pick them up, her gray work dress hiked up an inch or two, and my eyes automatically traced the shapely lines of her legs from ankle to thigh. That is when I saw it.

There, on her left leg on the back of her thigh was a prominent mole with what appeared to be an inordinately long black hair growing from it. I blinked my eyes and took a step closer, forgetting that there was a crowd of people awaiting my determination. She must have heard me move, or perhaps she felt my eyes upon her—I was staring so intently—for she turned before straightening and looked up at me. In that very instant, with an audible popping sound in my mind like a cork being pulled from a bottle of champagne the knowledge of the Physiognomy returned to me completely. My eyes again teeming with their old intelligence, I saw immediately that she was no Star Five, as I had been somehow duped into believing by her youthful, feminine beauty, but that those features seen anew brought back Professor Flock's original profile of the criminal: a tendency toward larceny and a religio-psychotic reliance on the miraculous. I remembered why the child the woman had begged me to read in the street that day had later on seemed so familiar. He had many of the same facial features as I now perceived Arla to have. The woman had, in fact, been her.

I turned to the crowd and said, "Ladies and gentlemen of Anamasobia. We have in our midst a thief." I stepped back and pointed at Arla, who was now closing the clasp on my bag. "It is Arla Beaton who has stolen the miraculous fruit of paradise."

She turned and stared at me dumbfounded. Garland sprang from his seat and made a move toward the altar with his claws out. With all my regained confidence, I stepped gracefully forward and kicked him in the head before he could jump me. As he landed on the bottom step leading to the altar, I took the derringer out of my pocket and fired a warning shot into the ceiling. Splinters of wood fell on those in the first row of pews, and the near riot subsided back to near silence.

Arla sat down slowly in the chair I had used for the past two days and stared, as if in shock, out over the heaving sea of physiognomies.

The mayor stood up and begged everyone to be quiet.

Then he turned to me and said, "This is a serious offense, your honor. Can you please explain for those of us who do not comprehend the intricacies of your science. If I may say so, this comes as a great shock to us all." For once, he wasn't smiling.

I wanted nothing better than to explain. "It is accepted among the learned," I began, "as certainly as the sun comes up in the morning or that Drachton Below is our munificent Master, that the visible structure of our physical features, when analyzed by the well-trained eye, reveals one's moral aptitude in general and specifically exhibits the details of one's personal foibles and virtues. If you take a look at the subject . . ."

Here I approached Arla, who did not move a muscle but continued to stare as if dead. I ran my finger the length of her nose and then pointed to the small hollow just beneath her bottom lip. "In these features, I have just pointed to," I said, "we find a combination of intrinsic signs that disclose a personality prone to reckless action."

I moved around her to the other side and pointed to the arch of her eyebrow. "Here we see an effect known to my colleagues and me as the 'Scheffler conclusion,' named, of course, for one of the fathers of the Physiognomy, Kurst Scheffler. What this effect denotes is, amazingly, both a tendency toward thievery and a desire to participate in miraculous events. There is also a mole on the left thigh, with a long hair growing from it, that nails shut this case once and for all." I stepped forward and brushed my hands together as if wiping the taint of crime from them.

By the number of open, expressionless mouths in the audience, I could tell that I had made my point. I bowed and applause broke out in the pews and along the walls. Father Garland had just then come to and was crawling back to his seat when the first cries of "death to the thief," were heard to echo through the hollow heart of the wooden Gronus.

11

"And what now?" asked the mayor.

We stood outside the church as evening fell. The stars and moon were beginning to appear, and the snow had stopped falling sometime in the day. The crowd had gone home, many of whom had thanked me personally for having apprehended the criminal. From the words of appreciation, I got the feeling that these simple people had, for their own reasons, always harbored a certain fear of this girl. As for Arla, she had been taken away to the one cell in Anamasobia—a small, windowless locked room in the town hall.

"I suppose justice must be served," I said.

"If you'll beg my pardon, your honor, you may have found the criminal, but the white fruit is still missing. How are we going to retrieve that if I have the girl executed?" he asked.

"Interrogate the prisoner," I said. "You must be aware that there are methods for making people talk. Search that hovel she lives in. My belief is that she probably fed part of it to her bastard child in order to offset its obvious physiognomical deficiencies."

He nodded sadly, which took me by surprise.

"Nothing to laugh at, Mayor?" I asked.

"Torture is not my strong suit," he said. "For that matter, neither is execution. Is there no other way to go about this? Couldn't she, perhaps, just apologize?"

"Really, now," I said, "the Master would not perceive such leniency with a kind eye. With that course of action, you might jeopardize the entire town's very existence."

"I see," he said. "It's just that I've known this girl from when she was a child. I knew her grandfather. I know her parents. I saw her grow up, and she was such a sweet, inquisitive little thing." He looked into my eyes, and I could tell he was on the verge of tears.

Although I met his gaze with complete silence, his words about Arla forced me to remember those things about her that had, for the past days, kept her constantly on my mind. I was now certain that it had not, after all, been the Traveler who had blinded my perception, but instead it was Arla's own special beauty and intelligence that had bewitched me.

The mayor, getting no reply from me, began walking away, and, with this, I experienced an unfathomable emotion, almost like sadness. I wasn't sure if it was because I also could not bear the thought of Arla's execution, or if it was that, although I had my thief, little had truly been resolved.

"Wait," I told him.

He stopped but remained with his back to me.

"There is something I might try."

He turned and came slowly back to stand before me.

"It is an experimental procedure that I am not sure will work," I told him. "I wrote a paper on it a few years ago, but it was not favorably acknowledged by my colleagues, and the idea died out after a few weeks of heated debate."

"Well?" he said as I searched my mind for the particulars of the theory. When I hit upon it, it seemed rather daring if not reckless, but in light of my newly regained powers, and the feeling of great inner strength their rediscovery gave rise to, I began to think that this case might be the perfect opportunity to test this untried method.

"Listen closely," I said to him. "If the physical features of the girl's face are an indication of the character traits she harbors deep within, then does it not make sense that if I were to rearrange those features with my scalpel, creating a structure that would indicate a more morally perfect inner state, would she not then be re-formed from the congenital criminal malaise, resulting in the willingness to reveal the location of the fruit and rendering her no longer in need of execution?''

Bataldo rolled his eyes and took a step back. ''If I am understanding you,'' he said, ''you are saying you can make her good by performing surgery on her?''

''Perhaps,'' I said.

''Then do it,'' he said, and like the lion lying down with the lamb, we each smiled for different reasons.

I made arrangements with the mayor to have her brought to my study at the hotel the next morning promptly at nine. He then asked me if I would join him for dinner at the tavern, but I declined, knowing that there was much preparation to be done if I was going to rescue her from herself.

For the first time since I arrived at Anamasobia, I truly felt at ease. On the way back to my quarters people greeted me with the deference befitting my station. Even Mrs. Mantakis, seeing me enter the lobby of the hotel, addressed me with a certain air of subservience that had obviously been lacking heretofore. I told her to send away all visitors and to bring me some of that blue wine and a light dinner. She told me she had prepared something special for me that evening that had nothing to do with cremat, and I couldn't believe myself that I actually thanked her. She purred like a cat at my grateful response.

Had I still been in the thick of the mystery, I would have been alarmed to see how little of the beauty I still had in my valise—only enough for three or four real doses, but with my new self-assurance that the case would be completely resolved by sometime the next evening, I took a full vial without a second thought.

Then I undressed, put on my robe and slippers, and had a cigarette. True to my old form, I was able, with the enhanced power of the drug, to readily envision Arla's face and the changes that would have to be made to it in order to save her life. I quickly got pen and paper and began sketching my vision of the new Arla.

It must have been hours after Mrs. Manktakis had delivered my dinner and wine that I finally finished making my plans. By now the town was perfectly quiet, a condition, after having come from the City, that I could never really get used to. The sheer beauty was still active in my system, bringing me intermittent visions of splendor. Not one paranoic image found its way into my head as I worked, but occasionally I would daydream vividly about my idyllic childhood on the banks of the Chottle River.

Finally I sat down on the bed to consider the fame this next day's procedure would bring me if it was successful, and that is when Professor Flock made his appearance.

"You again," I said.

"Who else?" he asked, now dressed in his teaching uniform and toting the dress cane with an ivory monkey-head handle it had been his practice to carry at official events.

"You're a traitor," I said to him.

"Did I not suggest the appropriate method with which to apprehend the criminal?" he asked, smiling.

"That you did, but I'm done with you. I'm going to banish you from my mind," I told him.

"That may be a little difficult since I am really you talking to yourself in a drug-induced haze," he said. "I can only say and do, can only be, what you desire."

"Well, what do you think of my plans for tomorrow?" I asked.

"Be certain that you cut some of the intelligence out of the poor girl; she's too smart for her own good. And, by all means, let's have a cut in the center of the chin to ward off those delusions that there is anything in store for her but the meanest existence here in this shit village at the end of the world. The rest of it seems quite good. I don't think I could have done better myself," he said, tapping the cane on the floor.

"Very well," I said, "I can't argue with that."

"My real reason for coming tonight is to bid you farewell. I don't think I will be seeing you again," he said. Then he held the cane up and out toward me, and the ivory monkey head came magically to life, screaming in its small voice, "I am not a monkey. I am not a monkey." As always, Flock left his laughter behind, and I bid him good riddance.

That night I fell into a deep sleep from which I struggled to escape. I revisited again my childhood, but this time what came to me were only the scenes of my father's unbridled anger and the resultant early death of my mother. I woke at sunrise, crying into my pillow as I had done so many nights of my early life. What a relief I felt when I finally opened my eyes and realized I was free of it.

After I bathed, ate a light breakfast, and dressed, the mayor and two of his miner thugs escorted Arla to my study. I greeted her cordially, but she said nothing and would not make eye contact with me. I had prepared the lab table with straps in order to hold her down in case she became unruly.

"I pray you are successful, Cley," said the mayor, a note of skepticism in his voice.

I stepped up to Arla and looked directly in her face. "I will do for you what I can, my dear," I said.

She looked now directly at me and spit in my eyes. I took a step backward and at this instant she brought her knee up into the crotch of one of her detainers. With the suddenness of it all, she was able to break free, and she bolted from the room across the hall into my living quarters with the other miner in hot pursuit. She almost got the door closed, but the man was, of course, stronger and was able to pry it open before she could lock it. We all followed immediately.

When I came into the room, she was wielding the knife that had come with the breakfast service and swinging my valise at the fellow who had managed to corner her. "Murderers," she was yelling. The mayor made a move for her, and she heaved the valise at him, hitting him square in the head. It was finally the miner whom she had kneed in the groin who was able to jump in after one of her lunges with the knife and subdue her. They dragged her next door, kicking and yelling for help. Quickly I prepared a rag with a strong general anesthetic and buried her screaming face with it.

The miners were helping me strap her to the table when the mayor appeared, rubbing his head. "Feisty," he said with a laugh, but I could see the ordeal had shaken him.

"Don't worry," I told him. "I'll cut that out of her, along with quite a bit more. By the time she awakens, she will be a new woman."

"Anamasobia was never so strange," said the mayor, staring at the floor.

Then I told them to leave and come back the next afternoon.

I put pads beneath her head in order to catch the blood that would result from my cuts, and then fitted her with a headband that had a long piece of cotton attached to it that could be flipped back over her skull while I worked and then brought down over the face in order to mop up the gore that might obscure the area of flesh I intended for incision. With this completed, I methodically laid out my scalpels and picks and clamps, and then brought out the drawing of the new Arla. Through the night, as I had worked on it under the gaze of the beauty, that picture had spoken words of love to me. I was determined for it to become more than an illusion.

The scalpel ploughed smoothly through the skin of her left cheek, and with this first pass, I could feel nothing but the ultimate success of the experiment. I whistled a tune that was popular in the Well-Built City just prior to my departure, a sweet ditty about endless devotion, as I leveled her willful lower lip. "There goes that vain intelligence," I whispered to her sleeping form while scoring the upper lids of her eyes. I relieved her nose of a weight of cartilage that I knew was at the root of her troublesome curiosity. There was no other choice with those haughty cheekbones but to employ the chrome mallet. My concentration became so intense that all I could see was her face, and it became like the topography of some untamed country that I manipulated from above with artistic finesse and a transcendent vision of perfection. It was all a matter of subtraction, and for a time I wished that the sublime mathematics would never end.

I had worked diligently through the morning and well into the afternoon, taking no break for lunch, when I began to lose my way. The map I carried in my head of where I wanted to end up, began to lose its clarity. My self-assurance flickered in and out like a flame in the wind. It was the telltale itching of my skull that let me know I was in need of the beauty. I reasoned that with the drug to bolster my innate genius, I could easily finish the job successfully by dinnertime. Besides, I could not go on without it, because the chills were beginning to run through me, making my sight wobble and my hands shake. I set down the scalpel and went next door for a fix.

I found my valise on the floor where it had landed after making contact with the mayor's head. The thought of that actually brought a smile to my lips as I opened it. I pulled out an unused vial, and to my horror found that it was cracked and empty. Frantically, I pulled out another and found it in the same condition. Then I noticed that there was a violet puddle on the floor. All of the vials were broken. I was without sheer beauty, and the pains of withdrawal were breaking out all over my body like the blows of an invisible enemy. I groaned, but my mind screamed and then dove straight down into a turbulent ocean of confusion and fear. The only thing that kept me from passing out was the thought that I could not leave Arla in the state she was. If I were to fail to retrieve the fruit, it would surely mean my life.

I staggered across the hall, determined to finish the job before I lost all my senses. My mind was already reeling so terribly I could barely stay on my feet. I held myself up with one hand resting on the lab table and with the other I lifted the scalpel and tried to concentrate amid the quaking of my internal organs. The first shivering cut I made I knew was wrong, but there was no erasing here. I pushed on in an attempt to make another cut that would offset the one I had just made. This became a trap, and I pictured myself running headlong, deeper and deeper into a labyrinth from which there was no possible escape. My earlier precise incisions now became a desperate slashing, and the blood flowed freely, sometimes spurting across my shirt. Droplets of it momentarily blinded me. They landed on my lips, and the taste of it brought me to my knees. I struggled back to my feet, fighting off the flashes of blankness that turned my mind into a ball of night.

I continued like this, basically unconscious for some time, before, far off at a great distance, I heard myself scream in agony. Then I fell through the nausea, the freezing and burning of the chills, the tearing of my brain, the silence of my heart to a place I supposed was death but unfortunately wasn't.

12

 I got an urgent message from the mayor that there was one more person I should definitely read before making my ultimate decision. "At this time of night?" I said to Mantakis, who was carrying his feather duster.

I put on my topcoat and took my bag of instruments. It was again snowing hard outside, and I only made the slowest headway down the street in the face of the fierce gales. The children had been out in the storm, I could tell, because the street was lined along both sides with frozen effigies of the Traveler. They appeared every now and then from behind the driving blizzard, staring down with cold eyes like a gauntlet of righteous judges. I trudged along for what seemed an eternity through the murmuring, twirling dark, and then suddenly I had arrived.

I knew I was going to trip and fall on the bottom step leading to the church and I did. Opening the big, crooked door that creaked with sounds of mirth, I entered. I took it slowly over the bridge, which seemed more unsteady than ever. In the altar chamber, only half the torches were lit. "Hello," I called, but there was no answer. The screen had again been set up, and the chairs we had used for the reading were sitting in the same positions.

"Hello," I called. In the dim light of the torches, the arms and faces of the hardened heroes appeared now to be flesh instead of stone. Either the wind outside or the echo of my own breath created a faint sound of breathing as if the church itself had life. The eyes of the painted God stared down on me.

From behind the screen came the sound of someone coughing.

"Hello there," I said. "Why didn't you answer?"

I set down my bag, took my coat off, and went to view the subject. As I stepped behind the screen, the torches blew out, bringing instant night. In a panic, I took a step forward. I felt two hands grab my wrists and pull me in. My hands were placed on a face and were made to glide over the features. At first it was all too unusual, but I felt the owner of the hands would do me no harm. Then the Physiognomy took over—math turning numbers to images in a most brilliant display of color in my mind. My body began to vibrate with energy as if I had become a machine.

Suddenly, the torches rekindled, shedding their blurred light. I found myself with my arms out, my hands manipulating thin air. This angered me greatly. In a fury, I put my coat on and grabbed my bag. Back out into the storm I went, muttering invectives at Anamasobia as I stumbled through another eternity.

I woke all too suddenly from the dream and could tell it was early the next morning by the bright light that streamed in through the window. I was shaky and nauseous and had a headache that nearly blinded me. Still, from where I sat in the chair by the small table Arla and I had shared dinner at a few nights ago, I could see her form. The cotton cloth that was attached to her head, now reddish brown with dried blood, was draped over her face. I could detect, by the gentle movement of her chest that she was still alive. I wanted to get up and see what I had done to her, but I was still too weak to move.

At first, I thought that it was all in my mind. Then I realized that the screaming voices I heard were not coming from the Mantakises but from out in the street. There was a great commotion going on somewhere, and if I was not mistaken there was the sound of either gunshots or fireworks. My first inclination was to think that perhaps the town was celebrating in their belief that the white fruit would soon be restored to the altar of the church. I wondered through the fog of my illness if perhaps I might not have been successful and that everything still might work out well, when I heard the sound of footsteps on the stairs leading to my rooms.

I had no time to try to get up before the door to my study burst open. It was Garland.

"My god, what have you done?" he said, seeing Arla laid out on the table, her head surrounded by the bloody pads.

I reached into the pocket of my trousers for the derringer, but then remembered that I had left it in my topcoat the day before. I was about to yell at him to get out, when another figure appeared in the doorway. I thought it might be Calloo, judging from the size of him, but then my eyes focused and I saw the Traveler bending his head down in order to pass through the opening. What made the scene even more fantastic was that the thin, brown creature carried in one arm a baby swaddled in blankets.

"What kind of a circus act is this?" I asked, trying to sound powerful from within the cloud bank of withdrawal.

Garland walked over to stand before me, but I paid no attention to him. My eyes were on the Traveler, the way he moved, his long braided hair, the unearthly look of calm on his face.

"Your Master, the great Drachton Below, is here in Anamasobia," said the father.

"What?" I said. Now Garland had my full attention.

"Oh yes," he said. "His soldiers are systematically murdering everyone. He has with him some wolfen creature that has torn the throats out of women and children. Hell has come to the territory."

"But how does this thing live?" I asked, pointing to the Traveler, who smiled gently at me.

"The fruit. I fed him one single bite of the fruit weeks ago when I first took it from the altar. Since then he has been recovering slowly. When you applied your ridiculous instruments to him, he was already well on his way back to life."

"So, Arla was right," I said. "The Physiognomy was right."

"When I ran at the altar and you kicked me, I was trying to confess, to spare her the consequences of having foolishly become involved with you. I can't waste my time on you," he said. "We are taking the girl and heading for Wenau. You, on the other hand, must go down and take your bullet. You're a vain, stupid, man, Cley. I would have killed you myself, but I think it more appropriate that your Master do it for me."

Everything was moving too fast for me to protest or even get out of the chair, and the sight of the Traveler paralyzed me with a fear, not for my safety but that the world could be so absolutely strange. They walked over, one on each side of the lab table. The baby began to cry and the Traveler softly touched the child's forehead, quieting it.

"Let's see what horror your nonsense has created," said the father. He reached out and lifted the cotton veil that covered Arla's face. The Traveler automatically brought up one of his huge hands to shield his sight as if the girl's visage were a blinding beacon. Garland was not so quick. Taking the invisible blast full in the face, it snapped his head back. He fell to the floor, and with a groan, expired, blood trickling from his nose and the corner of his gaping mouth. The holy man's face was transfixed with a look of absolute horror I had to turn away from.

With his free hand, the Traveler reached into a small pouch he wore around his waist and took out the white fruit. He gracefully brought it to his mouth and took a bite. Then he put the fruit away, took the piece from his mouth, and forced it between Arla's lips, all without casting a glance at her. Instead, he looked into my own eyes and told me silently but as clearly as if he were speaking that what I had wrought through my work was the very face of Death.

I cringed in my chair like a child, unable to look away from him. Then, I don't know where he found the strength in his willowy frame, but after replacing the cotton veil over her face he lifted her with one arm and slung her over his shoulder. Now carrying the baby in one arm and with Arla's form draped over him, he walked lightly to the window. There, he lifted one of his enormous feet and kicked the glass out with two well-placed blows. I could hear the shards breaking against the wooden sidewalk four stories below. With his passengers still secure in his grasp, he stepped up onto the windowsill and crouched so that his height fit into the opening.

"No," I said, knowing what he was about to do.

He turned his face to me and smiled.

I jumped out of my chair in order to try to stop him, my head pounding and my intestines tightening like a fist. I took three steps and then fell over the body of Garland. On my way to the floor, I watched them fall. I listened but did not hear anything hit the ground. With all my strength, I scrabbled to my feet and made my way to the window. Looking straight down, I expected to see them all sprawled like broken dolls on the walk. Instead, I saw nothing. They had vanished.

The fact that the ugliness I had projected onto Arla's face had killed Garland was too much for me to accept. I knew, even through the dizziness, as I staggered to the lab table and vomited, that he had been right and that, at this point, the Master would kill me as if I were just one more piece of human trash from the territory. My only chance was to try to make it out of town and hide in the surrounding forest. This seemed rather unlikely, considering the condition I was in. I had a feeling that it was over, the end of the line. I wanted to cry, seeing how far I had fallen in one short week. He was right: I was a vain and stupid man. One cannot serve a monster and expect not to be devoured someday. As I straightened up and cleaned myself off, my first thought was that worse than death would be my being sent to the sulphur mines. If I was to be brought back to the Well-Built City for trial, I would have to find a way to commit suicide.

I left the room and staggered down the stairs to the lobby. There, lying in the middle of the floor, beneath the broken-down chandelier, were Mr. and Mrs. Mantakis, dead in each other's arms. A pool of their commingled blood spread out around them. It looked as if they each had been shot no less than twenty times. I stepped past them and could not believe that I felt a pang of remorse. Unbelievably, actual tears were welling in my eyes. I ran past them and pushed through the front door, knowing that the gruesome tableau I fled was a fraction of what Garland had seen in Arla's face.

Outside, the morning sun blinded me for a few moments as I tottered down the street, reeling from the aching of my head and joints. The continuing pains of withdrawal were enough to make a bullet seem welcome. As my vision cleared, I saw bodies strewn everywhere in the street, fresh blood turning the fallen snow a deep red. Up by the church, I could make out the uniformed soldiers of the city. Gunshots sounded, and those without uniforms fell face first in a race to the ground. Flames billowed from the tops of buildings, devouring gray wood, and thick smoke spewed forth from the broken windows of the bank.

"Cley," I heard a familiar voice yell. I turned and saw the Master standing a hundred yards away. He was dressed in furs and wore a broad smile. Greta Sykes strained at a golden leash he held tightly. He waved to me. "It's been nice working with you," he called over the din of the mayhem. I saw him crouch down then, and he appeared to be whispering something in the werewolf's ear. Even from the considerable distance that separated us, I could see she looked exactly as she had in that vision or dream in which I had met them in the mines of Gronus. Then he unhooked her collar and she was dashing toward me.

I turned and tried to run, but at that very moment the coach and four came charging out from the alley between the bank and the theater. I lost all my will to live, knowing I was trapped. The breath left me in one great torrent as I prepared myself for the sharp fangs and long-suppressed revenge of Greta Sykes.

"Cley," I then heard another familiar voice call. I looked up and saw that the driver of the coach was not the Master's porcine henchman as I had expected but instead Bataldo. I thought I was going to be crushed beneath the horses' hooves and the wheels, but at the last moment, they swerved to my left and came to an abrupt stop. "Get in," said the mayor.

For a second, I could not move. When I did, it was to turn and see the werewolf push off the ground fifteen yards away, springing directly at my throat. The door of the coach opened and out stepped Calloo. He strode over and grabbed me with one hand, pulling me back out of the way. Then turning with a grace and precision I would not believe him capable of, he made a fist and drove it into the side of Greta Sykes' head, burying one of her metal bolts deep beneath the skull. She shorted out on the ground before my eyes, jerking, sparking, spewing yellow liquid as he dragged me to the coach and threw me inside. The door closed with a bang and the horses responded. We flew past the sound of whizzing bullets, children screaming, the Master laughing eternally deep behind my eyes.

13

We stopped briefly at the mayor's house to collect guns, ammunition, and warm coats and blankets. Calloo staved in the wooden wheels of the coach and turned the horses loose. He told me that it was held to be true that the demons of the wilderness had a special appetite for the flesh of domesticated animals, and the smell of the beasts would attract them like a magnet. Bataldo could not stop crying as he ran from room to room, setting the drapes and shelves of books, the bedding and the furniture on fire.

Outside, we stood for a moment at the boundary of the woods and watched the smoke pour from the open windows. The mayor told Calloo and me that he had watched as Drachton Below's werewolf ripped out and devoured his wife's intestines on the main street of Anamasobia.

"Why did you save me?" I asked as he wiped his eyes clear.

"It doesn't matter what we were, Cley. I was no innocent; none of us were. We will head for paradise. There is no room for hatred there."

Calloo simply nodded and then rested one of his huge hands on Bataldo's back as much to hurry him along as to comfort him.

We set out into that vast forest that the members of old man Beaton's expedition had referred to as the Beyond. I was still nauseous and aching from withdrawal, but I ran on and on, determined not to slow the others down, pacing myself a few yards behind Calloo, who seemed tireless. It felt good to run amid the tall barren trees, over the hardened snow. I felt like a child running away from my guilt. I did not care if I froze to death, if I was rent to pieces by demons, if I was caught and killed by the Master's troops. Had it not been for the elusive promise of Wenau, I probably would have sat down where I was and waited for Greta Sykes.

After running for an hour, the mayor collapsed on the snow, heaving for breath. We decided to stop and give him a few minutes rest. I could not have gone on much longer myself. From our position on top of a wooded hill, we could look back and see smoke from Anamasobia rising high into the air. Even as far away as we were, I noticed that a flurry of fine, black ash was falling around us.

In the valley we had recently traversed, we could see the troops in pursuit. Some carried rifles and some the special flamethrowers that had been invented by Drachton Below. He himself rode in another of his inventions, an automated, gear-work carriage with a small compartment for two riders and eight articulated legs like a spider's, that carried him over rocks and fallen trees. I pointed out to Calloo a soldier holding a leash attached to the straining neck of Greta Sykes. Although I was astonished at the speed of her recovery, the big man just shrugged and spat. Then the two of us went and helped Bataldo to his feet and offered words of encouragement.

"Leave me behind," said the mayor. "I can see I will only hold you two back." His face was flushed and his formal, raccoon coat was ripped here and there and covered with all manner of twigs and burrs.

Hearing this, Calloo walked up behind the mayor and kicked him hard in the rear end. Bataldo jumped and then the two of them broke out laughing. I had no idea what I was laughing at, but I joined them.

"All right," said the mayor, and we crested the hill and started down the other side. We no longer ran, for fear that Bataldo would give up, but we walked quickly, heading due north, pushing ever deeper into the Beyond. Each mile of forest we traversed held natural wonders never before seen by civilized man, but we could not slow to inspect any of them.

There were certain trees whose barren branches moved like arms, swiping at the birds that flew just out of their grasp. A species of diminutive deer, the very color of grass, moved in small herds off in the distance. We saw them through the trees, and when they saw us they ran away, emitting the cries of a woman with her hair on fire. Small red lizards with wings flitted from tree to tree like dragonflies, and the songs of birds we could not see, for they flew too high, were hauntingly human. We witnessed all this in utter silence until we came to a brook where Calloo said we could rest for a minute. Then the mayor wondered aloud if we might not really have died back in Anamasobia and were wandering in the next world.

I was leaning over, taking a drink of water to ease my burning throat, when the demons came swooping down from the trees and burst out of snowbanks we had never suspected. The mayor was the first to draw his gun and shoot. He hit nothing, but the explosion frightened our attackers, and both the ones on the ground and the ones circling above flew up to the highest of the tall trees. They peered down at us, hissing and dropping branches they had torn from their perches.

Calloo lifted the rifle he was carrying, took aim, and shot one of them. Its scream was like nothing I had ever heard. The piercing nature of it tore a hole in reality as the creature plummeted to the ground. There it writhed, its barbed tail slapping the snow. We did not wait to see more but started running as fast as we could. I bounded over the brook with an agility I did not know I possessed. Calloo made it over easily, but the mayor fell into the water, having twisted his ankle when leaping from the bank. By the time we could turn back to help him, two of the creatures had him by the arms and were lifting him toward the treetops. Even as they flew, one of them had sunk its fangs in Bataldo's cheek.

Calloo reloaded in seconds, put the gun to his shoulder, and fired. He hit one of the demons in the back. The shot wasn't good enough to kill it, but it arched its spine as it screamed, releasing Bataldo's face from its jaws and letting go of him. The other demon could not support the mayor's great weight by itself and dropped him. He fell kicking and screaming from a height of twenty yards, hitting the ground stomach first. I heaved a sigh of relief when he got immediately to his feet and began hobbling toward us. He wore an expression of complete terror and his right hand was thrust forward as if leading him. No less than a dozen of the creatures left their perches.

"Run," Calloo said to me, but I didn't. I watched as he feverishly loaded the gun. He took careful aim, but not at the descending monsters. The shot hit the mayor in the forehead and blood blossomed from the dark hole just as the first set of claws grasped at his collar.

We were off through the woods like a pair of creatures ourselves. For the longest time, I swore I heard demon wings beating above me. At any second I expected to feel a claw as hard as stone crack my head like an egg. Finally Calloo called to me that we had lost them, and I was able to stop and see there hadn't been anything at all behind me. We slowed our pace to a walk and went on till nightfall like that, never speaking.

Although Calloo knew how it was done, we did not dare to light a fire to warm ourselves. We found a spot in a thicket of trees that had grown above into an odd tangle that offered some insurance against attacks from the air. Calloo told me I should sleep first and that he would stand guard. As I lay down on the cold snow, wrapping one of the blankets we had carried around me, he began cleaning the rifle that had saved our lives. The noises of the wilderness, the weird mating calls and death screams, frightened me—but not enough to keep me awake. I fell instantly into a hard sleep.

Of course, I dreamt of Arla. Her face was clear of the ravages of my physiognomical quackery. We were in the wilderness, standing on a mountainside, gazing across a gorge at a tall craggy peak, at the top of which was a plateau where grew a resplendent garden that glowed brightly with golden light.

"Look," she said, pointing, "we are almost there."

"Let's hurry," I said.

"Once we arrive, I will be able to forgive you," she said.

Then we ran hand in hand down the mountain toward the mile-long rope bridge that reached across to paradise.

I woke suddenly to what I thought was the brightness of early morning but soon learned, after rubbing my eyes, that our thicket was ablaze with torchlight. I heard whispered voices and sat up slowly to see where they were coming from. As I moved, I felt the barrel of a gun press into my back. Across the clearing at the center of the thicket I saw Calloo, gagged, with his hands bound behind him and a rope tightened around his neck. Two of the Master's uniformed soldiers were leading him away.

"Get up," said a voice behind me. Once standing, I was made to put my hands behind my head. The soldier kept the gun pressed into my back as we followed the torchlight of those surrounding Calloo.

We stumbled through the night for a half hour before coming upon their camp. It was well lit by torches everywhere fixed to the trees. The Master stood before a large fire heaped high with kindling, warming his hands. Off to his left there was a metal cage containing a live demon. The thing hissed and barked and rammed its horns against the bars. The gear-work cart stood off to the right of a large tent. There must have been a hundred soldiers milling about and another fifty on the perimeter, standing guard with flamethrowers.

I was led to the Master, who sighed and said, "Cley, you are the embodiment of disappointment. It nearly breaks my heart to think of it. What do you have to say for yourself?"

"Kill me," I said.

"Sorry," he said, wrapping the cape he wore around him and shivering. "This territory is as bleak as your future, Physiognomist, First Class. You are going back to the City to face trial. Try to remember the frozen air here; it will be a pleasant respite from the heat of the sulphur mines."

Later, I was forced to watch as he turned Greta Sykes loose on the bound and gagged Calloo. The troops stood around them in a circle, cheering and laughing as the big man kicked at the nimble wolf girl. She took chunks of flesh out of both his legs before he toppled and she pounced on his chest. The metal bolts sparked as her snout burrowed down, shredding skin and cracking bone, to get to his heart. Every time I tried to close my eyes the Master would slap my face and make me watch. The gag prevented Calloo from screaming, so I screamed for him. Each time I bellowed, the Master would join me.

He had me ride along with him in the gear-work cart. We made our way out of the woods and were passing the charred remains of Anamasobia as the sun began to rise in the east. Our vehicle was surrounded on all sides by uniformed soldiers who marched in double time to keep up with its mechanical pace. Behind us rolled a wagon with at least three cages on it.

"Too bad you failed, Cley. It was a shame to have had to wipe out that town. Now I'm going to have to recruit new miners to work Gronus. I will mention at your trial that the increased heating costs this winter can be directly attributed to you."

I said nothing.

"Look here," he said, steering the cart with one hand. With the other he reached inside his cape and brought forth the white fruit. There were two distinct bite marks in it, but the rest of it was completely intact. The instant he brought it out, I could smell its sweet perfume.

"Where did you get that?" I asked, fearing what his answer might be.

"We had them before they even left the town," he said. "The girl and her baby and that big brown fellow."

"Are they alive?" I asked.

"Oh, I'm keeping all of them," he said. "The girl is worth her weight in gold with that face you gave her. Simply by staring at them, she took down ten of my best men before reinforcements could get a bag over her head. The Traveler, as I believe he is called, came peacefully when he saw that we had the girl. Him, I think I will put on display in one of the malls and charge two belows apiece for anyone who wants a look."

"What do you intend to do with the fruit?" I asked.

"First, I'm going to have it studied, and if it's free of poison and exhibits some proof for the outlandish claims made for it, I'm going to eat it to the core and plant the seeds." He put it away inside his cape and then took out his cigarette case. "Have one," he said and I did.

Pressing a button on the console, the glass canopy opened back and we rode along, smoking, in the fresh cold air of the territory. We continued on without conversation for a while, the Master whistling and I contemplating my fate in the sulphur mines. Then he suddenly reached back into his cape and brought forth a portfolio stuffed with papers.

"A little something for you, Cley," he said. "Let's say, a going-away present." He handed it over to me.

"What is this?" I asked.

"It was meant for you, but I hope you don't mind that I took a few minutes to peruse it. I nearly split a gut reading that thing," he said, smiling.

I took out the first page and saw that it was written in Arla's beautiful, rapid style. *Dear Physiognomist Cley,* it began. I soon realized that it was the notes she had assiduously been keeping on what she could remember having been told by her grandfather about the expedition. She had titled it *Fragments from the Impossible Journey to the Earthly Paradise.*

My trial took a week, there being fourteen physiognomists assigned to the case. Some of them had been my students and some my colleagues, but they all came forth to convince the public that I had somehow been marred by my experience in the territory. They all attested to the fact that my physiognomy had mutated into a symbolic representation of evil, which, of course, indicated that my personality was now irreparably ruined. The crowds in the Well-Built City called for my blood. I was to be executed by having my head inflated with an inert gas of the Master's discovery, resulting in its bursting like a grape.

At the scene of my execution, Drachton Below stepped in and commuted my sentence. Instead of being executed, I was to be sent to the sulphur mines on the island of Doralice in the southern latitudes of the realm.

14

I arrived at Doralice in the middle of the night, empty in both heart and head. As far as the official business of the realm was concerned, I was already deceased. My suffering in the sulphur mines was merely a formality that must run its course through the lethargic bureaucracy of torture. There was no moon, no starlight that night, so I couldn't make out any of the features of the island as we approached. I could tell from the pitching of the small ferry carrying myself and four guards that the seas surrounding my new home were angry. My keepers joked about how I would slowly, over a period of months, bake to a fine crisp and then suddenly begin to smolder, my body parts turning to salt and blowing away on the island winds.

We entered a small stone harbor that dimly glowed with torchlight. There was no welcoming committee, no soldiers to receive me. The guards helped me up onto the wharf and threw my meager bag of belongings up next to me. I was left standing there handcuffed.

"There will be someone along to get you shortly," said one of the men as the boat pulled out into the channel. "I hope you have a fondness for the smell of shit."

"He looks the type," said another as they drifted slowly away from me, waving and laughing.

I stood there on the dock that had been cut from limestone. A wind blew off the ocean and I breathed deeply to see if I could detect even the slightest molecule of the fruit of paradise. As I suspected, the place was devoid of hope.

Back in the Well-Built City, while I awaited trial in my jail cell, I had used up my prodigious reserves of self-pity, crying and discussing aloud with myself how I had been wronged and how it had led me to a state of ignorance in which I had wronged others. Now I was washed up on the shores of hell with no will left—"a blob of flesh," as I would so aptly have put it in my previous life.

I waited for ten minutes and still no one came to take me to my cell. For a moment, I entertained the idea of trying to escape but then realized that there was nowhere to go. The waters surrounding the island—I had been told by one of the guards who had brought me—were teeming with shark and kraken, and the uninhabited parts of Doralice were home to a ravenous breed of wild dog. Both possible fates seemed more appealing than the mines, but along with my loss of self had come a sense of fatalism that eschewed action.

At that moment, I heard footsteps approaching along the dock. I looked up and saw a man with shoulder-length white hair, wearing an old military coat, the left breast covered with medals and pins. He drew closer and my first inclination was to apply the Physiognomy to him. I fought that urge and simply saw a face of folds and pouches, the eyes sunken, the nose a testament to voluminous drinking. Although he carried a drawn saber in his left hand, he did not seem at all threatening. Instead, there was a certain weariness about him.

He smiled as he approached and offered his hand to shake, but then realized I was handcuffed and said, "Good thinking." He sheathed his sword and told me to turn around. I did as he said. Then he approached behind me, and I could feel that he was releasing my wrists.

"Good enough," he said as he pocketed the key and cuffs.

By the way he spoke, I did not think he would mind my turning back around. When I stood looking at him, he put his hand up and we shook.

"Corporal Matters," he said. "I am the corporal of the night watch."

I nodded.

"You are Cley," he said. "I suppose you can see now what a lot of rubbish that Physiognomy nonsense is?" He waited for a reply, but I remained silent. "Welcome to Doralice," he said with a tired laugh. "Follow me." He brandished his sword, and I followed him off the dock. We took a sandy path that led us through a thicket of stunted pine trees which reminded me of the Beyond.

"Excuse the sword," he called back to me over his shoulder, "but every once in a while one of those execrable wild dogs will be waiting for me here in the dark. Don't worry—I've gashed my share. Besides, they are usually at the other end of the island this time of year."

We continued on, clearing the pines, and then wound through a maze of enormous dunes. Beyond that, we came to a white beach where the ocean broke. We kept to the shore for about a mile and then walked up the beach, through another maze of dunes, at the center of which was a large, dilapidated inn.

"The Harrow House," he said, pointing.

I stood beside him and looked up at the ornate architecture in varying stages of decay.

"You know the expression 'Harrow's hindquarters'?" he asked, smiling.

I nodded.

"This was built by that Harrow," he said. "I could never quite figure out what that saying meant. Anyway, he built this inn here years ago, hoping that the island would attract visitors from the City. No one ever came, and Harrow swam out to sea one afternoon and was drowned or was eaten or something.''

"This is the prison?'' I asked.

The corporal pointed to his head and said, ''This is the prison.''

"Is this where I am to stay?'' I asked.

"Yes. I bet you were expecting much worse,'' he said. "Sorry to say, at this juncture, we have no other prisoners. You can choose any room you like, though. In the morning before dawn—for one of your punishments is that you should never again see sunlight—my brother, the corporal of the day watch, will be here to roust you out of sleep and drag you off to the mine, where you will work till sundown. Is that clear?''

I nodded.

"You will meet Silencio. He is the caretaker of the inn. There is a well-stocked bar on the back porch, and he loves to play at being a bartender,'' said the corporal.

"Thank you,'' I said.

"Remember something, Cley. My brother is not so accommodating as I am. The night watch is sleep; the day watch is death.'' Then he smiled and waved to me, heading off through the maze of dunes.

I stumbled through the dark inn, across the main barroom, and then up a flight of stairs where I thought the living quarters might be. On the second floor there was a long hall lined with doors. Halfway down that shadowy corridor, I could see that one of the doors was open and that a soft light shone forth.

It was room number 7. I stepped inside and saw that it had been newly cleaned. The linen on the bed was uncreased and the curtains were spotless. There wasn't one grain of sand on the polished wooden floor. The light came from a gas lamp, whose light could be lowered or brightened or extinguished by turning a keylike knob.

There was a bed, a nightstand, a dresser, and a closet of moderate size. Next to the closet was a small bathroom that, instead of a door, had a curtain that could be pulled across. Inside hung a mirror over the sink that was too large for my liking, but the walls were painted a soothing sea green. I lay on the bed and pushed off my boots.

The two windows had been left open, and the white lace curtains billowed. I could hear and smell the ocean cutting through everything. The salt air had sunk into me and turned me to lead. My eyes closed and I lay there for a second or two, grappling with the future.

A minute later it seemed, I felt a stick come down across my back. Someone kicked me in the rear end. There were hands on me, pushing me onto the wooden floor. It was completely dark and outside I heard birds screeching.

"Wear only your underwear," roared an angry voice. "You have two minutes in which to be out in front."

I was groggy and aching from the beating I had gotten, but I rose to my feet, stripped off my clothes, and followed him. On the bottom step, I stumbled and fell against my tormentor's back. He turned to push me off him and struck me with his stick.

"Get off me, you shit," he screamed.

He let the screen door slam in my face on the way out. I came to stand before him on the path that led through the dunes. Hugging myself against the early morning chill, I peered through the darkness and saw the face of the corporal of the day watch. With the exception that he had long dark hair, he was the image of the corporal of the night watch. He wore the same coat with the same pins and medals, but his face was atwitch with red anger and fear.

"Get down on the ground," he said.

I did.

"Draw me a circle in the sand," he said.

I did.

He hit me with his stick. "A bigger circle," he shouted.

I drew a bigger one.

Then he crouched down in front of me and showed me

a pair of dice he held in his right hand. I think they were red with white spots. He put his fist around them and brought them up to his mouth to blow on. Once this was accomplished, he shook them and threw them into the circle I had drawn. The white dots of a three and a four glowed in the dark.

"Seven pounds," he said, sweeping the dice up in his hand and standing.

I got up.

"You'll be digging seven pounds today," he repeated.

I nodded.

"All right, walk forward with your hands on your head," he called from behind me. I did as he said, and before I had gone one step I could feel the tip of his saber resting against my spine.

We walked a different route through the dunes, and within a half mile, over loose sand, mosquitoes biting my arms and legs, we came to the entrance of the mine.

A sick yellow light shone out from the timbered shaft, making visible the fumes that drifted up. I gagged several times at the smell. It was overwhelmingly corrupt.

"Breathe deeply," yelled Corporal Matters of the day watch. "You will become this stench in a matter of weeks." He paused for a moment. "I will issue you a pickax and a shovel. You will also be given a bag to carry your sulphur to the surface, one gourd of putrid water, and three moist cremat disks." He walked off into the shadows and soon returned with those items.

I put the shovel and axe over my shoulder and took the string of the gourd and the brown-wrapped package of food with my opposite hand to show the corporal that I understood.

"There are a few things that my prisoners need to know," he said, pacing back and forth in front of me.

I wondered if the Corporals Matters were really twins or just the same twisted fellow switching wigs. The similarities were unnerving.

"My first dictum," he shouted. "Every miner must dig his own hole. This means that you must find a barren piece of rock and create your own tunnel. You will be requested to chisel your name over your tunnel after you have been with us for six months. Your remains, whatever they may be, will be interred in your tunnel, proceeding your demise. You are your tunnel. Do you understand?"

I nodded.

"My second dictum is: the mine is the mind," he said, then suddenly reached out with the stick and whacked me in the shoulder. "Say it," he yelled. "Say it."

"The mine is the mind," I said in a near whisper.

"Say it again," he yelled and I did.

Then he stepped up to within an inch of my face, breathing his alcoholic breath on me. "The mine is my mind," he said. "While you work, you are in my mind, tunneling through my head and I see you always. My mind is always killing you as you dig through it. Dig hard. I will teach you a zest for the battle."

I nodded again and waited for my next order. He came at me, brandishing the stick and reaching for his saber. "To work, you idiot," he bellowed. "Seven pounds or I'll feed you to the kraken in the lagoon."

I turned and ran ahead of him, but not so far that he didn't catch me with the stick here and there. Into the sick yellow I went, toting my shovel and pickax, my gourd of putrid water, and cremat disks. I thought the odor of the sulphur would fell me, but after I realized that the corporal would not follow me in, I stood, bent over in the yellow mist, until my head and vision cleared.

"Seven pounds of sulphur," I thought. "What is seven pounds of sulphur?"

15

The walls of the chamber I entered had an ambient glow, some kind of phosphorous material mixed with the sulphur. I peered through the hazy light and saw, ten feet in front of me, a wooden bridge that passed over a small chasm and led to the opening of a tunnel. Shifting the weight of the tools on my shoulder, I advanced. The bridge swayed with every step, but I made it across, half expecting Garland to meet me on the other side.

I paused for a moment to shiver and gag through the stench. The evil odor was always present, but sometimes it was as if I was not paying enough attention to it, and then it would consciously swamp me like a wave. To imagine this aroma, think of all things scatological roasting with a viral fever and bury your face in them. In the tunnel it was cramped and dark, and the way seemed to wind inward like a coiled snake. The pickax kept striking the ceiling. My bare feet burned against the heat of the rock. I was on the verge of panic, when, eventually, I saw light up ahead and quickened my pace.

The underground chamber I stepped into must have been as large as the entire structure of the Academy of Physiognomy back in the Well-Built City. Before me was an enormous hole in the ground. I stepped carefully up to the edge and peered down and down. Its circumference was so wide, I could barely see across to the other side. All of it glowed a dull yellow through the mist, and I could make out a path that spiraled along the inner walls. Cut into these walls, at various points all the way to where the rising smoke obscured my vision, were the entrances to tunnels, which I assumed had been cut by the likes of Professor Flock and Barlow, the tepid poet. In relation to the immensity of the mine, these appeared the work of insects.

With each step I took down the treacherous spiral, the heat increased another degree as did the foul bouquet. I wondered, as I crept lightly along, how many had tripped and fallen into the mine and how many beyond that had simply flung themselves down. The narrowness of the path would make it very advantageous to hurry the construction of a personal tunnel.

I descended steadily for about an hour, trying to locate an unused portion of the inner wall. By the time I had found what I was looking for, I was gasping and drenched with sweat. My eyes burned so badly from the fumes that I could hardly see. I threw the tools down and placed my package of cremat disks safely away from the edge. Keeping the water gourd, I sat down on the path and cried. The tears washed my eyes out and this offered some relief. I took a sip of the water, and though it was putrid, it required great fortitude to keep from swallowing it all at once.

After another sip, I cocked my head back and saw the name that had been chiseled over the opening to the tunnel to my right. Cut deeply into the glowing sulphur were the letters F-E-N-T-O-N. At first this made little impression on me, but then the mine gathered up its stench and battered me.

As my head reeled, I remembered Notious Fenton. It was my physiognomical skills that had sent him here. I believe the charge was that he had harbored ill thoughts against the Well-Built City. He had been part of the roundup in the Grulig case. Most of the conspirators had had their heads exploded, and I could now see they were the lucky ones.

I got up and entered Fenton's tunnel. The light was very dim inside, but I could still make out the form of a skeleton, sitting on the ground, cross-legged, with a pickax resting on what had once been his lap. I remembered that during the trial, his wife and sons had been very vocal in their protests against the realm. Then one day I came to court and they were not there. In fact, they never returned. It was only later, after the Master had intimated to me in a stupor of beauty that it was he who had Grulig beheaded, did I find out that he had also had the Fenton family, as he put it, "permanently restructured" as a personal favor to me, assuring the smooth procedure of the case.

I stepped slowly forward as if the poor man's remains were potentially dangerous. Then I leaned over and said, "I am sorry. I am sorry." My hand came up of its own volition and rested on the collarbone of my victim. In a moment, it shattered beneath my touch, turning to salt and drifting to the dusty floor. I stepped back and watched as the process I had started in motion slowly spread like a plague through the rib cage and down the spine, disintegrating the entirety of Fenton until his skull crashed to the floor and disappeared in a shower of atoms.

Although there was some respite from the smell in there, I could not stay in his tunnel. I stepped back out into the horror of the mine and lifted my pickax. It required a firmer grip than usual, because the voluminous sweat that poured from every inch of me made the wooden handle as slippery as a fish. I brought the tool back over my shoulder, and then I struck the wall with a mighty blow powered by self-loathing.

I worked with an insane energy for about twenty minutes, after which, I collapsed against the craggy rock face I had torn away at. In a panic, I suddenly realized I wasn't breathing. The pick fell out of my hand onto the path. My eyes felt as if they had burned out completely. I could now no longer see. There was an intense pain in my head, and I could feel myself sliding down the wall, my hands and face being lacerated by the jagged stone.

Unfortunately, I woke a little while later. Breathing somewhat easier, I crawled over to where my food and water were. A big chunk of sulphur I had chipped from the wall had landed on my moist cremat disks, squashing the package to a disturbing thinness. I ripped the paper open. Moist was not the word for them, for I found no disks within, just brown cremat smeared upon the paper. I licked it off greedily and then downed it with some of the water.

When I was done, I rolled the paper into a ball and tossed it out over the edge of the pit. The rising steam prevented it from falling, and it floated for a minute or two before my eyes. Eventually the upward current overpowered it and carried it out of sight. I wondered what this phenomenon stood for in the mind of Corporal Matters of the day watch. If the mine was his mind, his mind was a hot stinking pit riddled with holes, holding the brittle remains of the dead. This struck me as humorous. But later, as I again dug away at the yellow wall, it dawned on me how accurate he had been.

The day was eternal. I passed out twice more and thought, once, that my blood was literally boiling. In my brain, I heard a constant sizzling sound. Soon after I had eaten, the cremat dug into my stomach like a demon and gave me no rest from its fury. In addition to these tortures, the abrasions I had received from sliding down along the sharp face of the wall stung from the salt of my sweat mixing with the poisonous air.

Finally, like a voice calling out of paradise, I heard my name echoing down through the emptiness of the mine. "Sundown, sundown, sundown," the corporal yelled. I gathered chunks of sulphur into the canvas sack I had been given and slung it over my back. On the other shoulder,

I hefted the shovel and pick. The string for the water gourd, I held in my teeth. The ascent was brutal. My legs ached beneath the weight, and my arms shook with weariness. I stopped three times to catch my breath, but I made it out into the open air.

It was dark outside, but the air was filled with a night breeze that carried the smell of the ocean. I would have traded ten vials of the beauty for just one gasp of it. The corporal propped his torch in a hole in the ground and weighed my load on an antique scale that operated somehow with shifting stones and springs. He beat me with his stick when he found I had brought up ten pounds instead of seven.

"Does seven sound like ten?" he asked me.

"No," I replied.

"You are a moron of the first water," he said.

I nodded.

"You aren't the first physiognomist I've seen reduced to ash. I remember a Professor Flock. Oh, how I flayed that idiot. It was rich. I blinded him with a beating one day. Taking his sight was like pulling the wings from a fly. When he eventually went under, I stole this from him," he said.

He held his stick out to show me the handle—a carved, ivory monkey head. "Some evening Harrow's hindquarters will not shit you out, and I will find you down there in a pose of agony, surrounded by the smell of baking flesh," he said. "Now get out of here. I will be by to fetch you early tomorrow."

The corporal took the torch with him and left me standing there in front of the mine. Above, the moon was shining and the stars were bright. My body stung all over as if I had a bad sunburn, and the cool night wind made me shiver. The abundance of fresh air caused me severe dizziness as I staggered forward onto the winding path that led through the dunes. It took me two hours to locate the inn.

The light was on in my room. The bed was made, and

someone had drawn a warm bath for me. For a moment, it was a battle between the water and sleep. I ended up opting for both. I lay in the tub in my underwear, feeling the warm perfumed water wash the mine off me as I fell asleep. I was awakened sometime later by a soft hint of a sound coming from downstairs. I tried to ignore it and continue with my dream of Arla, but it was as persistent as a mosquito. After a while, I gave in to it and discovered that someone was playing a piano.

After dressing in just my trousers, I went barefoot down the stairs, through the inn. I followed the sound of the music across the main bar, through a dining room toward the back of the place. A chair had been left in the aisle, shrouded by night, and I stubbed my toe against it. I held my voice, but the chair scratched along the floor and hit another one. With this collision, the music abruptly stopped.

At the end of the dining room, I pushed through a door and stepped out onto a large screened porch. Again, I could hear the ocean, and the breeze washed over me. The dunes beyond the screen were lit by the moon. Sitting before me was a small black piano, not very much bigger than a child might practice at. Across the empty plank floor, at the other end of the porch, was a polished wooden bar with shelves of bottles and a mirror behind it. As I stared through the shadows, it appeared to me that there was someone sitting behind the bar.

"Hello?" I called.

I watched the dark figure and saw it raise a hand and wave. Slowly, I made my way across the porch. When I was within a few feet of the bar, a match flared. I stopped but then saw he was lighting a candle and continued to take a seat before him.

"Silencio?" I asked.

He nodded and I saw his face. The caretaker appeared slight of build, a miniature old man with a wrinkled face and a long beard. My attention was momentarily distracted by something moving in the air behind him. Suddenly it became clear that what I was looking at was a long tail. Silencio was a monkey.

Seeing the look of recognition in my eyes, he reached below the bar and hoisted up a bottle of Rose Ear Sweet, which had been my standard cocktail at all political functions and social gatherings. With the other, he pulled up a glass. Putting the cork of the bottle in his teeth, he opened it. A smile grew around that cork as he poured me a double.

"Silencio," I said and he nodded.

We stared at each other for a long time, and I wondered if I had not died in the mines that day. "This is the afterlife, eternity for me—sulphur all day and a monkey at night," I thought. Then he nodded slightly as if he had been thinking the same thing.

"I am Cley," I said.

He brought his hands together and clapped twice. I was unsure if he was mocking me or letting me know that he understood.

I realized I didn't care. Taking up my drink, I sat back in the chair and sipped. He seemed to approve of my decision to stay.

"Thank you," I said.

With this, he hopped off his chair and went through a doorway at the end of the bar. A few minutes later, he returned holding a serving tray. He climbed back up on his chair and then laid the tray before me. It was a complete dinner of pig shank covered with pineapple slices. There was bread and butter and a separate dish of potatoes and garlic.

I did not realize until that moment how insane my hunger was. While I ate like an animal, Silencio got down from his chair, went around the side of the bar, crossed the porch, and sat down at his piano. It was the combination of the pineapple and the music that made me think of paradise. I gulped the Rose Ear Sweet and jammed potatoes down my throat as I saw the golden gates sweep open to let me in.

I was still at the bar when Corporal Matters of the day watch came for me. He beat me roundly but I was too drunk to feel it. Out in the sand, in the circle, the dice showed two sixes. I heard the corporal's laughter all day, spiraling down through the mine as I stood before my hole, swinging the pick. Even after I had passed out and was deep in a cool dream of salvation, it was there, like a cricket in an egg, threatening to hatch.

16

On Doralice, the days were near infinite and filled to the brim with physical suffering. The nights were a candle going out, a few brief moments of shadow-laden solitude, underscored by the persistent whisper of the ocean and the baying of the wild dogs. The moonlit pain was mental anguish, bubbling up from dreams in which my guilt was revealed both literally and symbolically. Sometimes, when the corporal of the day watch woke me with his stick across my back, I almost thanked him for retrieving me from some memory of myself in Anamasobia.

The only thing that seemed to change on Doralice was me. Over the course of a few weeks, I had become physically stronger from my efforts in the mine. Silencio was a wizard at curing my wounds when I returned beaten up or scorched or delirious from the fumes. He had large green leaves he sometimes dipped in water and then wrapped me in to ease the fire in my flesh. There was a certain herbal tea he prepared that increased my strength and cleared my head. With his hairy-backed hands he gently applied a blue salve to the places where the corporal's stick had landed and broken the skin. But even with all of his efforts, and the fact that my muscles were becoming as hard as the rock I worked, I could feel I was dying inside. Day and night, I thought longingly ahead to the time when I would exchange my haunted remembering for a complete forgetting.

I learned my lesson about going down to the bar at night after that first painful experience. From then on, after staggering back to the inn, I went to my room and stayed there. Silencio brought up a tray of food for me. Whatever type of monkey he was, he was most unusually brilliant— handsome too, with his various shades of brown and that long black beard that came to the middle of his white chest. He used his tail like an extra hand, and was quite strong in his wiry muscles. I could swear, when I spoke to him, that he understood every nuance of my conversation.

Sometimes, when I had finished eating, he sat on the dresser, picking ticks from his fur and cracking them between his teeth. I lay on the bed and revealed to him the depths of the vanity that had brought me to the island. Occasionally, he shook his head or gave a little screech as I related yet another embarrassing detail, but he never seemed judgmental. When I told him the story of Arla, and what I had done to her, he brought his fist to his eyes to wipe away tears.

One day when the corporal had rolled only a pair of ones, and I had plenty of time to myself down in the mine, I went exploring through the tunnels of my predecessors. Some of the names were familiar to me, either from having read about them in the city *Gazette* or having had a hand in prosecuting their cases. It dawned on me that most were political prisoners. Those who committed robbery or rape or murder were usually dealt with immediately by way of electrocution, firing squad, or explosion of the head. It seemed the ones who made it to Doralice were all individuals who had, in some way, questioned the authority or philosophies of the Master. In words or writing, they had professed a disdain for the rigid societal control of the Well-Built City, doubted the efficacy of the Physiognomy, or called the mental state of Drachton Below into question.

Above the entrances of the various openings, I found Rasuka, Barlow, Therian. They had all in their own cracked ways seen beyond the limits of the city to a place where brutality and fear were not necessary for the regulation of society. I remembered the Master laughing at Therian's plan to feed the poor of Latrobia and the other communities that had sprung up around the walls of the metropolis. "He's a whiner, Cley," Below had told me. "The stupid ass doesn't see that starvation is a way of thinning out these undesirables." And what did I do? I read poor Therian's head and found him dangerous to the realm. I can't recall if it was his chin or the bridge of his nose, but it didn't matter. Those two features, along with the rest of him, sat before me, a sizable pile of salt, barely visible in the dim, yellow glow of his otherwise barren tunnel.

Barlow's hole was filled with writing. He had used some implement to etch poetry into the sulphur walls. It was a sad thing to see that through all his suffering, he had never become any better a writer—here rhyming *ghost* with *host*, there, *trope* with *hope*, too many beats, too few images, all *love* and *lovely*. In the heat and stench of the pit, I wondered if that was important, or if there was not something I was missing about the passion that had literally consumed his life. What danger he was to the Master, I could not see.

Although I used quite a bit of energy I could have otherwise conserved in moving from tunnel to tunnel inspecting the remains of the dead, there was something fascinating about my search. The upward draft in the pit was doubly hot that day for some reason, but I continued on, wiping the burning sweat out of my eyes and peering through the mist. It was almost as if I was visiting these people, almost as if I was one of them. Here were my compatriots. This thought actually offered a modicum of solace until I moved down along the path, past my own tunnel, and found the name Flock, carved- above one of the openings.

Out of all the eternal homes I had visited that day, the most impressive one was my old professor's. Had I been able to put out of my mind that it was all hewn from sulphur, and been able to ignore the stench, I would say that Flock's little grotto was quite beautiful. The old man had a touch of the artist in him, for he had made his hole into a garden, having sculpted onto the walls reliefs of plants and shrubbery and trees. Tendrils and vines, leaves and blossoms were delicately rendered, showing detail and proper dimension. At the back of the tunnel, which was quite deep, was a small garden bench, carved entirely from what must have been an enormous boulder of sulphur. It faced the back wall.

I took a seat there, in Flock's garden, and stared at a row of life-size faces that he had shaped out of the yellow stone. The first was of the Master—an uncanny likeness. He was snickering, his eyes slightly rolled back as if he had just injected himself with sheer beauty. Next to him was Corporal Matters of the day watch, scowling jowls and deep pockets beneath the hateful eyes. Last in the strange gallery of the professor's tormentors was a visage I could not place, though I knew it to be familiar. It was certainly as filled with spite and menace as the other two. One might say it had some of the Master's own madness in it.

While I tried to remember where I had seen it, I noticed that beneath all of these rude heads had been carved the word *forgive*. Eventually, I lifted my pick and swung violently, smashing that last head from the wall. I beat it where it lay on the ground until it had been reduced to yellow crumbs. Then I shoveled it into my sack. "Two pounds," I whispered to the corporal's leering face.

That night, after bathing, I lay on my bed, simply staring. I should have left those other tunnels alone and not disturbed the dead. What I had found there had taken what little will to live I had left. Now it was just a matter of deciding how I would hasten the end of my life. "Should I leap into the pit, a graceful dive and never-ending fall into the bright yellow heat, my body disintegrating before I hit the bottom," I wondered, "or, like my dead host, Harrow, should I swim for it?"

"Have you seen the kraken?" I asked Silencio, who sat on my dresser with a worried look. All night he had been imploring me by way of looks and hand gestures to eat the tray of food he had brought up.

He pulled some nit off his fur and wiggled the fingers of his opposite hand around it before bringing it to his mouth and crunching it between his teeth.

I resumed my despondent gaze as Silencio jumped down from the dresser. I thought he had left the room, but a moment later I was recalled from my reverie when I heard him rummaging in the closet. A few seconds later, he was on the bed, hoisting up the travel bag I had brought to the island with me. I watched without interest or comment as he unfastened the snaps and reached inside. What he brought forth was a parcel wrapped in blue paper and tied with string. At first, I did not remember ever bringing such an item with me. Then the monkey kicked the bag back on the floor and, lifting the parcel in two hands, tossed it onto my chest. The next thing I knew, he had returned the travel bag to the closet and left the room.

I lay there looking at the package with both fear and wonder as if it were the tentacle of a kraken. Lifting it slowly, I ripped the paper away, and as I did, a very faint mixture of scents was released. One of these was that of parchment and ink and the other was distinctly the perfume of Arla Beaton. These were, of course, the pages of her notes on the memories of the story of her grandfather's journey. I tore away the rest of the blue wrapping and string, remembering that I had packed it in such a manner to protect it on the trip from the mainland.

Up till that moment, I had been unable to lay my eyes

on the manuscript without shaking uncontrollably. All the time I had spent in my holding cell while my trial was dragging along I kept the pages in the opposite corner from my bed, and if my gaze landed on them, I quickly averted my eyes as if I were seeing a ghost there instead. Now I did not have the same aversion to it. I held up the bulk of pages and read the first words: *Dear Physiognomist Cley*.

Soft piano music drifted up from the back porch of the inn, laying a melody over the constant bass of the distant ocean. The breeze lifted the curtains, and I began to read the *Fragments from the Impossible Journey to the Earthly Paradise*.

Dear Physiognomist Cley:
A number of days ago, at your request, I spent some time delving into the physiognomical attributes of my late grandfather Harad Beaton in an attempt to discern both his personal worth and any "secrets" he might have to reveal concerning an expedition he had taken many years past. My reading of his features, which have been turned to blue spire, merely confirmed that he was an ordinary man with a rather low physiognomical quotient. What is more interesting is that as I ran my hands over his hardened face, I began to remember snatches of the story of this journey he had related to me when I was a child. I began to write these down, thinking that they might be of some use to you.

Once I began, I could not stop. The memories turned into waking dreams, and, as I recorded them, I believe I was experiencing what some mystics call automatic writing. I wrote so rapidly, without looking at the page, it was as if some unseen hand were guiding my efforts. Although I did not re-experience the entire journey, I did experience quite a bit of it. There are gaps that probably will never be filled in.

When the journey did come to me, it was as if I were there with the miners in the wilderness, an invisible witness to their quest.

Seeing Arla's script, I could almost feel her hand moving across the page. Breathing in the vague scent of her perfume, traces of lilac and lemon, it was as if she were there with me in bed. These things calmed my mind and I began to grow weary as I continued reading. Her earliest fragment was a vision of the Beyond. There was great detail concerning the unspoiled beauty and strange vegetation and animals the miners saw as they headed deeper and deeper into those woods Bataldo, Calloo, and I had passed through. I could see them with their lantern helmets, their pickaxes slung over their shoulders, walking in single file, joking and laughing. Some of their names passed by me. Twigs broke and branches rustled as a herd of albino deer broke into a small clearing and bounded away through the trees. The moon was out at midday and Harad Beaton was longing for home.

The next thing I knew, I was scrabbling beneath the stick of the corporal of the day watch. My mind was so full of the Beyond, even his curses and punishment did not clear away the undergrowth and enormous cedars until we were well on our way through the maze of dunes. Before entering the mine, I had to ask him again what it was he had rolled that morning.

"Ten, you dimwit," he yelled, "a six and a four." He seemed like he wanted to give me another beating, but the night was beginning to lighten, so he pushed me toward the mine instead. "Perhaps you will die today," he said as I stumbled through the entrance.

His words caused me to remember that I had planned to do just that, but I never seemed to get around to it. I realized as I pounded into the rock of my tunnel, sweating, heaving for air, that I would have to stay alive at least until I had finished reading Arla's manuscript. I worked with great vigor that day.

Whereas Flock's tunnel was filled with a make-believe garden, my mind was overgrowing with images of a real wilderness. As I worked, I began to wonder if Beaton had ever made it to paradise. This thought, no bigger than the grains of sulphur that flew about me following each blow of the pick, buried itself in my mind like a seed with the potential to blossom.

17

I was lying in bed, reading aloud to Silencio a passage from Arla's *Fragments* concerning a demon attack the miners had sustained in a tract of pines on a steep hillside. My monkey friend sat by my feet, wide-eyed, grasping his tail with one hand and covering his eyes with the other. A miner by the name of Miller was being disemboweled by three of the filthy creatures amid a torrent of rhetorical description. Blood was flying, duodenum was drooping, groans from the nether end of hell were being loosed into the wilderness when I was interrupted by a knocking at my half-open door.

The sound frightened me, and I thought, "Could it be the morning already? I just began reading a few moments ago."

Silencio jumped down off the bed, bounded twice, and then leaped up just as Corporal Matters of the night watch entered the room. The monkey landed deftly on the man's left shoulder and strung his tail around the corporal's collar like a necklace.

"Good evening, all," said Matters, wearing a broad smile.

I had neither seen nor heard him since the night I had first arrived. Because of his absence, I had just assumed that he was really one and the same person as the corporal of the day watch. It was my theory that he had two wigs, one black and one white, and he would pretend, from reasons of insanity, to be two people. Now seeing him, though, smiling, reaching up to pet Silencio, I had to change my mind.

"Cley," he said, "it's good to see you. Sorry I wasn't by sooner to check up and see how you were getting on."

I said nothing but tried to drop the pages on the floor next to the bed, fearing a rule that might require him to take them from me.

"Thought you might like to join me for a drink down on the back porch," he said. At the sound of his voice, Silencio jumped down off his shoulder and scampered out the door.

I got out of bed, put my shirt and boots on, and followed him downstairs. As we were wending our way through the dark inn, I could hear the piano playing.

Later as we sat at the bar, sipping Rose Ear Sweet, he pushed his white hair behind his ear on the left side and said, "My brother is quite a fellow, isn't he?"

I shook my head. "With all due respect," I said, "he seems somewhat angry."

The corporal laughed wearily. "With all due respect," he said and shook his head, "he is the angriest person I have ever met."

"The mines are brutal," I said, feeling I could be honest with him.

"Quite," he said. "If it was up to me, I would not require you to go down there. I'd let you roam the island and live out your life here as you saw fit." He paused for a moment as if weighing what he was about to say. "I'm afraid you are going to die down there—you know that yourself already."

I nodded, staring across the porch at Silencio as he worked the keys of his miniature piano.

"The realm is corrupt," he said, "rotten to the core. I'd rather be out here on this island then in that ill City.

With all the death I've witnessed here, there is less suffering in the mine then there is close to Below.''

"Have you met the Master?" I asked.

"Met him? I fought alongside him on the fields of Harakun. You remember, no doubt, from your history lessons, the Peasant Revolt? Oh yes, the poor outside the walls tried to take the City. My brother and I both fought there. Knee-deep in slaughter we were.''

"I remember reading about it," I said, though I remembered very little.

"Three thousand men in one day. Five hundred of ours and the rest theirs," he said, then took a long drink. He wiped his mouth and continued. "My brother's troops and my own outflanked a large party of peasants just south of the Latrobian village. They were all that was left of the revolt. We butchered most of them but took more than fifty prisoners. It was that maneuver that finished the war. We were to take the prisoners to the City the next day to be executed in Memorial Park, but that night, while my brother slept, I relieved the sentries and let every one of the poor beggars go.''

"And you're still alive?" I said.

"Below blamed both of us. My brother was furious. He wanted to kill me. We were to be tried and executed ourselves, but since we had fought so bravely, and the insurrection had no chance of rekindling, the Master spared us, giving us permanent positions here on Doralice.''

"How long have you been here?" I asked.

"A good forty years," he said. "And I haven't seen my brother since the day we arrived. Soon after disembarking on the dock, we came up with this arrangement. He would rule the day, and I, the night.''

"Not even a glimpse of him?" I asked.

"My only evidence of him is the suffering of the prisoners," he said. "If I were to meet him, we would probably fight to the death. I know it will happen sooner or later. I live with the thought of it always.''

We sat quietly for a long time. Silencio eventually stopped playing and came over to refill our glasses. That beautiful breeze was at work, and I wished I could sit there all night.

"Is this not a remarkable monkey?" asked the corporal, as Silencio pushed a drink toward him.

"Remarkable is not the word for him," I said. "He has already saved my life on more than one horrible day."

"He came to us from the city," said Matters, "the result of one of the Master's intelligence transference experiments. Apparently they did not want to do away with him, but he was far too friendly to be of any use. We have become good friends over the years. My brother could not get him to have anything to do with policing the mine."

"I will never look at animals the same again," I said.

"Silencio has made friends with all the prisoners. He takes it very hard when one of them does not return from the mines at night. That is when he takes to drinking himself—Three Fingers with a shot of Pelic Bay is his poison. For a whole week he will be inconsolable," said the corporal.

"A comforting thought," I said.

He laughed. "It is all rather absurd," he said. "But you'd better be off to sleep. Mine-is-the-mind will be here in a few hours."

I put down my drink and stood. The corporal of the day watch shook hands with me, and I went back through the inn and up the stairs to my room. I was not drunk, but I felt calm and sleepy. Once in bed, I closed my eyes and let the images of the Beyond flood my thoughts. During the day, I hid the *Fragments* under my pillow so that Arla's scent would be with me all night.

When I picked up where I had left off, I discovered that there was with them now a foliate, a man of green, whom they called Moissac. It never said in the text how they had come upon him. He just appeared at the beginning of a long shard of the journey. He was friendly to

the miners and offered to take them to an ancient abandoned city by the shores of an inland sea. Harad Beaton
thought there might be evidence among the ruins sug-
gesting a path to paradise.

Moissac spoke to them through touch. He placed his
viney hand upon the side of a man's face and spoke flu-
ently. In his thatched, flowering hedge of a face there were
eyes like distant fires, but in the tangle of branches and
roots it was hard to see their exact origin. When he moved
through the trees and underbrush he was almost invisible.

At this point, there were only four miners left beside
Beaton. Even out beneath the open sky, they felt as if they
had been trapped by a cave-in. In the weeks preceding,
they had seen their companions devoured by demons, suc-
cumb to suicide, fall from some precipice, but they had
not lost the idea that they were on a divine mission. They
moved like ants through the immensity of the Beyond.

Before they entered the empty City, the foliate told them
it was called "Palishize." Other than this he could tell
them nothing about it. It looked from a distance like a
giant sand castle melting in the surf. Situated behind an
outer wall were high mounds punctuated by crude openings one could not exactly classify as doorways or windows. It appeared to be more the home of some prodigious
beetles than any human civilization.

The miners drew their rifles and clutched their picks
firmly as they walked between the sand and seashell pillars
of the main entrance. Moissac led the way, motioning for
them to move quietly through the already silent City. The
streets were cobbled with millions of clam shells between
which weeds had run wild.

The buildings of Palishize were tunneled dirt mounds
hiding an elaborate network of passages and small empty
rooms. The miners lit the candles on their helmets as they
explored the weird structures. They soon found that the
buildings were connected by long, underground hallways.

"There is nothing here," Beaton told the others after a

full day of traversing the maze of tunnels. "We had better move on."

All were in agreement, especially Moissac, who told them he felt a sense of doom pervading the stale air of the place. They bedded down on the street for the night, thankful that they did not have to stay in one of the mounds. The dark emptiness of them reminded Beaton of a grave.

Just before dawn, the foliate awoke them. He pointed to the sky where strange red lights slowly moved like fish in a pool. The miners knelt and prayed, believing now what they had already suspected—that they were dead and working toward salvation in some world between heaven and hell. The lights swam in their eyes and dazed them, so that when morning came, they did not want to leave Palishize. Moissac implored them, telling them through touch that something was wrong.

Beaton told him everything was fine and that they would stay one more night to see the lights. All day they moved through the tunnels again, searching for some sign of humanity. Near evening, Mayor Bataldo's uncle, Joseph, found something in one of the passageways. It was a small gold coin with an imprint of a coiled serpent on one side and a flower on the other. After showing the others, he put it in his pocket and joined them for some salted caribou meat and turnip root.

My head nodded more and more with fatigue as I continued with Arla's account until I must have fallen asleep reading, because it was precisely here that the words of the text suddenly swept up off the page, turning into the snaking arm of a sea creature, and pulled me down beneath the surface of paper and ink. There was a minute of gasping for air, and then I, Cley, stood next to the huddled miners asleep on the street of Palishize. Even Moissac, who was supposed to be keeping guard, was firmly rooted in dreams. I leaned over and studied the face of Beaton as a young man.

"Cley," said a voice a few feet down the street. At the curve where the cobbled shells disappeared around the base of a building, there was a woman. She wore a veil over her entire face.

"Arla?" I whispered.

She waved to me to come to her. I moved cautiously away from the miners. As I approached her, she reached out to me, and I instinctively took her in my arms. I kissed her through the veil and we fell to lean against the slope of the mound. She was breathing heavily as my hand ran up under her skirts, along her thigh, toward paradise.

The next thing I knew, we were standing in front of the sleeping miners and Arla was pointing down at Joseph.

"He has my coin," she said to me.

"What coin?" I asked.

"It runs my child," she said. "The Master has taken my son and automated him, made him into a penny machine. I was given four coins to put in a slot in his back. When the coins drop in, he will be alive for an hour. He moves stiffly and sometimes I can hear the gear work humming, but I love him. I foolishly have used up three of the coins already, and the one that man has is my last coin. There are no others like them; the Master poured the metal himself."

I tried to nudge Joseph with the toe of my boot, but it passed right through him.

"I don't think we can do anything," I said.

"Tomorrow, we can," she said. "I'll bring up the red lights for one more dawn, and then tomorrow night we will have him."

"What do you mean, 'have him'?" I asked.

She took my hand and put it to her breast. An instant later, it was the next night and she was relating her plan for me. I was to play a little flute she gave me and lure him awake and around the corner where there was a small alley. She would be waiting there.

"I can't play," I told her.

"Blow hard," she said.

I did, but heard nothing. Nevertheless, Joseph awoke from sleep, stood up, scratched his stomach, and then came toward me. Although I was amazed, I began backing up the street to where it turned into the alley. We were halfway there, when I saw Moissac sit up, crossing his legs in front of him. He watched intently but made no move to interfere.

Arla stood a short way down between the structures. As I brought Joseph around the corner, she stepped forward.

"My coin," she said, putting her hand out.

To my surprise, the miner turned and looked at her. He shared a strong resemblance to his nephew, only thinner from the rugged journey.

"I haven't got it," he said, bringing his hands together as if in prayer.

"Where is it?" she asked, the veil rustling slightly with the breeze of each word.

"I lost it," he said. "Today in the tunnels, I took it out of my pocket to look at so many times, I must have dropped it."

She stood like a statue. I could hear the distant waves of the sea. Then she lifted her arms and put her fingers to the bottom of the veil. As she lifted it, I closed my eyes and turned away.

I heard Joseph make a noise, a furious exhalation as if the breath were being sucked out of him. When I finally opened my eyes, the veil was dropping and the miner lay dead at my feet. There were as many holes in his flesh as there were openings in the mounds of Palishize. Arla vanished, sifting into the sound of the surf.

Somehow, I was still present in my ghostly form the next morning when Beaton and the others discovered Joseph was missing. They went in search of him. Moissac found him almost immediately and called to the men. Whatever spell the red lights had cast over the expedition, it suddenly vanished in the face of Joseph's wounds.

"Run, now," said the foliate, caressing Beaton's left cheek.

He yelled, "Run," and they did. As they dashed out through the gates of Palishize, they could feel the thing following them. They made their way back through the forest, moving like deer over the fallen trees and bursting through the undergrowth. Not until they had crossed a frozen river did they feel the invisible terror take its gaze from them. Once on the other side, they lay down on the bank and gasped for breath while all the time the frozen water snapped and cracked against my spine and the moving ice moaned, "Cley, you worthless fly turd, it's time to mine sulphur."

18

The gas lamp suddenly came up, casting out the darkness, and I staggered to my feet beneath a torrent of expletives. The corporal wielded the cane with a blind fury. As I undressed down to my underwear, my arms and back bleeding from the assault, I heard Matters say, "What is this nonsense?" I turned around to see him lift the manuscript pages of the *Fragments* off the bed where they had fallen through the night.

"This won't do," he said, gathering the pages into a pile and clasping it beneath his arm. "You'll dig double your roll for a week for this, you sorry ass of a dog."

"Drachton Below said I was permitted to bring these pages to Doralice," I said.

The corporal reached out with the cane and struck me hard on the side of my neck. The blow staggered me, and I went down on one knee. He had caught the bottom of my ear, and it stung unmercifully.

"Do you think that will prevent me from burning this in my fireplace tonight?" he said. "I don't even want to be touching it. There should be no room in your head for this air. The mine is the mind, and I don't want it littered with frivolity," he said, swinging the cane across my back.

I came up off the ground so quickly, he did not have

time to react. My fist, fueled by the thought of the *Fragments* reduced to ash, drove deep into his soft stomach. I could smell the Rose Ear Sweet as his breath exploded out. Before he could straighten up, I came across with my right hand and hit him squarely on the side of the head. Blood came from his mouth. He tottered for a moment or two and then began to fall. As he went down, I grabbed a handful of hair and the whole ratty coif came sliding off his scalp, his hat dropping next to him. Two more kicks to the head put him out, and over his face I dropped the black wig.

I dressed quickly and then set about turning the corporal over in order to fetch the manuscript. I rolled the pages into a tube and tied them with the piece of string they had come bound in. Instead of taking his sword, I grabbed the monkey-headed cane. Putting my fist around it gave me a sudden sense of power. I so wanted to thrash the slumped form of Matters, I had to grit my teeth in order to forgo my revenge. Instead, I bolted from the room, stumbled down the stairs, and fled the inn.

I tried to follow the sound of the ocean down to the beach, but I could never seem to get there, trapped as I was in the maze of dunes. Running through the sand was tiring me out, and I began to fear that the corporal would have awakened and would soon be on my trail. I stopped in order to think and listen more closely to the waves. That is when Silencio came bounding over a dune.

"I'm breaking out," I told him.

He stopped before me, clapped his hands, and did a back flip.

"Get me to the beach," I said. "My only chance is to go up the island."

He took my hand, and we began walking. In two quick turns, we were standing staring at the long expanse of beach that led down to the shoreline. The sky was beginning to lighten, and I could see flocks of white long-legged birds running back and forth at the water's edge.

I was a good way up the beach when I heard a faint scream and looked back to see Silencio waving. The horizon was hatching a brilliant red sun, and my mind was swimming with freedom. I hoped that in the daylight I would be able to think more clearly about my predicament. A few rash moments of action, and now there was no going back. Having smelled the Rose Ear Sweet on Matter's breath, and held the black mop of hair, I was convinced that the corporals were one and the same twisted individual. Not only had I thrashed him, but I had also exposed his charade. I was sure the punishment for this would be death.

As I strode along through the ever lightening day, watching the fins of the sharks circling a quarter of a mile from shore, I racked my brain for a plan of, first, survival, and then escape. "If there could only be trees at the other end of the island," I thought, "then I might be able to fashion a raft and set out for the mainland." I needed to return to the Well-Built City, to rescue Arla and make things right. I realized my suffering would change nothing. Action was the only thing that could eradicate my guilt.

The sun climbed in the sky, growing less red and more brilliant. Its warmth penetrated my bones and cleansed the persistent shadows from my eyes. Above me, the sky was perfectly clear and infinitely blue. Every now and then, I had to spin around in order to take in the full scope of the ocean and dunes. Although I was drunk on the beauty of Doralice, I kept it in mind to cut a path through the fringe of the surf so that it would quickly wash away my footprints.

Around noon, I left the beach and headed up into the dunes to find a place to lie down. The salt air was like a drug to me. I could hardly keep my eyes open. At the top of the tallest dune, I found a small plateau of sea grass, and in the center of it was a sandy depression, like the palm of a cupped hand. That is where I lay down and closed my eyes, resigning myself to fate.

Hours passed before I awoke. The sun was still high in the sky, the day still beautiful. The wind had picked up somewhat, and when I strolled over to the edge of the dune, I could see whitecaps on the ocean. I turned to look up the beach to see if anyone was coming and found it empty.

I had to hold tightly to the *Fragments* after untying the string for fear of the wind. Leaning back on my warm throne of sand, I fingered through the pile of pages looking for where I had left off. Matters had made a bitter mess of it, but it was not long before I found the image of the two miners and the foliate adrift on an ice floe in a near-frozen river.

Moissac was weakened by the intense cold. He lay on the ice, wrapped in a black coat, grunting and rolling slowly from side to side. All of his leaves had shriveled to brown, littering the surface of the floating island of ice. His face was barren bark, and the fire of his eyes was distant.

Beaton kneeled next to the foliate. Behind them stood Ives, the youngest of the original expedition. He held his rifle aimed, ready to fire, waiting for demons that weren't there. The wind blew fiercely. The sea was iron and the sky, dull.

"When I die, you must cut a hole in my chest. Inside, you will find a large brown seed with thorns. Take it with you and plant it in the spring," said Moissac.

Beaton wanted the foliate's thorny hand to release him.

"I will do that," he said.

"I have been to paradise," said Moissac.

"Tell me what I will find there," said Beaton.

"You will never get there; it is the paradise of plants. Humans have their own paradise."

"What is it like?" asked Beaton.

Moissac writhed back and forth wildly, and then a shudder began at his roots. Like a wind, it moved through his legs, his chest and extinguished his intelligence. Small trails of smoke came snaking up from his thatched sockets, but still he managed to say, "Like this," the words echoing up through Beaton's wrist.

He pulled out his knife and hacked away at the branches of Moissac's hand. The fingers still gripped him tightly like an elaborate wooden bracelet. It took him some time to chip and splinter the rest of it to pieces without cutting himself. When he was free, he plunged the knife blade into the chest of the foliate. Twigs cracked and flew as he sawed a hole in the chest. He lifted out the panel he had cut and found beneath it the promised seed.

That night the temperature dropped so fiercely that Ives could no longer keep the rifle in his hands. The ice floe came to a halt and Beaton realized that the river was freezing solid. He knew it was their only chance, a dash across the ice before the sun came up.

"Soon we are going to run," he told Ives.

"What about the demons?" asked the young man.

"There are no demons," said Beaton.

I rolled up the pages and retied them with the string. It was late afternoon before I got on my way, blazing a trail through the dunes. I swung the cane in my left hand and this helped me keep a brisk pace through the loose sand. For the first time, I felt some relief from the idea that Matters might hunt me down. I thought that if I was careful I could easily avoid him. The beating I had given him reminded me of some of those brutal encounters when I had been a Physiognomist, First Class, and it clearly brought back those dirty fighting skills. I was sure that in hand-to-hand combat, I was his superior.

The dunes of Doralice seemed endless. When night fell I finally just crawled to the top of one of the taller ones and lay down among the sea grass. The stars were magnificent, so perfectly clear you could see the space around them. I held the monkey cane across my chest and wondered what had happened in the mine that day, who had finally turned to salt and how it might have affected Matters's mind.

It was all very amusing until I heard the first howl. After the fifth howl, I could tell the dogs were drawing closer and closer from every direction and seemed to be converging on me. I grabbed the pages under my arm and held the cane up in a defensive posture. In moments, though, I could see the absurdity of my position. I had to get off the dune or I would be trapped.

I slid down the side and landed softly on the sand below. Once I had my feet beneath me, I began to run. The valleys of the dunes echoed with the barking of the wild dogs, and I had no idea where I was going. All I could think of was the demon attack I had been through with Bataldo and Calloo, and the sounds of the approaching beasts filled me with terror.

I expected at any moment that one would leap out of the sea grass at me as I rounded the turns in the sandy labyrinth. My leg muscles were burning, and I could hardly draw breath, but I fled until I tripped and landed with my face in the sand. I could see nothing, but I heard the low chorus of dogs begin to build around me.

As I stood, I waved the cane in front of me to ward them off. They began to snap and growl. Clearing the sand from my face, I saw what seemed a hundred pairs of yellow eyes bobbing in the shadows. Their upper incisors were like down-curving tusks, and their ears came to sharp points. They leaped forward. I shouted and swung the cane, and they jumped back. I had to keep turning inside their circle to try to stare them down all at once.

It became clear to me very soon that they were more than willing to let me stew there until I was weakened by fear. I had no choice but to comply. To make matters worse, a few had begun running laps around the outside of their circle, always counter to the direction I was turning. Trying to keep them in view made my head ache. I could hear them breathing heavily, a kind of weird, hungry laughter.

I turned for hours, to the right, to the left, and then I turned inward, spinning a glimpse of Arla moving amid the dogs. When I blinked she disappeared, but soon after her, I saw young Ives fall through the ice. I could feel the pack sense my confusion, because things got suddenly quiet. Trying to keep my sanity, I cut to ribbons with the cane a phantom of the mayor as he lurched out of the night, arm reaching forward, a perfect black hole in the middle of his forehead.

It leaped on my back, driving me to the ground. I could feel it snapping at my ear, trying to get to my throat. Covering my face with one arm, I rolled over and stabbed it with the end of the cane so hard I heard ribs cracking. It yelped and leaped off me. The next one was already on its way. I heard it running before I could turn to see. There was just enough time for me to hoist the cane up like a club and swing. The ivory monkey bit down into the dog's eye as my boot came up for the jaw.

I had sustained quite a few bites and scratches, and also wounded a good number of them, but near dawn, a shot rang out from the top of a nearby dune and the explosion chased off the dogs. I wasn't sure at first if it was another apparition or really Corporal Matters and Silencio coming toward me. The corporal wore no wig, and through his closely cropped hair I could see a suture that cut a longitudinal hemisphere across his scalp. He carried two pistols, both of which were aimed at my heart. Silencio followed close behind, carrying a rope.

"You've got a mother lode of sulphur to dig, Cley," said Matters. He looked down at Silencio and said, "Tie him up."

The traitorous monkey tied my hands behind my back and then wound the rope three times around my neck, leaving a long leash in front by which he could lead me. When he was done with the job, he clapped and did a back flip. Matters ordered him to bring the cane which was covered with dog blood. Silencio tugged me by the neck and brought the corporal his stick. I thought he was going to cry when he saw the condition it was in.

"I'd love more than life itself to beat you this very moment, Cley, but I'm saving you for something finer," he said, controlling his obvious anger. He walked close behind me with one of the pistols trained on the back of my head. Silencio led the way, the end of my leash over his shoulder.

"The monkey tracked you for a case of Three Fingers," said Matters. "After you're gone, he'll need it to console himself."

19

"What was all the business with the wigs, and the night watch and day watch?" I asked. I had nothing to lose. We trudged along the shoreline back toward the maze of dunes that held the mine. Silencio pointed out to sea, and I caught a glimpse of a kraken's tentacle as it curled beneath the waves.

"I'll give you some business," said Matters and shoved the barrel of the gun up under my ear.

"Your head has been tampered with by the Master, hasn't it?" I asked.

"If you consider a pound of brass gear work tampering," he said. "But tell me that your head hasn't been tampered with."

"I can't," I called over my shoulder.

"My brother's got the same setup, springs and the like, but his runs counterclockwise to mine," he said.

"What brother?" I asked.

He struck me across the back with the stick. "You think you're so smart, Cley. My mind is going to eat you alive," he said and swung twice more.

Silencio led us up through the dunes and, by some miracle route he knew, brought us to the opening of the mine in less than an hour.

"Now, Cley," said Matters, coming up close behind

me, "I've been having nightmares about demons and ice, and I expect not to have them this evening. By sundown you'll have literally baked to death."

I was going to plead for my life, but before the words could make their way out, the butt of the corporal's gun smashed the back of my head, and I found I was already gone. In the dark distance where I was huddled, I felt my body being dragged and then the unbearable heat of the mine enveloped me.

I woke, screaming, to find my feet and hands bound and each roped tightly to metal cleats that had been pounded deep into the sulphur of the path. I lay outside my miserable tunnel, my head on the down slope, my eyes looking up to see, through the mist, the upper rim of the pit. Halfway to the top on the spiral path, I saw the doll-sized figure of the corporal across the abyss. He stopped in his ascent, turned to me, cupped his hand to his mouth, and yelled something. I thought he was going to yell, "The mine is the mind," but he didn't. It had more syllables than that, yet came across as a frantic grunting that he kept up until he had breached the top of the mine and disappeared.

Without the benefit of being able to keep moving, the mine was an oven. The heat built up in me quickly, and it was not long before I could feel my skin begin to lightly sizzle on the hot stone of the path. The sweat bubbled away in pools of evaporating steam. My tongue and throat soon became parched.

I tried to think what I could do, but all my plans gave way to an overwhelming weariness. I soon reached a point beyond pain where I felt nothing. The mine was cradling me in its warmth, but I fought to stay awake by trying to read the inscriptions above the tunnels on the opposite side of the hole. I located Barlow and went on from there.

Then I heard something, the sound of a voice far off. I searched all around before staring straight up. There was Silencio, dancing on the rim of the pit. He was screaming and waving as if trying to tell me something. "The damn monkey is more insane than Matters," I thought to myself and could not help but laugh, drawing in great clouds of the noxious mist.

I watched from a distance as the miniature Silencio crept near the very edge of the hole. He moved suddenly as if he were tossing something out into the mine. I caught with my glance the falling object, something like a white log. Then the updraft hit it and it blew apart into a hundred separate white birds that flapped and circled.

For the longest time I watched, enchanted, as the thin flock soared through the sulphur wind, rising and falling. One swept down and flew past my face before being carried out and up in a hellish gust. That is when I realized that what Silencio had tossed in had been the *Fragments*. I caught one last glimpse of the monkey, leaning over, looking down at me. He made a brushing motion with his hands, as if washing them of the scene, and then turned and was gone.

When I lost sight of the pages, the pain returned, instantly becoming unbearable. It was difficult to breathe, and I could no longer keep my eyes open but for short intervals. The hair on my arms and back began to singe. To avoid suffering, I journeyed inward, searching desperately for paradise, and soon caught sight of Beaton in my eye's-mind.

Beaton walked alone now along a dry riverbed that wound through a willow wood. After the deaths of Ives and Moissac in snow country, he had given up all hope of ever reaching paradise or home. He had with him the rifle the young man had continuously aimed but had never had the courage to fire. This would help him to survive for a few more weeks in his wandering.

Harad Beaton was numb with adventures and oddities. He had no wonder left. The things he had witnessed in the Beyond had made an ardent believer of him. What he had come to believe in was the invisible energy that connected the trees, the plants, the creatures of the wilderness. Now that he was alone, he would catch the whisper of its low hum moving beneath the wind in the branches. It was definitely there in all its awesome power, but he could not see what good knowing about it had done him. He was an outsider to it, a germ to be eradicated.

That afternoon, he sat on a tree stump next to the dry riverbed and ate some venison from a deer he had killed two days earlier. He drank from his water skin and judged that he should do some hunting that day. When he was finished with his meal, he left his blankets and provisions, his helmet and pick by the stump and took along only the rifle.

He entered into the willow wood, parting the long branches. There were cool shadows under the whips of foliage, and he could hear small animals and birds moving about. He wanted a rabbit, even though in the Beyond they had the pink, fleshy faces of pigs. The taste of them was unusual too—earthy and birdlike. He was still not sure that he enjoyed it, but he was always happy to have one skinned and turning on a spit.

It wasn't long before he spotted a pheasant, pecking around the base of a willow twenty or so yards ahead of him. He pulled the gun up and took aim. The shot would be difficult because of the layers of branches that separated them. He took his time, feeling for the drift of the breeze and calculating the location of the bird's heart. That is when he felt a hand come down lightly on his shoulder.

"Are you looking for Wenau?" said a voice behind him.

He spun around and there stood the Traveler, full of life, as I had seen him back in Anamasobia. Beaton backed up three steps and turned the gun on the creature.

"No harm," said the Traveler, holding up one of his webbed hands.

"You speak?" Beaton said.

"I heard you moving through the Beyond. I saw, in the

reflection of water, your friends die. At night, while you sleep, you cry like a child and none of the beasts of the Beyond will come near you,'' he said.

"But how do you know the language of the realm?'' asked the miner, unsure whether to lower his gun.

"The language was in me; I discovered it after having overheard your conversations in a seashell,'' he said.

Beaton shrugged. "I've got no reason to doubt you,'' he said and lowered the gun.

The Traveler stepped forward and handed the miner a piece of wood with a picture etched in black on it. It was the portrait of a young girl with long hair. Beaton had no idea at the time, but I could see over his shoulder that it was a likeness of Arla.

There was something about the strange man that Beaton liked right away. It had something to do with the sense of calm he exuded, something about his smile and eyes. The miner reached in his pocket to find a gift to exchange. He came across the seed first, but as its thistle poked his finger, he remembered his pledge to Moissac that he, himself, would plant it. Down below the seed, he found the coin he had seen Joseph drop in the tunnels of Palishize. As he placed it in the large brown hand, he wondered why he had never given it back to Bataldo.

"The flower and the snake,'' said the Traveler.

"Have you been to Palishize?'' asked Beaton.

"People came out of the sea and built it,'' he said. "They worshiped this flower, a yellow blossom from a certain tree that weeps when it is cut. This represented possibility. The coiled snake was forever. Palishize was abandoned before the forests of the Beyond had begun to grow.''

"What is Wenau?'' asked the miner. "Is it the Earthly Paradise?''

The Traveler nodded.

"Is death there?'' he asked.

"No death,'' said the Traveler. "I will take you.'' He

put the coin away in a pouch he wore on a leather strap about his waist. Then he reached up to a large fruit pit he wore like a pendant on a necklace. Miraculously, the thing opened on tiny hinges that had been carved into it. From within the pit, he pulled out two red leaves that had been folded over many times in order to fit. When opened all the way, they were the size of a man's hand and tissue thin.

He ate one of the leaves and handed the other to Beaton. "Eat it," he said.

"What will it do?" asked the miner.

"Give you courage," he said. Then he pulled the double-bladed knife from his belt and led the way.

Beaton began to feel asleep on his feet as he chewed the sweet red leaf. Things became visible to him that he had not noticed before. Small bright lights of various colors streamed down the path they took and passed right through them. Sparks of energy leaped off the ends of the Traveler's hair and fingers. Ghostly creatures poked their heads through the undergrowth to watch them pass. I hid behind a tree for fear that I could now be seen by them.

"We found one of you in Mount Gronus," Beaton tried to tell his guide, but the Traveler motioned for him to be quiet.

An instant later, Beaton perceived the Traveler was wrapped in deadly combat with a white phantom of a snake. Again and again, he plunged the double-bladed knife into its scaly back. White blood poured from the wounds, but still the creature kept tightening its stranglehold. The suddenness with which it happened shocked Beaton. It was almost as if the Traveler had always been fighting the snake.

Beaton finally came to his senses and lifted the rifle. He fired once, a direct hit through the jaw and into the brain of the monster. Then it was gone, disappearing like a memory forgotten, and they were walking calmly along again. The Traveler was smiling. His knife put away, he was smoking a long, hollow twig. How he had lit it, Beaton never saw. He passed it to the miner, who inhaled.

That day they forded streams and rivers, crossed vast barren tracts of snow and ice, climbed mountains, and walked along the shoreline of another inland sea. As the sun began to set, they came upon a village in a clearing in the woods. It was situated between two rivers, like an island.

"Wenau," said the Traveler.

People came streaming out of the simple dwellings and over the earthen bridge to greet them. There were children and women and old men, all made like the Traveler. Beaton was brought into the center of the village and fed a dinner of fruit and boiled grain. Stories were told, some in another language, until the rest of the inhabitants of Wenau discovered the language of the visitor.

Beaton was told he was welcome in the village, and they helped him to build a shelter for himself. He soon came to know all of the children and men and women. In the days that followed, he traveled throughout the island between the rivers, taking samples of all the myriad strange plants and flowers that grew there. Wenau always had a beautiful scent of spring to it. The days were always clear and warm and peaceful. One night, when he wandered by himself just outside the perimeter of the village, he planted Moissac's seed in a small stand of violet, flowering trees.

He marked his time in Wenau by the progress of the tree that grew up from the spiny brown seed. It grew rapidly and by the end of a few weeks, it was the size of the Traveler himself. The miner brought his friend to see the growth of Moissac's offspring one day. By then, it had brought forth on one single branch a white fruit like the one that had sat on the altar at Anamasobia.

"The fruit of paradise," Beaton said to his companion.

"Where did you get this seed?" said the Traveler.

Beaton told the story of the foliate, and as he did the Traveler shook his head.

"But the fruit holds immortality," said the miner.

"Come with me," said the Traveler.

Beaton followed him back to the village and then to a particular hut. There, on the floor in the main living quarters lay an old emaciated woman, gasping for breath. Two young women sat by her side, holding her thin hands, the webs now cracked and brittle.

"But she's dying," said Beaton to the Traveler.

"No, she is changing," he said. "The white fruit that grows from the seed of your friend disallows change."

"But she is physically dying then," said Beaton.

"I understand what you mean," said the Traveler. "I wasn't sure at first. This word *death* is a difficult idea. If you want to reach the land where there is no death, you must travel due north from here, a twelve season journey. I will show you the path, but I will not go with you."

"Then I haven't reached paradise?" said Beaton.

"What is paradise?" asked the Traveler. "That white fruit is an unchanging dream. It is death, as you call it. Now I must take it back to the world of those like you. We cannot have it here."

"You mean you will journey back with me to Anamasobia?" asked the miner.

"No, your people will discover me one day in a sealed chamber beneath a mountain, holding the white fruit," he said.

"But we already have," said Beaton.

"There are trails through the Beyond, if you know of them, that can take you back in time or ahead into the future. I will show you one to take that will return you to your town in two days' journey. Now I must hurry so that I can get to the mountain before the slow buildup of blue mineral seals the chamber three thousand years ago. There I will wait to meet you again."

Back out in the Beyond, I lost track of them, though I

tried to stay close. I was exhausted and lay down on the ground beneath a bush whose tendrils curled and uncurled in the breeze like the arms of a kraken. As I closed my eyes on the wilderness, I opened them to see the face of Silencio. It was night and I was back in my room at the inn, lying on my bed. Every inch of me was in exquisite pain, and the monkey had just brought a glass of Rose Ear Sweet to my lips.

20

 I sat up in the bed, extra pillows behind me. The sun streamed in the window, and the ocean breeze rolled through the room. I sipped at a cup of herbal tea. Silencio had applied his leaves to me through the night and saved my skin from anything worse than blistering. The most dangerous of my afflictions was dehydration, which the monkey had also cured over a period of hours by administering water, cabbage juice, and Rose Ear Sweet.

Corporal Matters of the night watch, with his winning personality and long white hair, stood before me with a nervous look.

"You say your brother has run off?" I asked him.

"Yes, he came by my place yesterday afternoon. I was working in my garden on the veranda overlooking the sea, when he suddenly appeared from behind a potted shrub," said the corporal.

"Was there violence?" I asked.

"None at all. He implored me to go to the mine to release you. He said his mind was full of paradise and that he must journey out into the wilderness. I think he has finally gone mad," said Matters.

"He said he'd been tampered with by the Master," I said.

"That's what they all say," said the corporal, sitting on the end of my bed.

"He told me that you too had been subject to some invention on Below's part," I said.

"Nonsense, Cley. It's all lies. Why are you willing to believe a lunatic who tried to kill you?" he asked.

"I saw a scar," I said.

"That scar," he said, "was made by a saber blade on the fields of Harakun."

"I had a suspicion that you and your brother were one and the same Corporal Matters," I told him.

He laughed. "Forget about that oaf. He's gone down the island. I doubt he will ever return. I'm in charge now, always. My first edict is no more mine. My second is, Silencio, go get us a bottle of Sweet and three glasses."

We drank, but I did not drink a lot. How could I not be leery of the corporal? He seemed to be truly the affable fellow of the night in broad daylight, but I knew I would have to watch him closely. Where Silencio stood, as an enemy or friend or maybe even the instigator of my salvation, was hard to tell. He seemed to have some personal agenda I couldn't yet figure out. Still, I was alive, and these two were the ones who had cut the ropes and dragged me from the mine. I gave myself up to the moment and conversed with the corporal about the fine weather.

It took a few days before I could get on my feet. With the constant attention of Matters and Silencio, I made a full recovery. As soon as I was up and about, I began spending my mornings down along the shore and my afternoons going to see certain sights suggested by the corporal. One day he and Silencio accompanied me to a lagoon that cut into the south shore of the island. It was surrounded by palm trees and flowering oleander. The monkey walked down to the water's edge and began doing a dance, flapping his arms over his head and screeching.

"Watch closely," said the corporal, who sat next to me on a blanket up the beach a way. As he spoke, I noticed that the birds, who had been squawking and chirping, suddenly fell silent. Now Silencio stopped moving and also quieted down. Although he had his back to us, I could tell he was staring intently into the clear waters. Off to his right, what I had thought to be an eel slithered up onto the shore, but when it kept coming, growing out of the water, and I could see the circular cups that lined it, I realized this was the kraken.

"Watch out, Silencio," I yelled and got to my feet, but the monkey had already begun to move as the huge, slippery arm swept the beach for him. A series of back flips brought him clear of the danger. Later that day, as we sat eating radish sandwiches and swilling Three Fingers, we saw the kraken surface. Its bulbous head, three barrels wide, had a single eye that watched us as its numerous tentacles undulated through the water.

We spent the nights sitting at the bar out on the screened porch. It was these times that almost made me forget that I had nearly been cooked alive a few weeks earlier. There seemed to be an endless supply of alcohol, and Silencio wouldn't take no for an answer on the refills. Sometimes we played cards by candlelight. The monkey invariably won, but we had decided to play for points—demarcations on a sheet of paper that stood for nothing owed. Many times, we did not go to bed until the sun was coming up.

On a morning after we had turned in rather early, the corporal came to my room and invited me to join him on a trip to the center of the island. He told me that we would have to bring guns in case of wild dogs, but that they probably wouldn't bother us in daylight. I agreed to go, seeing that all the sites the corporal had so far taken me to had been interesting. It was also my desire to know the island as well as I could.

When Silencio found out where we were going, he declined an offer to accompany us. This made me somewhat suspicious. The idea of the corporal toting a gun reminded me that the issue of him and his brother had never been sufficiently settled. Ever since my rescue, though, I had seen no sign in him that he was anything but what he professed. We had actually become good friends and companions. It was an effort to remind myself to be wary.

On the way to the center of Doralice, we did encounter a rogue dog who jumped for my throat from off the side of a dune. The corporal felled it with a rapid shot from his pistol. Very close to the spot of the attack, Matters showed me the bones of an enormous sea creature that had crawled ashore in a storm one night and died in the dunes. We continued on, passing through a valley in the sand that was a small oasis. There was a clear pool at its center, and fruit-bearing trees grew all around it.

"Sometimes I come here and think about my brother," said the corporal as he picked a lemon off an overhanging branch.

"What do you think?" I asked.

"You know, it all goes back to your mother," he said, biting into the fruit. Its aroma was one half of Arla's perfume.

At almost exactly midday we came over a particularly tall dune and saw below us an enormous wall constructed of seashells, behind which were tall mounds with openings, like sand castles melting in the surf.

"Palishize," I said to Matters.

He looked quizzically at me. "Very ancient," he said. "Once I found some writings by Harrow up in the attic of the inn. His theory was that it was built by people who came out of the sea."

We walked through the streets and, as in my vision, they were cobbled with large clam shells, backs to the sun. I found the experience so startling that as we wound around the bases of the mounds, I told the story of Beaton's journey to paradise. It took me the entire return trip to the inn to recount all of the adventures I remembered, and I finished up on the back porch at midnight, drunk on Rose Ear Sweet.

The corporal just shook his head when I finished. A

few seconds later, his eyes closed and he fell off his stool onto the floor. Silencio soon came with a pillow for him. The combination of Three Fingers and the Beyond had been too much. We threw an old blanket over him, and I stepped outside to see the stars. As I walked through the dunes, I thought about Arla and how I would get to her. I saw the Well-Built City in my head, but its vicious power scared me. I decided to simply think first about getting off Doralice.

I stopped in the path and looked up at the sky. As I traced the lines of the constellations, I heard someone approaching on the path. I thought it was Silencio, since, back at the inn, he had signaled to me as he finished his drink that he might join me on the beach. That is when two hands grabbed me by the shirt collar. I looked down into the face of Corporal Matters of the day watch. The scar that ran through the center of his head split my vision.

His breath was foul with alcohol, and, as he spoke, he spat all over me. "Cley," he yelled, "I order you to paradise." He pulled on my shirt, trying to drag me along with him. "I've located it; it's here on Doralice."

"Where is it?" I said, though I was still dazed by the suddenness of his appearance.

He stopped and loosened his grip on me somewhat. His eyes wandered as if he were trying to remember.

"I was there," he said and tightened his grip.

I poked him in the eyes with two fingers of my left hand, and he instantly let go of me. His scream echoed behind me as I ran at full speed through the dunes, back toward the inn. I had to see if the corporal of the night watch was still asleep on the floor. Either I had him or I didn't, but at least it would settle these matters.

As I came through the screen door onto the back porch of the inn, Silencio was playing a somber nocturne. I was gasping for air from my run, but I pushed on across the porch to the bar. There, I found Corporal Matters asleep where I had left him. I poured myself a drink and sat down and stared at him. It seemed to me that the white hair was rather askew, that he appeared to be breathing heavily for someone asleep, and that the blanket no longer fully covered him as it had before. On my second drink, I was not so sure of these things. By my third, I began to believe that the corporal of the day watch was really out there, searching for paradise.

The next day I told the corporal, as he sat nursing a hangover, that I had had an encounter with his brother.

"He's not in paradise yet?" asked Matters.

"He was out in the dunes," I told him.

"There's some bad business," he said.

"He ordered me to go to paradise with him," I said.

"He's run aground," said Matters. "I wouldn't be surprised if the wild dogs make a meal of his sagging flesh quite soon."

A few mornings later, Silencio came to me, screeching and motioning for me to get out of bed. The sun was barely up and the night had left a chill in the room. Corporal Matters of the night watch came through the door, looking worried.

"There's a boat in the harbor with soldiers on it," he said. "You'd better strip down and get over to the mine, while I go see what they want."

I immediately did as he requested, and, in less than a half hour, I was down there in the heat and stink again, sweating and gagging and chipping away at my tunnel. "One more reminder of hell," I thought, wishing it were true. I began to become concerned after I had been in the mine for more than two hours. I started to wonder why the soldiers were there. "Perhaps they are bringing another prisoner," I thought.

It was still an hour beyond that when I heard the corporal calling me from the rim of the pit. I gladly threw down my pick and scrabbled up the path. Outside in the afternoon heat, I found the corporal and three uniformed soldiers, carrying rifles.

"Cley?" said one of the men.

I nodded.

"Come with us, please," he said.

I looked over at Matters, who shook his head slightly to indicate to me not to address him. We followed the soldiers through the dunes, down the beach, and to the harbor where there was a steamboat waiting.

"Corporal Matters," said one of the soldiers as we stood on the wharf next to the boat.

The corporal stepped forward.

"We are taking Cley," said the soldier.

"As you wish," said Matters.

Then the soldier pulled something off his belt and applied it to the side of Matters's face. The object was a black box with two steel prongs sticking out of one end. The corporal screamed in intense pain. This lasted for a full minute until his eyes turned to jelly and black smoke poured from his ears, nose, and mouth. He fell in a heap at my feet.

"What?" was all I could ask.

The soldier proudly held the device up to me. "It melts gear work. It's an easy way to put them down when they've become obsolete. Now, if you'll kindly step aboard, Physiognomist Cley, we have been ordered by the Master to escort you back to the Well-Built City. You have been pardoned."

Just like that, dressed in my underwear, I stepped aboard the boat. I felt bad about leaving Silencio alone, but this was the only way to get back to the City. They sat me by the side so I would have a good view. One of the soldiers brought me a blanket and wrapped it around my shoulders. I couldn't believe I had been pardoned.

Later, as we cruised down the north side of the island, four soldiers came and held me down. One of them brought forth a syringe of sheer beauty and jabbed it into my neck. The drug exploded in my head and showered its violet glow throughout me. The soldiers begged my pardon, then lifted me up and put me back where I had been sitting.

The beauty wrapped me tightly against the winds and I stared, lost in daydreams. Before the boat turned away from the island, we passed its western tip. At somewhat of a distance but still visible, I saw Corporal Matters of the day watch on a small spit of sand that jutted out into the breakers. Behind him the beach was crawling with hungry wild dogs, waiting. I waved to him and called his name. He looked up and out to sea at me. "I've found paradise," he called over the water.

21

News of my return was all over the *Gazette*. The headlines hinted that a terrible mistake had been made in one of the more intricate calculations leading to the final equation of my guilt. As far as the general populace was concerned, they were to have no fear of the efficacy of the Physiognomy for themselves, since their features were obviously much cruder, hence, easier to read. There was a quote attributed to myself, which, of course, I can never remember having given, to the effect that the whole mix-up was totally understandable. The Master was quoted as saying that he was relieved that one of his most trusted subjects could now be pardoned and return to a fruitful life in the City. Following this nonsense was an in-depth recounting of my life and the numerous high-profile cases I had prosecuted. Every one of these represented to me a tunnel tomb carved in sulphur.

When I opened the door to my apartment, all was exactly as I had left it on that afternoon, months ago, when I had set out for the territory. The only exception was a giant bouquet of yellow flowers on my desk along with a small package which turned out to be a month's supply of sheer beauty and enough syringes to carry it to my veins. The soldiers, who had brought me from Doralice, had injected me every eight hours on the return trip, so that I was once again dependent on the drug.

I cannot say that I did not breathe a sigh of relief getting beneath the covers of my own bed and sleeping deeply, but once in dreams, Arla, Calloo, Bataldo—even Silencio—came to me to remind me that I had covert, unfinished business with the realm to attend to and that I could not allow any measure of comfort and warm welcome to deter me.

After I awoke from a nightmare of demons, I stayed up and tried to think clearly through what I would have to do. I smoked thirty cigarettes between then and dawn, in an attempt to forgo an injection. I soon realized that, in my secret self, with my new knowledge, I was as much a stranger in the City as I had been in the territory. The title of Physiognomist, First Class was merely a disguise for me now. Somehow I would have to outsmart the Master, stay two thoughts ahead of him. The only problem was that his thought process was less than linear. "I will have to think around him," I whispered, but then regretted my words, remembering the time he had told me, "I don't read, I listen." It was all too much, too suddenly. The morning sun brought tears to my eyes as I rolled back my sleeve and tapped a vein at the crook of my arm.

The next day a messenger appeared at my door to inform me that a coach would be by in an hour to take me to Below's offices at the Ministry of Benevolent Power. I bathed quickly and dressed in my lime silk suit with matching vest. Plucking one of the yellow blossoms from the bouquet, I affixed it to my lapel as an outward sign that all was right with Cley, that his confidence in the Master, the realm had been fully restored. I knew that the order of the day would call for both a good measure of groveling and a certain self-assurance when it came to discussing my future. I was sure that there had been some ulterior motive behind my pardon. As I heard the driver knock at my door, I decided to allow things to develop as they would, all the while staying keenly observant for a spark of insight that might lead to a plan.

As the coach wound through the streets of the City, I marveled at that complexity of design I had not witnessed in so long. My last stay there had been spent between my prison cell and the courtroom. The black bag, which had been thrown over my head during the transport between them, had prevented me from seeing the citizens bustling to and fro beneath the spires and domes. The pink coral buildings, the glass, the crystal would probably have made Beaton think he had stumbled upon paradise had he taken a wrong turn in his wanderings and landed here. I did notice a greater presence of uniformed guards on patrol. They carried flamethrowers, which was unusual.

The coach pulled up before the enormous crystal structure of the ministry. I got out and made my way up the steep steps and through the front door into the lobby. A young woman came up to me as I advanced toward the elevators.

"Physiognomist Cley, welcome back to the City. The Master awaits your arrival," she said.

I nodded to her and smiled, but she was only the first to greet me. People I didn't even know stopped me in the lobby to wish me well. Behind their smiles and open palms, I knew there had been an order from above requiring affability. I stayed calm until I had nodded to everyone and then took the elevator up to the tenth floor. When the doors opened and I entered the long hallway that led to Below's office, I was astonished to see that it was lined on both sides with the blue static forms of hardened heroes from Anamasobia. Among them I spotted Arden, holding his mirror. On my left, Beaton leaned in a static pose into the aisle, the fingers of his hand slightly parted, proffering his invisible message.

When I entered his office, the Master was sitting behind his desk, a flat, smooth piece of quartz the length of the coach that had brought me. There were stacks of paperwork on it, which he was in the process of throwing into the blazing fireplace behind him.

"Cley, welcome," he said, nodding for me to take the seat across the desk from him. "I don't think I'll ever get through this paperwork. It is the bane of the Master."

He threw a few more stacks in and then turned, folded his hands on the desk, and stared into my eyes. I returned his stare for as long as I could and then looked away toward the miniature replica of the City that sat on a table in the corner.

"I see you have brought back souvenirs from the territory," I said, pointing over my shoulder toward the hallway.

"The territory, the territory, the people can't get enough of it. The papers are filled with tales of the territory. I've made a fortune on the few things I was able to bring back. Demon horns are selling for seven hundred belows apiece. I disseminated the lie that when taken in its powdered form it would induce week-long erections and orgasms that would leave one washed up at the gates of paradise." He laughed. "Some fun for the people."

"I wanted to thank you personally for my pardon," I said, trying to seem as cowed as possible.

"Well, Cley," he said, leaning back, "I missed you. You were always so damned conscientious. The memory of you riding next to me in my cart, bespattering your trousers over the consequences of your crimes against the realm, made me feel . . . shall we say, like a father who has lost touch with an errant son."

"Master, you honor me with the analogy," I said.

His eyes darted back and forth beneath that one contiguous hedge of eyebrow as if he were unsure whether he had gone too far. "How was Doralice?" he asked.

"Well, I met your old war companions, Matters and Matters," I said.

"Oh, those two. Fuck them, the monkey runs the show on that island," he said. "What did you think of the monkey?"

"Silencio. He was remarkable," I said.

"One of mine," said Below and clapped for himself.

"I also came to the conclusion that I had sinned and that it was just punishment for me to bake in the mines," I told him.

"Very well then," he said, and began manipulating the fingers of both hands in front of me. I knew that one of his parlor tricks was to follow, and, sure enough, the yellow flower I had been wearing was now cupped in his palms.

I looked down at my lapel to find it empty. "Miraculous," I said.

He nodded in agreement with me. "Listen, Cley, I can't have you come back to the City and not have some work for you. I know you love your work. I've got a new project for you."

"Will I be employing the Physiognomy?" I asked.

"Your rank has already been reinstated. I need someone of your intensity to carry out this special mission I have. You see, I noticed while wandering through the streets in disguise the other day that my divine creation, this amazing metropolis, was getting too crowded. Believe it or not, I heard rumblings of unhappiness from the citizenry. When I looked closely at these malcontents, I began to notice that their physiognomies were less than sterling. Many of their faces could have passed for the rear ends of animals. So I began to devise a plan to thin out the population."

"I am at your service," I said.

"I knew you would respond with fortitude," he said. "What I want you to do is round up ten people a day, read them all, find the ones with the least favorable visages, and send their names to me. In ten days, we will bring these people in and have them eradicated. My plan is that we hold public executions in Memorial Park. We'll see how much grumbling there is afterward."

"A splendid plan," I told him.

"The word is out that you have full power to detain and read any subjects you see fit with the exception of my personal staff. Remember those idiots who prosecuted you? They are open to investigation, if you see what I mean," he said, laughing. "In any event, I want ten warm bodies in ten days, but it is important for you to read as many as you can. I want these investigations to touch as many people's lives as possible."

"Understood," I said. "I will proceed immediately."

He was not ready to let me go just yet, though. He brought out two vials of the beauty. I wanted to decline, but I could see that it was a test of my loyalty. The Master went for the vein in his tongue.

"It's my special mix," he slurred as he pulled the needle out of his mouth.

We sat there for an hour in the throes of the beauty, and he did card tricks and sleight of hand with coins. Below's special mix was certainly special. I couldn't move. The graceful motion of his hands as he performed was hypnotic. Pigeons, fire, a tiny man fashioned from his earwax did somersaults across the table. Finally, it all came so fast and furiously, I thought I was going to pass out. Then he jumped out of his seat, came around the table, and ushered me toward the door.

"Tonight, Cley," he said, "I have arranged for a dinner in your honor. I want them all to kiss your ass for a night. It was a shame that I allowed them to talk me into sending you away."

"As you wish," I said.

"You'll need this to get in," he said and put one of the coins he had been performing with into my palm.

I said good-bye and walked down the hall of hardened heroes. Once outside, I stopped on a bench and tried to catch my breath. Not even on Doralice had I perspired so much. That batch of the beauty had given me the worst case of chills I had ever experienced. In addition to this, my nerves were frayed by the immensity of the future.

Eventually, I pulled myself together by walking around one of the outside malls. In a temporary ring, at the center of the walkway, there was a battle match taking place between two of the Master's hardware-enhanced citizens. I tried not to pay any attention to the brutality, but at that time of day the mall was relatively empty. There was only a young mother and her two daughters present.

When my breathing had returned to normal, I turned my attention to the contest in the ring. One of the fighters had snapping metallic claws for hands and a set of steel corkscrews protruding from his head. The other fellow whirred and clanked with the noise of his defective inner workings, but he was very large. There were crude skin grafts across his neck and chest. He had no odd features save for life itself, but he carried in one hand a pickax and in the other a net.

The metal claws snipped through the net as if it were lace. When the big man swung the pick and missed, the other drove forward with his head and gored an arm. I saw no blood, but the skin tore fiercely. It ended with the pickax in the claw man's back. The sound of applause filled the mall from speakers mounted on the buildings. The big man bowed stiffly as the cleanup crew came to take away the vanquished. The mother and daughters lost interest and wandered off to something else. I walked quietly up to the side of the battle ring behind where the winner stood.

"Calloo," I said.

He stood perfectly still, staring off into the distance.

"Calloo," I called.

At the sound of his name, he turned and looked down at me. He stared for the longest time. I thought I was making some deep contact with him, but then I realized that he had broken down. When I looked up, I saw a large spring protruding through the skin at the back of his neck.

I ran through the mall and out into the park. I wandered through the City gardens for an hour or so before I finally made my way across town to my office. After having seen Calloo, I was more determined than ever to undermine the realm in any way I could. As soon as I got to my desk, I dashed off a letter on official stationery to the Minister of the Treasury, requesting a complete inventory of all the items the Master had brought back with him from the territory. If I was lucky, my message would never even get to the minister but would be handled by one of his underlings. I was afraid of being caught, but in this situation it was as dangerous not to act as it was to. I thought I might find a clue in the official records that would show me the way to Arla.

After dispatching the note with a messenger, I stood by the window, staring down across the street in front of the Academy of Physiognomy. I wanted to yell out the window to the passing crowds, "There is madness here," but I could tell they were too busy thinking of what official connections they could massage in order to procure a snort or two of demon horn.

22

My dinner was held at the Top of the City, beneath the crystal dome. When I tried to give the guard at the entrance the coin that Below had handed me, he refused it. He welcomed me back from Doralice as I stepped through the doorway. The sun was setting behind a mountain range off to the west, its red beams refracting through the translucent roof of the candlelit restaurant. I immediately went to the bar and ordered a drink.

The circular room was a hive of ministers and dignitaries from the realm's matrix of bureaucracy. They moved around between the tables, methodically chasing one another and running away, talking from one side of the mouth, laughing from the other, all the while gritting their teeth. Big cigars were being smoked, and I caught snippets of conversation, all revolving around status and the acquisition of belows.

The moment it was known I had arrived, a long line formed before me. They came at me one at a time to shake my hand, welcome me back, perhaps ask some tidbit about the territory or the sulphur mine. I yessed them and thanked them and told them all how much I had suffered. The alcohol flowed freely, and many of my well-wishers were drunk. I, myself, had downed three Rose Ear Sweets before half the line had gotten to me. I remembered my days of Physiognomy and how many lines of faces I had been through. The same now as then; I did not expect to find anything remarkable.

That thought had just left my head, when a drunken young woman came staggering toward me. She was unescorted, probably one of the young women the Master hired at these events to "fill out the crowd." Her eyes were half closed, and she wore a smirk on her face. I could smell Three Fingers before she got within four feet of me. She threw her arms around my shoulders and kissed me full on the lips, pressing her tongue between my teeth. Those behind her in the line applauded.

I drew away and she put her lips to my ear and said, "How's that leather glove?"

"Do I know you?" I asked.

"No," she said. Then she released me and stepped back to the person behind her in line, a tall fellow with a striped suit and a well-trimmed mustache. "He pinkied me one night wearing a leather glove over in Memorial Park," she said.

The man laughed and nodded. As she moved off into the crowd, I saw him turn to the man behind him and tell him something. The second man looked up at me while he listened and then he too began to laugh. I watched with a sick feeling as the description of my dalliance made a visible wave through the crowd. Some of the inebriated put on their gloves to shake hands with me. I grinned and told them how much I had suffered.

After I had been accosted by everyone present, the Master made his appearance. He was dressed in a living suit made of some trailing plant that grew from pockets filled with soil. The thing covered him like a hedge and made a sort of hood above the back of his head. In a half dance, he moved to the center of the room and called for silence. Quiet descended like a rock, for everyone knew that even to sneeze during one of his orations could mean dire consequences.

"I have been to the territory," he said, staring up through the dome at the gathering night as if looking for something.

Everyone looked up until they realized it was merely a dramatic effect.

"And," he continued, "I have brought the territory back to you." With this he clapped his hands and attendants began moving tables and chairs aside, creating a wide path that led from the double doors of the kitchen to a large, circular clearing. When their work was finished, the Master announced, "Behold the demon."

They brought it through the doors of the kitchen with its hands chained behind its back and a rope around its chest, folding down and holding fast the wings. Two soldiers accompanied the creature—one leading it by a chain attached to a metal clasp around its neck and the other following, a flamethrower trained on its back.

The demon hopped more than walked, all the time flashing its fangs and growling at the guests. They shrank back as it tried to lunge at them. The soldier pulled hard on the leash and brought his prisoner away from the crowd. It was led into the circular clearing, and its chain was shortened considerably and attached to a clamp in the floor.

The demon roared and fought against the restraints. Muscles across its back flexed, swelling the wings a pitiful half inch beneath the rope. The Well-Built City's elite stayed clear of it for five minutes, and then seeing that it could not escape, they inched closer and closer. Soon the taunts began. They threw crumpled cocktail napkins at it. They crept up until they were just out of its reach and yelled threats to it. The Master walked up to me where I still stood next to the bar.

"You're a smart man, Cley," he said to me, turning to keep an eye on the spectacle.

"How's that, Master?" I asked.

"You are interested in investing in some of the relics of the territory, I believe?" he asked.

"Well, I'm not sure," I said, taking a drink to disguise my confusion.

"The Minister of the Treasury has informed me that you requested an entire list of items brought back from the territory," he said.

"Oh, that," I said. I smiled, then laughed, then scratched my head. "I thought a demon horn might be a wise investment, seeing as how if it were ground up and sold by the snort, one could charge quite a bit, making fourteen hundred out of seven," I said. "Of course, I got the idea from you this morning."

"I knew that is what you had in mind," he said. "I'll send you one as a gift."

I was going to thank him, but there was some commotion going on in the crowd. The guests suddenly fled backward, tripping over the legs of chairs and sprawling across tables. It seemed the demon had been able to catch one of its tormentors with a horn to the forehead. I looked up just in time to see the poor victim slide to the floor with a blood-drenched look of total surprise beneath a gaping wound. The demon immediately descended, snapping down with its powerful jaws on the now screaming face.

The Master stepped forward as the soldier with the flamethrower tightened his finger on the trigger. "Hold on a second," he called as the man writhed beneath the fangs of the demon. "Who is that on the floor there?" he asked.

A few of the people turned and said, "It's Burke from the Ministry of the Arts."

The Master laughed. "Forget it," he said to the soldier, and the man lowered his weapon. Then Below snapped his fingers and the music began to play. Waiters entered from the kitchen, carrying bottles of absence and trays of chived cremat. "Delicacies from the territory," he called out over the rush to grab them.

Later, I had to sit on a dais at the north side of the dome while ponderous speeches were made about my brilliance, my dedication to the realm, the perplexing elegance of my physiognomy. I smiled and nodded inanely, and the crowd applauded, laughed, and cheered in all the right places. When I was asked to speak, I merely gave the standard salute to Below and said, "Long live the City, the realm, and the Master." I looked down at the crowd, and after their response died away they looked at me, none of us knowing what should come next.

The Master was then beside me, shaking my hand for all the dignitaries to see. I was escorted back to my seat on the dais by one of the attendants as Below addressed the guests.

"Watch this," he said, and grimaced. White flowers popped into existence at the ends of the tendrils that made up his hood. The guests were beside themselves. I preferred to watch the attendants drag the remains of Burke away from the demon with an eight-foot steel hook.

"Get your résumés in for the minister of the arts position," said Below. A wave of laughter welled up from the crowd, but once things had quieted down, the Master struck a more sober pose. "It is only fitting that we honor Physiognomist Cley tonight," he said, "for he embodies the ingenuity and insight of the territory. You all love the idea of those strange, wide-open places, and I have done my best to bring some of that to you tonight. But beyond this, I see the territory as a symbol of my new campaign to revitalize the City. In doing so, I propose two measures. First, I have ordered Cley here to round up physiognomical undesirables for execution. In ten days, in Memorial Park, you will witness the survival of the fittest, or should I say the perishing of the unfit, a phenomenon borrowed directly from the wilderness."

The guests clapped madly for this announcement, as if in the energy of their applause, the Master might notice they were worthy of survival.

"As a result of this campaign, you may lose a relative, a spouse, a child, but never let it be said that Drachton Below takes without giving back. A new exhibit from the territory will open in ten days. The location of this spectacle will be kept a secret until it is announced after the executions in the park. This display will be called 'Anomalies of the Territory,' and in it, you will see some of the strangest sights any City dweller has ever beheld. It will be fun for the whole family. The demon there is merely a pathetic creature. Wait till you see what I have brought back,'' he said.

He moved the fingers of his left hand as he had that morning and produced a small coin out of thin air. ''All of you were given one of these,'' he said. ''Save these special coins, for they will admit you and a loved one to the exhibition for free at the grand opening.''

I followed suit as the members of the audience began searching their pockets for the coins. When I pulled mine out and held it up in my palm, I saw that it had an image of a coiled snake on one side. I flipped it over and there was a flower.

The mess that was Burke had been whisked away by the time dinner was served. I sat at a table with the Master and the Minister of Security, Winsome Graves. The moment we were seated, Graves began toadying, blathering on about the grandeur of Below's Territory Campaign.

''Shut up,'' Below said to him.

''Yes, of course,'' said the minister with a forced smile.

In keeping with the theme of the evening, roasted fire bat and old-fashioned cremat dumplings were the main course. I could barely keep from retching when my plate was set down before me. The Master looked over and saw that I wasn't digging in like the other guests, some of whom were already inquiring about seconds.

''Cley, don't you like the meal?'' he asked.

Graves looked across at me and smiled, his mouth full of dumpling, waiting to see what would happen.

''It's the excitement, sir. I am overwhelmed by this outpouring of acceptance,'' I said.

"Well, I don't blame you," said the Master. "I don't see how they can eat that shit."

He, of course, did not have a serving of the foul repast set before him, but as he finished speaking, a silver tray with a domed top was brought. "Here is real sustenance," he said as he lifted the top to reveal the white fruit of paradise.

"Begging your pardon," said Graves, "but is it wise to eat that? Who knows what effects it might have."

"I've had it tested over the past few months," said the Master. "There is a laboratory rat, now in the Academy of Science, who was fed a morsel of it. The little beggar has been brought back from death's door by it. Though he was dying of rat old age, he is now virile, resilient, and runs mazes, I dare say, with more intelligence than you would, Graves."

"May you taste paradise," I said to Below as he lifted the fruit to his mouth and began eating, its pale juices flowing down his chin. The aroma of it wafted around me, bringing me back to my visions and dreams and obliterating the stench of the cremat. The Master's vegetal suit reminded me of Moissac, the foliate, and fragments of the *Fragments* of Beaton's journey came back to me. When I looked up from my thoughts, I saw the core of the fruit, a gnawed hour glass, revealing black pits at its center.

"Quite edible," he said, as he wiped his hands on his leaves, "but I hardly feel immortal." He snapped his fingers and his private servant moved up next to him. "Take this away and plant the seeds as I have instructed," he said.

The night wore on as I minced and bowed and nodded. I kept a close watch on the Master to see what kinds of changes the fruit might make in him, but nothing remarkable came to pass. When he got up to dance with the young lady who had revealed to the others my sexual techniques, I pumped Graves for any information he might have about the exhibit the Master had referred to. He told me some of his men had been pulled from their usual assignments in order to guard the thing, but not even he knew where it was being built.

"We can only know what the Master tells us," he said, smiling.

I considered paying him a visit the next day in my new, official capacity and ordering him in for a reading. I wondered how many deaths he had been responsible for over the years. As I pictured his head being filled with inert gas before a crowd in Memorial Park, swelling to match his sense of self-importance, I caught myself. "You are hating again, Cley," I told myself. I remembered the word carved into sulphur in Professor Flock's tomb—"forgive." It was a struggle, but before long, I could see that Graves was simply trying to survive. He had his own disguise, like me, like the rest of them. We were all trying to hide our true selves from Drachton Below, waiting for his "glorious dream" to finally come to a close.

The affair abruptly ended when the Master entangled two young ladies in rapidly growing vines, like spiderwebs, and left through the double doors of the kitchen. The minute he was gone, the music stopped, the lights came up, and the attendants began cleaning up. The demon was then led away. Guests were wrapping up the delicacies of the territory in napkins and pocketing them to take back to their families. I was quite drunk but relieved that I had made it through the evening.

The coach was waiting for me outside on the windy street, but I told the driver to go on without me. I walked the City for an hour or so, trying to sober up. It was down on the Boulevard of Montz along the man-made lake of floating lilies that I realized I was being followed. I first heard the footsteps in syncopation with my own. Finally, I spun around and saw a shadow clumsily dart into a doorway on the other side of the street.

I went directly to my apartment, locked the door behind me, and listened with my ear to the keyhole. When I had established that there was no one there, I rushed to my desk and prepared a vial of the beauty. My skull itched terribly, and I was beginning to quiver on the edge of withdrawal. I took it in the head and called on Flock, but he would no longer come. The floor and walls wavered and sparked, the yellow flowers wept, and before I dozed off, of all people, Frod Geeble, the tavern owner of Anamasobia, appeared before me and spent a half hour belching.

23

 The next morning I was up early, filling out
appointment cards for those unlucky citizens I
would decide to read. Of course, I had no intention of turning ten people over to the Master
for execution. Whatever it was I was going to do, I had
ten days in which to do it and then figure out some way
to flee the City. For now, though, I would need to follow
through with the charade by requesting that certain individuals I encountered through the morning come to my
offices in the afternoon for a reading.

I left my apartment before the crush of workers on the
way to their jobs could choke the streets. My first stop
was to be the Top of the City, where I had dined the
previous night. I took a circuitous route, doubling back,
stopping in passageways, passing through the Academy of
Physiognomy and then out the back door. I had not noticed
anyone following me, but if someone was, I felt confident
that I had lost him.

When I got to the restaurant, the cleanup crew was just
opening the doors to the elevator that led to the dome.
They tried to prevent me from going up, but I told them
who I was and asked them if they would like to stop by
my office for a reading that afternoon. When they instantly
lost all interest in detaining me, I realized that my new
power would come in handy. I didn't bother to give any

of them cards, and they smiled thankfully at me. I smiled back as the elevator doors closed.

The restaurant was empty, save for a cleaning woman, who entered soon after me and was trying to scrub the blood of poor Burke from the middle of the dance floor. She ignored me and I her. I could see the sun coming up beyond the dome, and the room began to glow with its warmth. My plan was to use the tower as a lookout point in order to see if I could spot any signs of construction going on throughout the city. I walked the rim of the crystal, staring down, watching carefully as the insectlike inhabitants scurried purposefully along paths and through holes in the coral structures. "Palishize," I thought to myself.

I spotted nothing. All seemed as it always had on the City's skyline. There were no great depressions in the earth, no accumulation of building equipment, no scaffolding. As I spied from my perch, I noticed that the woman had walked up next to me and was also looking down.

"Can I help you?" I asked.

"Was wondering if you were looking for the demon," she said.

"The demon was here last night," I told her. "That mess you are working on is the fruit of its labor."

"I know that," she said and smiled through missing teeth. "But I guess you haven't heard about what happened last night. As soon as they took it through the kitchen over there, it managed to burst out of its chains. They tried to flame it, but they ended up flaming each other. The ones that were left were killed by it. It's out there now, hiding in the City," she said.

"That is not good," I said.

"I read in the paper where one of the Master's experts said that it must be hiding underground during the daylight hours. They said there shouldn't be a problem until the night comes."

The news was frightful, but I did not miss the fact that

there was much information to be garnered from listening to the populace. I thanked her and she seemed genuinely happy that I had acknowledged her help. She went back to the stain, kneeled and continued scrubbing.

Having found nothing in the visible topography of the City to indicate the construction of the exhibit, I left and went immediately to a newsstand to purchase a copy of the *Gazette*. Sitting down with it in front of a steaming cup of shudder at the outdoor café by the park, I turned to the second page and read the headline DEMON LOOSE. I sped through the story, which told me little more than the cleaning woman had. "Since when has Below begun admitting to mistakes?" I wondered. In the past, this incident would never have been reported. This was something I would try to ask him about at our next meeting.

The shudder went down well, and I ordered another cup. I sat contemplating the thought that an ally of some kind might be helpful, but who was I to trust? The cleaning woman seemed the only one I had met since my return who didn't appear to have any ulterior motive behind her words. I thought about her and then recalled her telling me that the demon was probably underground somewhere. It struck me that not only was the demon hiding beneath the surface but also that was probably the location of the exhibit.

I remembered from my student days when I had had to be across town to attend a reading or fetch reports from the Ministry of Security in a hurry. I had traveled underground to avoid the busy hours on the streets. When the foundation of the City had been laid, Below had ingeniously built in a vast network of underground passageways, tunnels, and catacombs that he himself had used as a means of traveling unseen from location to location. "Surprise is my meat, Cley," he had said to me on one occasion, referring to that very network. Officials were allowed to use it but rarely did, not wanting to be found down there by the Master and raise his suspicion of some hidden plot.

"Beneath the surface," I said to myself, and wanted to go and investigate right then. Instead, I kept my revelation in check and got up and passed out appointment cards to the other patrons of the café. They thanked me in pitifully weak voices. I could see how frightened they were, but I had to keep a severe gaze as I took down their names.

On the way back to the office to keep those appointments, I passed through the mall where I had witnessed Calloo battle the claw man the day before. There was another match going on and quite a bigger crowd of onlookers. Belows were exchanging hands, and the audience was calling for gears and springs to be scattered across the ring. Luckily, the participants were not familiar to me.

I walked up to a soldier who stood behind the crowd, holding a flamethrower. One of the automated gladiators had just lost his head to a battle-ax blow. "What happens to the ones that are defeated or broken?" I asked him.

"None of your business," he said.

"Do you know who I am?" I asked him in a pleasant voice.

"You're about two seconds from being burnt beyond recognition," he said. "Move on."

I handed him an appointment card. Seeing it, he immediately understood the gravity of his mistake.

"Your honor," he said.

"Perhaps we could discuss it in my office this afternoon," I said. "By the way, has anyone ever read that forehead of yours?" I shook my head and grumbled a little.

"A million pardons, your honor," he said. "The ones who are defeated are taken back to the big warehouse behind the munitions factory. If they are beyond saving, they are incinerated after the brass and zinc parts have been removed. If they are salvageable, they are outfitted with new pieces and sent back for another battle match."

I snatched the card from his hand. "You are very helpful," I said.

As I walked away, he called after me, "Welcome back from Doralice."

I spent the afternoon at my office, reading those who I had made appointments for. They were all just simple people of the realm, and I did not make them undress. Instead, I played around with the calipers and the lip vise, every now and then jotting down a bogus note or two as I had done back in Anamasobia. No matter how deficient the Physiognomy told me they were, I lauded praise on their features and encouraged them to talk. At first they were wary, unused to having so important a member of the realm seem friendly to them. I believe they each reached a point where they intuited that I would do them no harm, and then they told me everything—about their children, their jobs, their fears concerning the demon. I nodded and listened attentively even though I was itching for the beauty.

Then the last of the fellows who came through my examination room, a young gardener, whose main job was keeping the tilibar bushes blooming in the park, mentioned something that I found interesting. He had heard I had been to the territory and wanted to let me know that he too had been there.

"I was sent out to the wilderness beyond the boundary of the territory about a month after the Master's expedition had returned, a few weeks after you were so wrongly sentenced," he said.

"Interesting," I said.

"I was ordered by the Master to bring back a variety of species of plants and trees—a great quantity of them. The operation was immense," he told me.

"What did you do with them?" I asked.

"It was the strangest thing," he said. "We brought them back to the City and were told to deliver them to the western side of town, over by the sewage treatment plant and the waterworks. We dropped them off in the middle of the street, and they nearly filled the whole thoroughfare. Then I was dismissed from the detail and was sent back to the park to my tilibar bushes. The next day, after work, I went to see what they had done with them, and they had all vanished.''

He wanted to then tell me about his fiancée and his plans for the future, but by then the chills were running through me, and I needed a fix desperately. I ushered him to the door as he was still talking, assuring him that he was a great asset to the realm and wishing him well in his marriage. The instant he was outside, I closed the door and went to my desk to prepare a syringe. Through the years, I had become so good that I had that needle in my neck in less than three minutes.

Since I had been able to quit the beauty once, it seemed to know that I could do it again, and because of this it did not treat me so roughly as it had back before my imprisonment. I would still hallucinate, but there was less of it, and that overwhelming feeling of paranoia was replaced by long stretches of deep thought. That afternoon, I daydreamed about rescuing Calloo from his mechanized, walking death and enlisting him to help me. Then I watched out the window the illusion of the City melting in a fine black rain that fell beneath an opulent sun.

I knew none of it was real, and yet I continued to fantasize, this time about Arla. How I would rescue her and she would forgive me and fall in love with the new me. It all seemed so simple, so absolutely necessary. I had my arms around her and was just about to kiss her, when there came a knocking at my door that scared me so by its suddenness that I nearly fell out of my chair.

"Package for Physiognomist Cley," a voice said.

My head spun as I got up and walked shakily to the door. I opened it just enough to let the package in and then closed it. "Thank you," I called, but there was no response. It was wrapped in brown paper and tied with a string. There was no name on it, no return address. I laid it on my desk and then just sat staring at it for some time. Finally, when the effects of the beauty had nearly worn off, I opened it. The first thing I pulled out was a note written in the Master's hand.

> Cley,
> *Here is the demon horn I promised you last night. Try to stay away from the ones that are attached to a head. If you can't, I have enclosed something to help you protect yourself. Do not go out at night until the crisis has been abated.*
>
> Drachton Below,
> *Master of the Realm*

Inside the package I found the hard black horn of a demon. Holding it in my hand, I realized that with its weight and sharp tip, it would make an adequate weapon. Beneath it, though, wrapped in tissue paper, I discovered something far more effective—my old derringer, fully loaded, along with a box of bullets. When I put on my topcoat that evening to leave the office, I had the gun, the horn, and a scalpel, each in a different pocket. None of them was a flamethrower, but I did feel a little safer as I stepped onto the street beneath the starlit sky.

I moved with some confidence amid the sea of home-bound workers. When they recognized me, they gave me that curious one-fingered salute. Upon seeing it, I smiled and lifted my middle finger to them as a show of solidarity. To my annoyance, they did not smile back, but dropped their gaze and moved off, looking disgusted. It was then that I wished I was one of them, a nobody in the crowd, living a simple life like the gardener and his fiancée.

24

The streets had emptied completely by the time I got to the munitions factory. This was one of the older parts of town that did not have gas lamps on every corner. There were no stores there to light the way with glowing signs. It was a district of manufacturing, where the Master's ideas were transformed into brass and zinc. There hadn't been a war in over thirty-five years, yet the munitions factory had triple shifts. One of the Master's greatest feats of sleight of hand was how he stored all of the rockets and bullets that were made there. As I passed by, I could hear the machines banging out shells, and the glow from the windows was as vague as twilight.

Two blocks behind the factory, I found the warehouse I thought the soldier in the mall had been talking about. It ran, windowless, nearly the length of a full block and was deep to the point where I could not see beyond it. The entrance to the place was two huge wooden doors with a loose chain attaching them. I could easily slip through the opening between them. I took out my lighter and my derringer and went into the dark crevice.

I could barely make out the rows and rows of large cribs that lined the aisle I suddenly found myself in. Next to the cribs were rolling trays of tools, gears, and wires. My lighter went out for a moment, and it took me too long to get it going again. When I held it lit over one of the cribs, I saw a near-human Below creation of metal and flesh, half open and completely asleep.

It took me over an hour to check all of the faces for Calloo's, but I found him. He seemed to have been patched since his contest in the mall. In fact, he looked much better. The scar tissue I had noticed on his neck and chest was greatly diminished, and his arms looked as powerful as they had in the territory. I put the lighter down near his open eyes to see if there was any movement. At first I noticed nothing, but then—and I nearly burned his lashes to see it—his pupils began to contract. Then his eyes began to rapidly jiggle ever so slightly from side to side.

Five minutes later, muscles all over his body began twitching, and then the lighter went out for good. Through the darkness I heard a great commotion of rolling and quaking from the crib. I almost ran, afraid someone might hear. Suddenly it stopped and there was quiet.

"Calloo," I whispered.

There was no answer. I tried the lighter, but it was spent. I whispered his name again and again. "It's me, Cley," I said. But the longer I stood in the dark, the more frightened I became. I was ready to bolt in an instant when I heard his voice. The horrible sound of it set me off, and I was stumbling back down the pitch-black aisle of cribs, ramming into their corners and slamming against trays of tools. I groped along in desperation as I heard him behind me now, yelling the word he had whispered. "Paradise," echoed through the warehouse, and I heard some of the Master's other inventions begin to stir.

Eventually I found my way back to the crevice between the doors and slipped out. The first thing I did upon gaining my freedom was throw that damnable lighter across the street. I began walking very quickly, and my breathing rushed to catch up with me. In my confusion, I took the wrong street and walked for two blocks before I realized I had not passed the munitions factory.

I tried to turn back but I was totally lost by then. Though I had changed direction and decided to push on, I had a sinking feeling in my stomach that it was one of those situations where I was heading in the exact opposite direction. I thought I saw the lights of the center of the City ahead of me, but I couldn't be sure.

It seemed as if I had walked all night when I came upon a bar with a glowing sign in the window on the corner of an otherwise unlit street. The sounds of voices and music drifted out through an open window. The sight of it so relieved me, I didn't care if I was spotted after hours in a less than reputable place. I went through the door, went up to the bar, and ordered a Rose Ear Sweet with which to erase the memory of those mockeries of life, squirming and squealing with a rudimentary electromechanical awareness.

Some of the people at the bar waved to me and I waved back. I sipped my drink and tried to relax. The bartender asked if I was from the manufacturing district. I told him that I was from the center of the City.

"I thought so," he said. "You're Cley, aren't you?"

"Physiognomist, First Class," I said and took a gulp of my drink.

"I read about you," he said. "You were in the territory."

I nodded.

"I heard paradise was out that way," he said.

"Yes," I said.

"I also heard that the women in the woods outside of Latrobia have three tits," he said and laughed.

"I've been there too," I said. "But I couldn't tell you one way or the other."

The bartender liked my answer and bought me another drink on the house. He had to go and serve the other customers then, so I took to staring into the mirror behind the bar.

My nerves needed considerable calming. I was on my third drink when a woman came running into the bar, screaming, "The demon, the demon."

The bartender rushed around to her and tried to calm her. "The demon is coming up the street," she said.

To my surprise, most of these citizens were armed. Ownership of a gun by workers was strictly prohibited by the realm. When I saw them brandish those weapons, though, I drew my derringer and followed the crowd into the street. We instinctively formed two rows, one kneeling, one standing. I had a position in the middle of the front row. Ahead of us we could see the thing's shadow approaching.

"Hold fire," said the bartender, who stood to the left of us, sipping from a bottle of twenty-five-year-old Schrimley's. "Wait up until we can all hit him," he said.

The creature methodically advanced as if it had no idea we were there. I heard the sound of his hidden machinery before I saw his face. Calloo had followed me. With a sick recollection of the favor he had once done Bataldo, I aimed for his forehead. The bartender raised his arm in the air and yelled, "Ready."

He was no more than ten yards from us when we fired. The volley hit him straight on and forced him backward three steps, but he did not fall. We heard him grunt, as if the volley had merely awakened him suddenly from a nap, and then he began advancing again. The bartender yelled, "Reload," and that is when I stood and told everyone to hold their fire.

"This is not the demon," I told them.

"What is it?" one of them yelled.

"Just another man in search of paradise," I said. At that, they put down their weapons and Calloo came to stand next to me. He had about twenty holes in his City-issue overalls, and there were definite wounds, though bloodless, in his chest and arms. His face was untouched.

The patrons of the bar came over and shook his limp hand. "We're sorry," they said and Calloo stumbled in place and grunted. Before we headed back toward the center of the City, I gave the bartender the demon horn that Below had given me.

"Powder it and give each person here tonight a snort," I said.

He passed me his bottle as I handed him the horn. I took a drink and passed it to Calloo. The bartender said, "You don't snort this shit, you shoot it." I wasn't sure if he was speaking literally or figuratively, but we had no time to ponder it. Calloo moved slowly, and it was a race against the sun to get him back to my apartment before the streets filled with workers.

It was entirely bizarre, but the only person we passed on the way happened to be the cleaning woman from the Top of the City. She smiled and waved, and I waved back. "Up early, your honor," she said, and then gave me a sign with her left hand, an *O* formed by the thumb and middle finger. I returned the sign and Calloo tried.

After that encounter, I prodded him to move a little faster. We made it to my apartment just before the streets filled with workers. I led him to my bedroom and had him lie on the bed.

"How do you feel?" I asked.

He said nothing but blinked his eyes.

"I have to go out to work," I said. "Do you understand?"

He blinked again.

"If anyone comes to the door, hide in the closet. If they discover you, kill them. Do you understand?" I asked.

He blinked.

As I made out the new day's appointment cards, I noticed that he was blinking quite a lot and began to question whether he had actually understood my instructions. I got dressed and armed myself with the derringer. I was just putting on my topcoat when someone knocked at my door.

"Who is it?" I called.

"The Master requests your presence," said a voice. "There is a coach waiting."

I looked into the bedroom and saw that Calloo had not moved off the bed. "Get in the closet," I said.

"Paradise," he mumbled but remained still.

I left with the coachman, and it seemed only minutes before I was across town in an elevator on the way up to the Master's offices. As I walked down the hall of hardened heroes, my mind was ablaze with fabulations and excuses for Below, but when I pushed through the door of his office, they twisted together and strangled each other. I stood, empty-headed before him. He sat with his elbow resting on the desk and a hand clutching his forehead. The expression he wore was grimmer than Calloo's.

"Sit down, Cley," he said, waving me into the chair.

There was a long pause, in which he closed his eyes.

"Did you hear about the demon?" he finally asked.

"Yes," I said.

He started to laugh. "That's right," he said. "I sent that note to you."

"Have you captured it?" I asked.

"Captured it," he said, "I was the one who let it go. I realized that change requires access to random possibility, so I released the demon into the City. He is your competition. As you methodically gather the unworthy for expungment, he kills them as he sees them. I'm thinking big, Cley, very big."

"Brilliant," I said. "By the way, I much appreciated your gifts."

He waved his hand at me and shook his head. "What I've called you here for is to discuss these headaches I've been getting ever since I ate that white shit of the wilderness. My, was that a mistake. Stomach pains and these blasted headaches.''

''I have some familiarity with chemistry,'' I said. ''What were the ingredients your researchers found in it?''

''Who knows,'' he said.

''Can you describe the pains?'' I asked.

''Like a fist squeezing my brain,'' he said. ''I can feel that it is projecting energy from my head. Never before has the Well-Built City of my imagination seemed so inextricably tied to the physical City we now inhabit. These attacks make it hard to distinguish between the two.''

''I can't think of what that might be,'' I told him.

''How is your special assignment coming?'' he asked.

''I read a group yesterday afternoon and already have some participants for the Memorial Park affair,'' I said.

''Excellent work,'' he said, clutching at his head again. When he didn't speak for quite some time, I started to get up to leave. As I made for the door, he stopped me.

''Cley,'' he said, not looking up, ''keep that leather glove of yours clean.'' He began to laugh, but soon it quieted into a wince.

By the time I got to the office, the morning was gone. I had just enough time to send out some appointment cards by messenger. I gave instructions that they should be distributed to the Minister of the Treasury and all the members of his family.

I longed for the beauty, but I did not take it. Instead, I smoked and stared out the window, trying to wrap my mind around the Master's gibberish about random possibility and the demon being my competition. He did not appear well at all, which was a blessing for me. I knew I would have to take bolder and bolder steps to get where I wanted to be, and to have Below distracted could only be beneficial. Then the Minister of the Treasury and his family arrived.

The minister was heavy and sweating profusely as I put him through his paces. Calipers, cranial radius—every tool

I had in my bag. As I worked away, I praised his features and told him he was remarkable. He spoke of his accomplishments and his importance to the realm. I duly noted in my book the elegance of his third chin. I offhandedly questioned him about the treasures brought back from the territory.

"I am not at liberty to divulge that information," he said.

"Good," I told him. "You have passed the test. The Master will be pleased with your reliability concerning the subject."

He left smiling.

With his three daughters and their mother, it hardly took any praise at all to get them to talk. I barely even scratched the surface and they each separately told me how much they despised the minister. "I can see what you mean," I told them. His wife got so carried away that she spat on the floor. I gave her a tissue which she used twice more. Even his youngest daughter, little more than a baby, gave the thumbs-down when I asked her about Daddy. I wondered where, inside all that flesh, he was hiding. When they left my office, they went quietly, calmly, with the minister in the lead.

Now it was time for the beauty. I went to my desk and prepared a full dose. Later, when I came out of it, I could hardly remember anything from the experience. Moissac had made a brief appearance, and Silencio had perched on the windowsill, picking ticks from his fur and crunching them in his teeth. The sun was going down, and I had to leave immediately. I had plans for Calloo and me to go on an expedition.

25

Even under cover of darkness, trying to be inconspicuous with Calloo was an effort. I had dressed him in a rather large topcoat of mine, the sleeves of which came nearly to his elbows and the bottom hem to mid-thigh. In addition to this, I shoved an old broad-brimmed hat onto his head and folded the front down to cover his face. He lumbered along behind me as I navigated a path through the alleys to the western side of town. It was clear to me that somewhere in his scrambled, gear-work head, he understood most of what I had told him, because when I arrived home from the office, I found him huddled in my bedroom closet. "We're going for a stroll," I had said to him.

I spoke quietly as we walked along through the shadows, but I could not stop from telling him everything that had happened to me since I last seen him. I was not sure how much of an asset he would be to my plans, but it didn't matter. He was to me what I needed most, a coconspirator, a friend to plot with. I had the courtesy not to mention his ghoulish condition, and I got the feeling he was thankful for this. Occasionally, he would mutter some words in his deep mechanical voice, and though I could not always pick up what he was saying, I tried to respond with a likely comment. He said my name once or twice, and when he did, I turned and smiled and patted him on the shoulder.

I could see that the duration of my companion's strange life was in some question, considering that there were times when his inner workings screeched and whined so badly I thought he was going to explode. Then he stopped walking and began to sway back and forth. Sparks were visible in his eyes and puffs of smoke drifted from his open mouth. A minute or two later, these episodes passed and we continued. Calloo was, for the most part, no different than the Minister of Treasury and the Minister of Security, his true self trapped somewhere deep within. The one thing that set him apart from them is that even in the condition he was in the voice that moved him was the one in search of paradise.

It took a good hour or so to traverse half the distance to the sewage treatment plant, and I realized after walking so far, that I had not eaten anything all day. My head was light, and I began to feel weak. I knew I should get some food, since I might be required to run or fight before the night was over.

"Hungry?" I asked Calloo.

He grunted and I took that to mean yes.

"We'll go up onto the main street, but whatever you do, don't talk to anyone, don't look at them," I said.

He put his hand up to scratch his beard, and a clump of hair sloughed off his face and came away on the ends of his fingers. I wasn't sure if that was a sign that he understood or not. We made our way out of the alley and up onto Quigley Boulevard, one of the less traveled thoroughfares of the city. I knew there were a few restaurants there.

I chose a small place that had dough-gummels to take out. The man behind the counter was extremely talkative, extremely inquisitive. It was just my bad luck that he, like the bartender the other evening, knew who I was. He welcomed me back and asked a lot of questions about the territory as he waited for a rack of the pastries to come out of the oven.

Calloo stood behind me, weaving in place, now and then sounding like an automatic water pump with a stone caught in it. The man behind the counter turned away from me to check the oven, and when he did, I turned to check Calloo. The big miner was having one of his seizures right there in the restaurant. There were few patrons in the place, probably because of the demon scare, but those who sat at tables eating were now staring over at us. I smiled and waved to them. When the smoke started issuing from Calloo's mouth, I reached into my coat, brought out a cigarette, lit it and stuck it in the corner of his lips.

"Is your friend all right?" asked the man behind the counter when he turned his attention back to us.

"A few too many Rose Ear Sweets," I said.

He nodded. "I've been there."

Not a moment too soon, the pastries were done and he had bagged them for us. Then a strange thing happened. When I tried to pay him, he refused the belows I held out. He simply waved his hand in the air, as if to say there was no charge, and gave me that signal the cleaning woman had—the middle finger and thumb forming an *O*. When I gave him a surprised look, he leaned across the counter and whispered, "See you in Wenau."

I was stunned. I backed away from the counter and quickly made for the door. Once outside, I leaned against the wall as I tried to understand how this man could have known anything about Wenau. My first thought, of course, was that the Master was on to me, toying with me, as I made and carried out my less than cunning plans. Then I wondered if there was some conspiracy at work in the City. Below had told me that there were grumblings among the populace. Perhaps that is why the soldiers now carried flamethrowers. I ran through this dizzying list of possibilities in moments, and then realized that I had left Calloo back in the restaurant.

When I turned to go fetch him, I found him standing

behind me, chewing on the lit cigarette. Fearing for the safety of my fingers, I plucked most of it from his mouth exchanging it for one of the dough-gummels. He simply continued chewing, but it couldn't really be said that he was eating. The pastry was turned to crumbs in his mouth, and eventually just fell out onto my old topcoat. Seeing this almost made me lose my appetite, but I forced one of the gummels down for the sake of the expedition.

For the rest of the journey, I spoke to Calloo. I told him about a possible conspiracy against the Master. He made a sound like someone passing wind, and I took this to mean that he was as excited as I was by the prospect. After that, I boldly admitted my love for Arla Beaton. I knew I had talked too much, though, when I had slipped and mentioned the mayor. Calloo was walking behind me, and I heard him stop moving for a second. I thought I heard a muffled cry, and I wanted to believe that if I turned around, I would find tears in his eyes, but I merely slowed and waited for him to catch up.

The sewage treatment plant and the waterworks were separated by a wide avenue. One of the buildings was white marble with columns and a dome, the other was gray, crudely resembling a beehive. Entering the hive was like stepping back into the mines of Doralice. The stench was poignant and the lighting dim. There were no guards, but this was not unusual, considering what they would have been guarding. We passed through the lobby and then down a set of concrete steps. The first level we came to underground was comprised of a vast lake of human waste with a catwalk spanning the middle of it.

Calloo actually held his nose against the rippling air as we crossed to the other side of the tarn. Passing beneath the walk were giant yellow-white spheres of grease that rolled as they floated by. Things were moving below the surface, stirring the brown sea, and occasionally a bubble or two would rise through the muck and pop.

"Paradise," Calloo called to me.

We descended level after level of concrete steps, following the waters from above as they became waterfalls that dove into large pools and then became a swiftly downward-moving river. It took us some time to manage the stairs because of Calloo's stiffness of gait, but he forged ahead as I gave him constant encouragement. By the time we reached level ground, it must have been a half mile under the street. I noticed that the water appeared to have turned clear. It rushed along madly beside us and we followed its path.

After walking for another few minutes we came to a place where the river tunnel opened up into an enormous concrete cavern. A hundred yards away from us, in the middle of the structure, was a clear crystal bubble of a size my imagination could not readily accept. It sat there like a giant's holiday paperweight, and I could see inside, a forest growing. Somehow there were clouds floating in the blue sky beneath a miniature sun. Exotic birds flew from tree to tree, and off around the southern rim of it I thought I saw a herd of green deer moving through the tall amber grass that bent to and fro in a subtle breeze.

It struck me more forcefully than it ever had before that Below was playing God. Those physiognomical features of his that had concerned me with their indication of pride beyond all bounds, though a fault in men, were perfect for the deity he perceived himself to be. That is why he had no problem utilizing the Physiognomy as his golden mean. When he looked in the mirror there had never been a discrepancy.

I quickly pulled my wonder in check when I noticed that there were soldiers standing around the base of it, sporting flamethrowers. We were too far off for them to clearly see us, as we still stood within the shadows of the tunnel. I grabbed Calloo and moved him up against the wall with me. We stood there as I tried to think of what to do next. I considered simply walking up to the guards and letting them know I was on official business, but then the Master would hear of that. For a second, I considered rushing them, derringer in hand, but I already knew that Calloo wasn't rushing anywhere. Then, I didn't have to worry about it, because I could hear someone approaching down the tunnel.

I took out the derringer and the scalpel and whispered to Calloo to get ready. Peering through the dim light, I tried to see how many of them there were. That is when Calloo took a step in front of me, blocking my vision.

"Pardon me," I whispered to the miner as the demon slammed into his chest with both horns.

The suddenness of it stunned me, and I dropped both scalpel and gun. I couldn't move as I watched the miner grapple with the creature. Its wings beat furiously as Calloo grabbed it around the throat and pulled its horns out of his chest. Then he reached up, took one of the vicious points in his huge fist, and snapped it off as though it were an icicle. The demon screamed and raked Calloo's jugular, or where it should have been, with his fierce claws. The big man responded with a hammer blow across the beast's face, sending it crashing into the wall.

Behind me in the concrete cavern I could hear the soldiers rushing toward the tunnel. I bent over and picked up my derringer and aimed it at the demon's head. It whipped its tail around Calloo's legs and spun him into the path of the shot as I fired. The bullet struck him in the forehead and a shower of diminutive brass gears flew from his open mouth as he fell back against the wall. Then the demon came toward me. I waited to feel its claws rip through my face, but before it could reach me, Calloo lunged onto its back, landing between its wings and taking a stranglehold around its neck. The demon spun to throw Calloo off, and its tail caught my ankles and lifted me off my feet. I fell backward and, as I did, I fired the second shot from the pistol into the monster's face.

The fall seemed inordinately long as I waved my arms

at my sides, trying to catch myself. When the water came up around me, I realized I had been knocked into the river. The force of the current was remarkably strong, but I reached out and grabbed a small outcropping of stone with my left hand. This allowed me to bring my head above water for a minute. In that time, I heard the soldiers arrive. There were shouts of "Harrow's hindquarters" and "I'll be a winking minch" before the tunnel above me exploded with fire. I heard the screams of the demon as I let go of the wall and gave myself up to the river.

I worked desperately to keep my head above water, but it moved so swiftly, tumbling me and dashing me against the sides and bottom, that I had very little control at all. I could feel my topcoat being torn off me by the action of the rapids. As it flew away beneath the foam, I managed a last breath before I hit my head against another out-cropping. Then I sank into unconsciousness, immediately dreaming that I was dead and that Corporal Matters of the day watch was sliding my body into its tomb.

There was an eternity of blankness in which I could feel myself becoming a pile of salt. When I finally opened my eyes, I stared up at a dreamy blue sky. There was a warm wind blowing, and I could hear birds calling in the distance. I felt thankful that death had been easy. I was tired and every muscle in my body hurt from the drubbing the river had given me. I lay there half asleep and just stared into the sky thinking, "Had I only known it was going to be like this."

I dozed for a minute or two, and when I woke again, the sky was eclipsed by something. A pale green piece of cloth fluttered over me. I concentrated and saw that it was a veil, covering a face.

"Arla," I said.

"Yes," said a voice, and I could tell it was hers.

"I love you," I said.

She leaned back so that I could see her whole body now, kneeling above me. Her beautiful hands came into view, and I watched them move like a pair of birds in the blue sky. They came to rest against my neck, and her touch thrilled me. I was about to reach up, when her fingers tightened around my throat.

26

 When I woke again, I was lying on the ground near a fire beneath a vaulting green canopy of leaves. That same beautifully warm breeze enveloped me, bringing the sweet scents of tree blossoms and wildflowers. I rose up on my elbow and saw Arla sitting across from me, holding a baby in her arms. Next to her, on the ground, sat the Traveler with his legs crossed in front of him. When he saw that I was awake, he smiled at me. I noticed now that in addition to the bumps and bruises that had been supplied by the river, my throat hurt terribly.

"Arla, I've come to rescue you," I said as I sat up. My head suddenly got light, and I fell onto my back again.

They laughed as I scrabbled back to a sitting position.

"You're lucky you're not dead," she said, her voice cold and flat, the veil moving slightly with her words as it had in my dream of her. "I would have killed you, but Ea came and made me stop choking you."

"Where am I?" I asked.

"Somehow, you came through the river into the false paradise. I found you washed up on the bank," she said.

"Arla," I said, then paused, trying to consider the best manner with which to present my case. Before I could employ any scheme to make my plea sound less trite, the words blundered forth with the power of the river that had nearly drowned me. "I've been waiting for a long time to ask you to forgive me for what I've done to you. I have suffered greatly, but somehow I managed to stay alive in order to find my way to you."

"You needn't have stayed alive on my account. What am I to forgive you for? Butchering my face? Making me a sideshow exhibit? Or just being a pompous prig, convinced of your own superiority?" she asked.

"I am changed," I said. "I have been to the sulphur mines. I am surreptitiously fighting against the Master in order to save your lives," I told her.

"Would you like me to remind you of what you were before this miracle you mention?" she said and began to lift the bottom of her veil.

I readied to cover my eyes, but here the Traveler held up his hand and spoke. "I can see in him that he is different now," he said to her.

"Unfortunately, my face is still a weapon," she said.

He put his hand out and touched her shoulder. "Even this, you will eventually forgive," he said in his calm voice.

After this, she let me speak, and I told them my sad saga and how I had come to see the evil of my actions. "All I can do now is try to rectify what I have done," I said.

She asked me about the fate of Calloo and Bataldo, and I wanted to tell her that they were free, heading through the wilderness toward Wenau, but that veiled face required more truth than any set of piercing eyes. She wept when I explained the fate of her people.

"I've got only a limited amount of time in which to get us out of the City," I told her. "In a few days, the Master is going to ask me for a list of citizens that he intends to execute as part of the gala event revealing this bubble of paradise to the people. If I have not been successful by then, it will be me who will be executed, for I will not turn over any names to him."

The Traveler asked me what I had in mind.

I told him how it was that I had come inside the bubble and suggested that, though it was dangerous, we could probably leave the same way.

"No," said Arla, "Ea is weak because of having to live beneath this counterfeit sun. The river almost killed you. He will never make it, and if he could, the baby couldn't."

"There are no other exits?" I asked.

"They built the place around us. It is hermetically sealed, a supposedly self-contained environment. It's a wonder you happened upon the entrance you did. We hadn't thought of that," she said.

"It is an egg ready to hatch," said Ea.

"Where did you learn the language?" I asked him.

"From the woman," he said, pointing to Arla.

"He is brilliant, Cley," she said. "He is so advanced, it was a miracle I could teach him anything."

"I remember," I said to the Traveler, "that you fed a piece of the white fruit to Arla before you left my study in Anamasobia."

"Yes," he said, "to preserve her life. She would have died otherwise."

"I thought maybe it would reverse the effects of my scalpel," I said to Arla.

"That will never change," she said.

"The fruit," he said, "does not do what you might expect it to always. That small bite of it helped her not to die, and it also burnt away some of her ambition for the power that you once held. If someone were to eat of it who was not so innocent as her, this could be trouble."

"Is it truly the fruit of paradise?" I asked him.

"It is not," he said. "It does cause seemingly miraculous things to happen, but they defy nature. They obscure what is important in life. Thousands of years ago, it came to Wenau, where my people lived. They began eating of it, and it caused many monstrous changes. The good things it caused cheated the people of a true life. The evil things it caused cheated them of hope. Finally, the elder of my people saw the truth about it and ordered the tree on which it grew to be burned. I was to take the last piece of fruit and find a spot to hide it that was so remote, it would never be found. We could not destroy it, because it had been made by the forest, and we did not have the right to obliterate it from the world. When I found such a spot, I was to take a mix of herbs and roots, prepared by our shaman, that would put me into a perpetual sleep. I was to guard the fruit and ensure that no creature ever tasted it again."

"But you were fed it by Garland, and then you gave a piece to Arla," I said.

He nodded and smiled. "I would have awoken from my slumber eventually without it. When the man gave it to me, it caused some change in my person. I should not have given it to Arla, but seeing her there in your room, I felt I could love her," he said. "The change it made in me is that I was able to see her beauty, though she was so different from my people. I went against the spiritual law of Wenau for the promise of love. I am a criminal both here and in the Beyond."

"What do you mean?" I asked.

"He means we are in love," said Arla.

"In love," I said, "as in the usual sense?"

"In every sense," she said, and I could almost hear her smile behind the veil.

The Traveler reached over and held her hand the way an old man might his wife's. I felt an instant surge of jealousy. "How could they be in love," I thought to myself, staring at them. "They are like two different species." I shook my head and tears came to my eyes, but when I cleared them and looked again at the couple, holding hands beside the fire, a transformation seemed to have taken place.

Where I had always seen the Traveler as some kind of

prehuman animal with outlandish features, I noticed now that he looked as much like a man as any I had encountered in my life. He was tall and his skin was dark, but other than this I saw no difference. In fact, when I looked closely, I realized that his fingers were not webbed as I had always believed, and his nose was a nose and not merely two holes in his face.

"Look," said Ea to Arla, dropping her hand and pointing, "he is seeing me."

She put her arm around him and held him tightly. "Cley," she said, "if you can save us, I will forgive you. Just help me get him back to the world before he dies. I love him."

"I will try," I said.

"You must think of some way to free us. We've beaten at the crystal with rocks and sticks. We've tried to tunnel under it, but found that the sphere reaches down below the ground. Ea has searched every inch of it for a flaw or some vent or opening. He has tried to dream an escape, but has been unable because of his waning strength," she said.

"I'd better go," I said, grimly considering the prospect of another swim. "You'll have to take me to where the river leaves the paradise. There is no way I can swim upstream against that current."

"I will show you," said Ea, rising slowly to his feet.

I got up and walked over to Arla and held my hand out to her. "I'm sorry," I said. She did not take my hand but sat silently, rocking the baby. The veil moved and I thought she was about to talk, but then I saw that it was just moving in the breeze. "I will come back for you," I said.

Then we left the little encampment and journeyed out across the false paradise. As much as it was a sham and a prison for Arla, her child, and the Traveler, Below had created something amazing. There was no way I would have known, had I not earlier been outside the bubble, that I was not walking through one of the forests of the Beyond. There were all manner of animals and birds and even insects trapped in the crystal. I could not imagine how he had made the sun and clouds. For the first time in thirty-five years, I again wondered why the sky was blue.

When we reached the spot where the river flowed beneath the crystal wall, I turned to Ea and took his hand.

"Watch for me," I said.

"I saw you coming in my dreams," he told me.

I wanted to say more, but the silence we shared was sufficient. Stepping up to the bank of the river, I tried to decide if I should jump directly into the swiftly moving water or ease in off the side. That is when I felt his hand on my back, pushing me. I plunged in and was immediately swept along. This time, though, I did not roll and tumble, but I continued to feel that hand on my back, guiding me, as I sped away from paradise.

Sometime later, I am not exactly sure how long, I felt the current quickly abate and knew that I had entered some larger body of water. Swimming to the surface, I noticed from the white marble ceiling above and the columns that lined the walkway a few yards off, that I had entered a holding tank in the waterworks. How it all came to be, I had moved too rapidly to tell. I swam to the side and pulled myself out onto the walkway.

Although I was soaked to the skin and my boots were squishing tiny geysers of water out of the seams with each step, I made it to the street before the workers arrived to begin the day. The sun was coming up as I fled from the entrance to the waterworks and down the first eastbound alley I could find. As I ran, I shivered and mourned the loss of Calloo for the third time. What was far more difficult was trying to come to terms with the fact that my dream of Arla's love was never going to come to pass.

When I finally crawled up the steps to my apartment, I was completely exhausted, and, now that all of my adrenaline had been depleted, the beauty was calling. I fixed a dose even before undressing and plunged the needle into my wrist. My vision began to blur, and I became unsteady as I tried to strip off my wet pants. At least the violet drug brought me some warmth. More than anything, I needed a few hours sleep before I could make my next move. I got into bed and fell headlong into a feverish beauty dream that swept me along like the river leaving paradise.

I saw Calloo and the demon wrapped in combat while the soldiers shot their flamethrowers, burying the two enemies in a wall of fire. Then I just saw the fire and it burned and burned forever. When the fire suddenly stopped, there was nothing left of either of them except what appeared to be one glistening droplet of water that fell to the cement path, making the noise of the highest key of a piano, struck once. I walked over and picked this droplet up, discovering it was really made of crystal.

It came to me that I was now outside, under a deep blue sky. In the newfound light, away from the river tunnel, I could see something moving inside the tiny crystal. Putting it up to my eye, I could see a minuscule forest growing inside. A wind blew then, like someone breathing, and I looked up, past the blue, and saw a giant eye staring down on me as if through a distant wall of crystal.

Everything shattered and I came awake. It was mid-afternoon. I went to my closet to get dressed, half hoping that I might find Calloo jammed in there, but there was nothing but clothes. I did not bother with a bath, seeing as I had spent most of the previous night in the water. When I was dressed, I made out some appointment cards for later that evening and went out to give them away.

My first stop was a café, where I bought a *Gazette* and ordered two cups of shudder to get my eyes completely open. The headline read: DEMON KILLS THREE AT SEWAGE PLANT. I went on to read that three armed soldiers were attacked and killed by the demon. There was no news of the remains of Calloo, nothing about a topcoat found floating. The story was brief, giving few details beyond the names of the unfortunates. I wondered if Calloo could still be alive out there somewhere, tottering around, springs poking through his flesh. For some reason this ghoulish thought brought a smile to my lips. I leaned back and drank my shudder and noticed that on page three there was a small piece announcing that the Minister of the Treasury had accidentally fallen out of his bedroom window and broken his neck.

I distributed my appointment cards at the open-air market, handing them out randomly. As soon as that was accomplished, I returned to my office, hoping to get a few more hours of sleep before the subjects came to be read. I had just eased back in my chair, settling my aching body in a position that would hurt the least, when someone knocked at my door.

"Who is it?" I called.

The door opened and in walked the Master. As the door closed behind him I caught a glimpse of armed soldiers taking up sentry positions in the hallway. Below carried a brown paper bag with him. He looked completely exhausted, and his hands were shaking. I whipped my feet off the desk and straightened to attention. He sat down in the chair across from me, reached into the bag, and pulled out two cups of shudder. Then he reached back in, took out a shiny object and threw it on the desk in front of me. I instantly recognized the scalpel I had dropped in the sewage plant when the demon had attacked Calloo.

27

 I did not hesitate but an eye blink before reaching out and grabbing the scalpel. "Where did you get this?" I asked. "I haven't seen one of these in years."

"It's a scalpel, Cley," he said.

"Yes, but it's a Pierpoint. The old-timers used to use these," I said.

"It's not the type you use?" he asked.

"I use a Janus, double head," I said. "The cut is cleaner and it is easier to slice cartilage with. But, I'll tell you, in the hands of someone like Flock or Muldabar Reiling, these were very effective."

"I want you to find out whose it is," he said, looking skeptically at me.

I put the scalpel back down on the desk. "I'm just waiting for another group of subjects," I told him. "The list is slowly growing. I've unearthed a nice selection of miscreants so far."

He nodded wearily.

"Cley, the headaches—I can't shake them," he said. "They come more frequently now with weird results."

"What do you mean?" I asked.

"My physicians have told me that they think certain foods I eat might set them off or make them worse. They have told me not to drink shudder, but, Harrow's hindquarters, how can a man with my busy schedule get by without a few jolts every day?" he asked.

"Perhaps it might be good to lie down for a day or two," I said.

"You have no idea what is happening. Last night, at a certain bar in the manufacturing district, my soldiers went in to check for a runaway gladiator and had a gun battle with the patrons. How can these workers have guns? My men finally just bombed the place, killing ten citizens. Then they rushed into the rubble and shot the rest of them. But this is bad business. There is a malaise of ingratitude among the people that even I was unaware of." He fell silent for a moment and shook his head. His eyes had dark crescents beneath them. "Things are falling apart," he said.

"Perhaps you should not drink this shudder you have brought," I said, trying to sound sympathetic. He did look rather pitiful and weak sitting there, but I could only gloat at the news he had brought.

"No," he said, "I've brought it to drink in front of you so that I can show you the effect these headaches have on me. I need your help, Cley. I don't trust anyone."

"I'll do everything within my abilities to serve you," I said.

He gave a weak smile and then reached out and took one of the cups in his hands and removed the lid. Bringing it to his lips, he dashed it off in a few seconds.

"It's the white fruit. I need something to reverse its change in me," he said as he put the cup down on my desk.

"What is this change?" I asked.

"Just wait," he told me, "you can't miss it."

"You said there was a runaway gladiator?" I asked.

"One of those wretches I use in the battle matches," he said. "I can't imagine that he will present much of a problem, but when you put it all together, there's just too much random possibility out there now."

"It must be difficult for you," I said.

"It's a lonely thing, being the Master," he said, looking over to stare out the window. "At the same time, I cannot give up. I don't care if I have to kill every last citizen— they will not take my City from me. My life has been the Well-Built City. I am this City beyond mere rhetoric. Every inch of coral, every pane of crystal is a memory, a theory, an idea. My mentor, Scarfinati, taught me how to turn ghosts of abstraction into specific imagery, but I did him one better, turning imagery into concrete actuality. These streets, these buildings are the history of my heart and mind."

I nodded.

He winced but the unseen pain did not prevent him from continuing. "My trouble began when I tried to turn the people into a magnificent equation whose sum would be perfection. Instead, they have become a virus that be-clouds my vision. Their ignorant simplicity corrodes my complexity. Order is needed to return viability to the mechanism of my genius in the same way I employed the Physiognomy to neutralize the chaos of abstract religion, the illness of faith." When he finished, he looked at me as if it should now all be perfectly clear.

"I will help you," was all I could say, my head swimming in the attempt to follow his meaning.

"I know," he told me. "It is the reason I brought you back. I realized when you were gone that you were really the only person here who could grasp the immensity of my vision."

"Your genius is beyond me," I told him.

"Somewhere along the line, someone has gotten the foolish notion that a city is its people instead of its magnificent structures," he said.

"Inane," I conceded.

He leaned over in the chair and grasped his head with both hands. His face became a closed fist of anguish. "Watch," he said as he rocked. Then, as if an invisible assailant had struck him in the face, he flew back in the chair. There was a moment in which the air in the room became heavy and a low crackling sound could be heard. The next thing I knew, the window glass shattered outward with a terrific explosion.

I leaped out of my seat and backed against the wall. The Master took his hands from his head and peered up at me, his pallid face forming a smile.

"It's over, Cley. You can sit down," he said.

I did as he told me.

"I had such a severe episode in my office the other day, the power, or whatever it is, blew apart one of the heads of those blue statues from the territory out in the hallway. It's growing in intensity," he said.

"Rest, Master. You've got to rest. Get off your feet. Let the ministers run the City for a few days," I said.

"Cley, I appreciate your concern, but those asses couldn't run a cart into a brick wall. That would be like turning my life over to a retarded child," he said. "I'd be better off putting the demon in charge."

"What can I do?" I asked.

"Find out which one of your illustrious colleagues uses a scalpel like that and be available for me to confer with you," he said. "What I need is your confidence. I can bring things under control if I just have someone to rebound my ideas off."

I had to help him to his feet when he was ready to leave. As I moved him in the direction of the door, he placed his hand over mine, which supported his elbow. "Thank you," he said. The words almost had the same effect on me as did his headache upon the window.

"I'll send someone by to repair your glass, there," he said with a laugh. Once outside in the hallway, he straightened to his full height. "Let's go, you laggards," he said to the soldiers. They surrounded him as he took the stairs to the street.

I rushed through my appointments late that afternoon in

order to get back to my apartment and go to sleep. I felt
the way the Master had looked. As I walked along the
night streets of the City, I thought about Below and actually felt bad for him. All around me were the incredible
designs of his creation—the lights, the spires, the incessant
commerce. He had built a kind of crystal sphere around
himself and was now vaguely realizing it was a trap. For
me, my exalted position of Physiognomist, First Class had
been the sphere. It had protected me for quite some time,
but it had also blinded me to the rest of life. I could sense
that things were going to change, and this was remarkable;
but in an odd way, there was a certain sadness to it. Still,
I knew that if I had to, I would take Below's life in order
to save Arla and Ea and the child. Like Moissac, the foliate, I would leave behind a seed, and it would be this
family.

Part of the next two mornings, I spent wading through
official documents in the basement of the Ministry of Information. I was intent on finding some design of a crystal
sphere in the literature of the Master's early writings. Although all of his inventions had been committed to his
strange memory system, he had written quite a few of
them out as shorthand blueprints for his engineers to follow. I could not believe that such an ingenious creation
as the false paradise could have been the work of a moment's free thought. There was nothing there in the collec-
tion that resembled what I had seen that night beneath the
sewage treatment plant, but there were notes for all manner
of exotic inventions, some of which had come to pass and
some that were probably still in the works over in the
manufacturing district. Seeing written evidence of all the
Master's brilliant theories and musings was daunting, but
it gave me the sense that it was, in a way, somewhat less
than human. It was as if he could not help himself tinker-
ing with nature.

I don't think anyone had bothered with these papers for

the longest time. They were yellowed and poorly filed, and the dust did not shower from them but rolled in tumbleweeds onto the floor. I also noticed, while down in the musty chamber, that some sort of winged insect had taken up residence amid the moldering dreams of the great Drachton Below. After the early morning rush out on the street had abated and there were no longer the sounds of footsteps and coach wheels, these six-legged interlopers sent up a chorus of chirping that often drove me to distraction. In all, my time there had been wasted.

I was loath to think that I had basically sat through two whole days. Of course, I kept up with my official duties and went on coach rides through the entire city every night searching for any signs of Calloo. I wanted more than anything to return to Arla and Ea with news of their deliverance, but it was too risky to go for a visit without some definite plan for escape. I had made a vow that when next I returned to them, I would take them away with me. I wished I had more time, a commodity I was quickly running short of. It was now less than a week until the executions were to take place.

My next brainstorm was a gift from the beauty. I was riding through the city the evening after I had given up on the Ministry of Information, looking out the coach window into all the shadowy doorways and as far down the alleys as I could. The driver had been instructed to drive slowly and to keep a lookout himself for a big hulking man, moving slowly.

I had not had time that day to catch a fix of the beauty and the symptoms of withdrawal were plaguing me worse than usual. Right there in the coach, I took a vial full and sat back for a few minutes to think. I saw the crystal bubble of the false paradise in my eye's-mind as if at a distance. Then I began to wonder how it had been put together. Arla had said that they had built it around the two of them.

If it was not blown, like a glass bowl, than it must have

been constructed in pieces and fitted together, which meant that there had to be a seam somewhere. I kept drawing a blank when it came to envisioning the plans for it, but I did see in my daydream, from a great distance, men at work on it, like a colony of ants swarming over an egg.

I banged on the ceiling of the coach and the driver answered me. "Your honor?" he said.

"Drive me around to the south side of the park, to Engineer Deemer's residence," I said. "Do you know the location?"

"Very good, sir," he said.

Pierce Deemer had been the Master's head engineer throughout the years of the construction of the Well-Built City. Some said he was every bit as brilliant as Below. He was an old man now, but still very active in working on municipal projects for the City. I knew he had children and that his children had children, and I was counting on the fact that he cared for them.

Engineer Deemer was a wiry, severe-looking man with short white hair. He allowed me into his house but was not pleased by my presence. We went into his study, a small comfortable room with a drawing board and books lining the walls. He was a powerful figure in the City, but even his influence, I knew, could not supersede my authority to detain and read him or any member of his family. I did not play coy but went straight to the heart of the matter.

"I need some information," I told him as I sat down in one of the plush chairs attending his desk.

"Everyone needs information," he said snidely.

I took out a handful of appointment cards and threw them on the desk. "Give one of these to each of your grandchildren," I told him. "I hope for their sakes they are all excellent physiognomical specimens. Have you heard about what the Master has planned for the park in a few days?" I asked.

He stared at the cards and then eventually nodded. "Are you threatening me, Cley?" he asked.

"Their heads will pop like grapes," I said. "All of those towheaded little minchs of yours, exploding for the glory of the realm. It will certainly be a spectacle," I said.

"The Master will hear of this," he said.

"Very well," I said and got up to leave.

"Wait," he called just as I was going out the door.

I turned and walked back to the desk. "The crystal sphere that houses the false paradise, how was it constructed?" I asked.

"You know of it?" he asked. "It's supposed to be a secret."

I pulled out another appointment card and threw it on his desk. "Have your wife come by my office also," I said.

"It was not constructed," he told me. "Crystal grows. The Master grew it in an elliptical mold that was made of a substance of his invention that eventually, over time, turns to pure oxygen. The solution was poured into the mold, the crystal grew, and the mold then disintegrated. A very rapid process," he said.

"Are there entrances or exits?" I asked.

He shook his head.

"Can it be cracked?" I asked.

"We tested it with flamethrowers, bullets, hand grenades. They didn't make a scratch. But why do you need to know?" he asked.

"It's a secret," I said.

"Has this been sanctioned by the Master?" he asked.

"No," I said. "If he hears of my visit to you, you can plan on your family line being snipped short."

"You're one of us, aren't you?" he said, and then held up his hand and made the sign of the O.

I nodded and gave him an O in return.

He smiled and showed me to the door. "If I can think of anything, I'll let you know," he said.

As I rode away from the park, I felt uneasy about having exposed my position to Deemer. I could only hope that he really was part of what appeared to be a City-wide conspiracy. "These unknown allies might be my last and only salvation at the end," I thought. But things were rarely what they seemed in the realm. On my way back to my apartment, I continued to search the streets for the only person I could definitively trust—a gear-work giant with a pinprick of paradise in his head.

"An egg waiting to hatch," was how the Traveler had described the sphere. In my mind, I hit that egg with a hammer, kicked it with my boot, rode over it with a coach wheel, and sat on it like a hen, but nothing could crack it.

Finally, I gave in to the comfort of the beauty for the second time that evening. Corporal Matters of the day watch appeared in my bedroom, flailing away at a crystal egg with the monkey-headed cane. When he reached a state of near exhaustion, he rolled the dice on the end of my bed and announced, "Zero."

28

"The conspiracy is real," I told myself as I stepped out onto the street the next morning and, scanning the horizon, saw that there was no longer a top to the Top of the City. The long column that was the enclosed elevator that led to the domed restaurant had now a jagged end. The dome was absolutely gone and there was smoke issuing from the open shaft. I stopped the first person who passed me and asked what had happened.

"Explosion last night," the man said. "There and over at the Ministry of Security—a whole wing was taken out."

"Who is responsible?" I asked.

"They are saying that there are evil forces at work in the Well-Built City," he said.

I thanked him for the information and hurried on to the café where I again bought a *Gazette*. EXPLOSIONS ROCK CITY was the headline. The story gave information on the loss of life, which was considerable in both instances, and made note that the Master was offering a hundred-thousand-below reward for information leading to the capture of the terrorists.

Things were heating up. The people of the *O* apparently were not waiting for me to move. I supposed that they knew about the upcoming executions in Memorial Park in a few days and were reacting violently to the idea of them, or perhaps this was in retaliation for the attack on the patrons of the bar the other night.

I had barely gotten into my first cup of shudder when a coach pulled up at the curb in front of the café. The driver got down and came walking over to me.

"There is an emergency meeting of the ministers this morning, your honor, and the Master requests your presence," he said.

"Very well then," I said. I paid for the shudder and took my cup and napkin and accompanied him to the coach.

The meeting was to be held in the Master's office at the Ministry of Benevolent Power. As we rode across town, we had to pass the Ministry of Security. I witnessed the aftermath of the destructive blast. The entire west wing of the building was now no more than a pile of rubble. The pink coral had crumbled like stale bread. Arms and legs and pipes and shards of windowpane poked out of the mess. Soldiers in riot armor patrolled the cordoned-off area. "These people aren't fooling around," I thought to myself.

We turned past what was left of the building and headed uptown toward the Master's office. As we went along, I finished off my drink and brought the napkin up to wipe my mouth. Out of the corner of my eye, I saw what I thought appeared to be writing on it. I brought it directly into my line of vision and discovered that there was a note penned on one side. *Cley,* it said, *it is easier to break an egg from inside out than from outside in. If you want to find out more, come this evening at eight to the Earth Worm at the western side of town. P.D.*

I crumpled the napkin up and remembered to throw it in the trash can outside the ministry before entering. As I rode up in the elevator, I wondered if the message had really been from Pierce Deemer or if it was a ruse to flush me out. To make the appointment would be very chancy, especially in light of the recent explosions, but it was an opportunity I couldn't let pass.

As I strode down the hallway to the office, I was disappointed to see that it had been the head of Arden that had succumbed to the Master's strange affliction. He stood there with his mirror, posing the same as ever, only now his body ended at the shoulders. The sight of it brought back to me a memory of Mantakis and his wife, and the last thing I thought before entering the Master's office was the sight of them clutching each other in a pool of blood in the lobby of the Hotel de Skree.

The ministers stood before the Master's desk in a semicircle. Seeing me enter, Winsome Graves, Minister of Security, said, "I thought this meeting was only for ministers."

"Shut up," Below said to him.

"Excuse my tardiness," I said to the Master, and he merely nodded to me and told me to take a position with the others.

He looked more worn and ragged than ever as he sat there in his chair. "We have a crisis on our hands, gentlemen. No doubt you know all about the explosions that ripped my City apart last night."

They all nodded.

"We have a conspiracy on our hands," said Below. "I want action on this. I want to see the culprits' heads brought before me by this time tomorrow morning, or you are all going to be out of a position in the worst way. Do you understand?"

They all nodded.

"Minister Graves," he said, "step forward."

Graves straightened up in military style and came forward, saluting the Master.

Below opened his desk drawer and pulled out a pistol. He hardly aimed before squeezing off a shot. Graves fell like a cut tree, straight onto the carpet, his face obliterated by the shot. Blood covered the jackets of the ministers standing next to him.

"One of you a day," said the Master, "until this thing is settled."

I noticed a yellow puddle forming beneath the new Minister of the Arts. The others were visibly shaken. They nodded and yessed and hailed to the realm. Then they stood there staring at Below who stared back.

"Get going," he yelled and fired the pistol into the ceiling. "Take that piece of dung with you and drop him off at the dump," he said, motioning to Graves's corpse.

The bureaucracy of the Well-Built City had never moved so swiftly. As soon as they were gone, he told me to pull up a chair. I did, trying to position it away from the gore that remained.

"I heard about the explosions, Master," I said. "Who do you suspect?"

"I know exactly who it was, Cley," he said, putting the pistol back in the drawer.

"But who?" I asked.

"It's me," he said. "I was up all night with headaches that were like seizures. I'm telling you, whatever has gotten inside me from that fruit has some kind of consciousness. It is determined to destroy my City. From my bedroom window I have a view of most of the skyline. I began to get one of the attacks, and then, in my mind, I saw a building I had lovingly designed so many years ago. The next thing I knew, my eyes were forced shut from the severity of the pain, and I heard an explosion. When the episode passed, I opened my eyes and could see outside that the building I had pictured was in ruins with flames leaping from the rubble. I won't even mention the damage I did to my own residence. My personal servant is a million flecks of flesh right now, spread across the ballroom of my palace."

"Is there any hope of a cure?" I asked.

"My researchers are working on something derived from the leaves of the tree growing where I planted the seeds of the fruit. It has just begun to sprout, and we hope the sap might counteract the effects of the fruit. I am still a day away from having my hands on that serum," he said.

"Why did you tell them it was a conspiracy?" I asked.

"What was I going to tell them? The Master is systematically destroying the City?" he asked.

I nodded.

"It's killing me, Cley," he said. "I can feel it inside me, plotting my demise. Here, in my veins, is where the conspiracy is." He shook his head in what appeared to be genuine sadness. "You know, there was a room in the Ministry of Security—perhaps you remember it—whose ceiling was made of tin embossed with the image of a pelican. That design was a mnemonic device for remembering the face of my sister, who died when I was ten. Now, after last night, I can no longer see her. That room has also been destroyed in the City behind my eyes."

Just then, he was flung back in the chair with another of the attacks. He grasped his head and cried out, "Here it comes. To the window, Cley. The Ministry of Education. They're going to take it in the rear entrance." His words turned into a prolonged groan.

I watched from the window as the back of the building he had mentioned suddenly turned into a pillar of smoke, shards of crystal, blocks of coral went flying into the air and rained down onto the streets below. In addition, I could hear blue spire heads popping down the hallway, and a bookcase just to my left cracked and splintered, the volumes falling in an avalanche to the floor.

I turned back to the Master, who was now drenched in sweat and breathing heavily. "I'm all right now," he said weakly. "Fix me a syringe, would you?"

I prepared a dose of the beauty for him. He took it and shoved it into the vein in his left temple. As he pulled the needle out, he breathed a sigh of relief. "My lovely beauty," he said. "It's the only thing that does any good against the pain."

"What more can I do?" I asked.

"Nothing," he said. "I just had to tell someone who would care. Keep your ears and eyes open for me, Cley. This is a dangerous time with me so under the weather."

"You can count on me," I told him.

I didn't hand out any appointment cards that day. I knew I was going to have to act within the next day or else there might be nothing left of any of us. The streets were in turmoil, rescue workers heading toward the Ministry of Education and citizens fleeing in the other direction. Soldiers were trying to keep the peace by aiming their flamethrowers at unruly crowds who were threatening to crush one another in human stampedes. I went back to my apartment, took a needle myself, and lay in bed, thinking. Somewhere amid the long dream of the beauty, I heard another explosion and stumbled out of bed to look out the window. The Academy of Physiognomy was on fire. I smiled and lay back down for a while more.

As soon as the night came, I got up and dressed. The streets were quiet now, though the smell of smoke was still in the air. I took the same route on which I had led Calloo to the western side of town. The Earth Worm was a dirty little place I remembered from my student days. Not that I ever visited it, but I knew many who did. I kept to the shadows and stayed off the main thoroughfares as much as possible.

A few blocks away from the place, I thought I heard someone following me. I looked back but saw nothing. With the whereabouts of the demon unknown—whether he was alive or dead—I was somewhat scared, not having my trusty derringer with me. I quickened my pace and did not turn around anymore, though I still thought I heard the sound of someone tailing me at a distance.

The Earth Worm was a small ramshackle establishment. There wasn't much light inside, only candles on a few of the tables and one glowing sign for Pelic Bay hanging over the mirror behind the bar. Three patrons sat together, drinking quietly in front of it, leaning against the splintered wood. The bartender dozed on a stool in the corner beneath an advertisement for Schrimley's. Over in the back, through the shadows, I saw Deemer's white hair. He was sitting at the last table, bent over a glass of wine.

I approached and took a seat in front of him. He did not look up. I cleared my throat to get his attention, but he didn't move. I thought that he had fallen asleep waiting for me, and leaned over and touched his shoulder. Then I noticed the bullet hole in his shirt, half hidden by his topcoat. At almost the same instant, I saw my derringer sitting on the table, next to his glass of wine. Behind me the three stools were scraping across the floor as the men stood.

I turned around and there were two soldiers holding rifles aimed at my heart. The Master stood between them, making the sign of the *O* with his middle finger and thumb.

"They've been fishing some strange items out of the containment pool over at the waterworks lately, Cley," he said. "In addition to that derringer, they also found a topcoat that looked very familiar to me."

"I can explain," I said.

He held up his hand. "I trusted you, Cley. I let you get close to me, and you betrayed me just like the rest of them. When the gun and coat were brought to my attention, I began inquiring as to your whereabouts. It seemed you had paid a visit to the engineer last night, so my men and I paid him a visit this afternoon. My head verily destroyed his study, but not before we found revolutionary writings. I had his whole family executed on the spot."

I looked over at the bar and realized that the bartender was also dead. "You can kill me," I said, "but at least I'll die knowing that you and this City won't be far behind."

"No more vacations to Doralice for you," he said. "I think we'll just inflate your head."

"Was it just the derringer?" I asked. "Or were you on to me from the beginning?"

"I found it rather peculiar that you never inquired about the girl. I didn't want to believe that you were hiding something, but when they came to me with the topcoat and gun today, I knew," he said. "What was your plan?"

"I wasn't after you," I told him. "I just wanted to free the girl."

"A shame. Take him outside," he said to the soldiers.

They came and each took me by an arm. As we started for the door, Below clutched at his head. I thought he was about to have another headache, but then it seemed to pass and we continued.

Out on the street, there was a coach waiting. "To the execution chamber," Below called to the driver. The soldiers took me to the coach and one of them opened the door. As it swung back on its hinges, something shot out and hit him in the face so hard his grip was torn from my arm by the force of it. The other soldier brought up his weapon, and as he did I hit the ground to get out of the way of his shot. He managed to get off one round into the coach, but as he aimed to fire again, Calloo, or something like Calloo but badly burned and popping springs, lunged out at him and grabbed him around the throat and snapped it as easily as he had taken off the demon's horn. In that same instant, Below was pulling a pistol from his belt. But Calloo's massive fist was faster, hitting him right in the face and sending him to the ground.

I leaped to my feet and moved around to the front of the coach to get to the driver before he could escape, but I soon saw his condition was similar to Deemer's. Calloo moved up behind me and put one of his hands on my shoulder. His inner workings were a cacophony of grinding gear work that I could barely hear over the dangerous hum of an overload. A good portion of his overalls had been scorched, and his left side, face, and arm had been blackened. There was a bullet hole or two more in him, but I think he smiled at me. A croaking noise came from his throat, and I interpreted it as a greeting.

29

I closed Calloo in the cab of the coach, begging him not to kill Below, who had only been knocked unconscious. I then climbed up into the driver's seat and pushed the lifeless body of the driver onto the street. Lifting the whip out of its holder, I cracked it over the horses' heads, realizing only then as they sped off that I had no idea how to drive the contraption. I pulled back on the reins and tried to slow them, but it seemed they had taken my initial command to go a little too much to heart. We rounded a few corners on two wheels and dashed the back of the cab against a lamppost, but in a few blocks, I was able to get them to slow to a moderate trot.

In the heat of the events that had transpired so rapidly, I had formulated a plan, or I should say it was more like one leaped into my head. I drove on and then looked around for the place Calloo and I had stopped for dough-gummels the night we had discovered the crystal sphere. It took all my strength to bring the four horses to a standstill at the curb outside the small store. As soon as I was sure they were not going to bolt without me, I leaped down from the driver's seat and ran across the sidewalk to the door.

Luck was with me, because the same man, a member of the conspiracy of *O*, was behind the counter again.

"Greetings, Cley," he said and made the sign to me.

I reached across the counter and grabbed him by the collar. "Listen," I said, "I need ten cups of shudder to go." When I looked around, I saw that there were a few patrons sitting at tables. I turned back to the counterman, whose shirt I still had hold of, and told him, "Tell your people I have kidnapped the Master. If they are going to do anything, tonight is the night. Do you understand?"

He nodded to me, and I released him. He set immediately to work, pouring cups of shudder and snapping lids on them. He arranged them neatly for me in a cardboard box. Again, he charged me nothing. As I ran out the door, he yelled after me, "See you in Wenau." Behind him I heard the patrons join in with a chorus of "Wenau."

I got back up on the coach and set the box next to me. We were off in a flash. The horses seemed now to be part of the conspiracy, because it was almost as if they knew that I was headed for the sewage treatment plant. Minutes later, we rounded a turn, and the white marble building of the waterworks came into view. I veered to the left of the street and brought the coach to rest outside the gray beehive.

As soon as we stopped, Calloo emerged from the cab, carrying Below over his shoulder. I jumped down and joined him in the street. After retrieving the box of cups, I grabbed the whip and cracked it over the horses' heads again. They took off down the street with the coach in tow.

We entered the building and followed the same route we had the first time. If Calloo was slow before, his scrambled clockwork now had him lurching along at a snail's pace. It seemed to take forever to get down to where the river tunnel hit level ground. There was nothing to do but wait for him. I couldn't complain, seeing as how he had saved my life so many times I could no longer keep count.

We walked along the tunnel until we came to just before the spot where it opened up into the concrete cavern that held the false paradise. I motioned for my friend to lay the Master down. He half put him and half dropped him, so that Below leaned back against the wall in a sitting position. I kneeled down and began smacking the Master lightly to try to revive him. It was a good thing he had been weakened by the poison of the fruit, otherwise he might have already escaped from us by use of his magic.

After a few slaps to the face and my shaking his shoulders, he began to come around. As soon as I saw his eyes open, I popped off the lid to the first cup of shudder, tilted his head back, and poured the liquid down his throat. He took half of it before I stopped, fearing I would choke him. When I tried to follow with the second half of the cup, he had by then reached full consciousness and spit it out all over me.

"You'll never get away with this, Cley. My men are right around the corner. All I have to do is scream, and they will come running," he said, gasping for breath.

"The minute you make a noise, my friend here is going to put his boot in your mouth," I told him. "If you want to live, you'll start drinking. There's a lot of shudder to down before we continue."

"Sorry, my doctors have prohibited it," he said and laughed. He closed his lips tightly and would not open them.

Calloo looked placidly down on the scene, whirring and chunking. I suppose he grasped part of what was going on, because he lifted his leg and kicked Below in the stomach. It wasn't as powerful a blow as he could have delivered, but it was enough to get the Master's jaw to unhinge and leave me an opening for the shudder. I poured down two more cups before he fought me off again. Calloo came at him with the boot, and we repeated the procedure. Finally, he grudgingly acquiesced and took the last few cups without fighting.

When I was done force-feeding him, he asked. "What is your plan, to drown me with shudder and leave me in this tunnel?"

"No," I said, "I need you to hatch an egg for me." With this, I told Calloo to lift him to his feet, which the miner did with the ease of a bear lifting its cub.

"Ingenious," Below said to me.

"Do you think it will work?" I asked him.

"I'm afraid you won't find out, since you and this hulk-ing wreck will be burnt to a cinder within minutes," he said.

"Feel free to have a headache anytime," I said.

Calloo kept his hand squeezed tightly around the back of Below's neck as we walked the remaining few yards to where the tunnel entered the chamber. I peered out of the shadows and saw the soldiers, four of them standing guard around the base of the sphere. The false paradise again filled me with wonder as I gazed upon it.

I wished I had thought to bring the rifles of the soldiers from the Earth Worm. We needed to get closer to the sphere without the guards interfering. "How did you make that sun?" I whispered to Below.

He began to give me an answer, but his words trailed off into a real cry of pain. I first thought that Calloo was squeezing his neck too hard, but I soon saw that the shud-der was having the desired effect. At the same time, I could see the soldiers had heard and were coming to inves-tigate. I was paralyzed with fear from the uncanny sense that this had all happened before.

"There goes the Ministry of the Treasury," groaned Below.

I felt a tremor run through the tunnel, accompanied by the very distant sound of an explosion. A moment later, chunks of rock blasted off the wall a few yards behind us. The force of the shock almost knocked me into the river again. As soon as I had my bearings, I looked out and saw the soldiers had stopped advancing for a moment, trying to figure out what was going on.

"Over here," yelled Below.

They heard his voice and instantly began advancing again.

I readied myself to spring out of the shadows at them. I didn't know what good that would do, but I thought in the confusion I might be able to subdue at least one of them. I was praying that Calloo still had a few more rounds of fight in him.

When I looked back, I saw that the Master was again grimacing with pain. He brought his hands up and clutched his head. "Not my palace," he croaked. We felt another tremor, heard another explosion, and a moment later out in the cavern the floor erupted and geysers of rock and steam shot straight up. It wasn't enough to kill the soldiers, but it was more than enough to scare them. They fled in the opposite direction, abandoning their posts and disappearing around the other side of the sphere as pieces of the cavern ceiling gave way and showered down.

As soon as they were out of sight, I motioned to Calloo to bring Below. We made our way across the uneven concrete floor, wending around the craters and watching for falling debris. Two more blasts occurred before we drew close to the base of the wondrous structure. The Master was drifting in and out of consciousness as the place came apart around us. The crystal sphere rippled in the explosions like a real soap bubble, but I saw no sign of its cracking.

Inside the paradise, I could see Ea and Arla, looking out at us. She held the baby, and they were waving to me. "Bring him closer," I yelled to Calloo. My intention was to mash his face right up against the shell of crystal. I ran ahead and motioned for the prisoners to move away. As I ran toward them, I saw a flash of bright light reflected. I turned in time to see Calloo detonate and burst with a deafening bang, the parts of him flying out behind the Master. Gears, springs, rotors, flesh spread out across the cavern like confetti in a high wind. Below fell forward, unharmed.

I rushed to him before he could get away and lifted him to his feet. My adrenaline was pumping wildly, and I had unusual strength. I forced him over to the crystal wall and shoved his face against it. Three more explosions blasted out of him, again furiously rippling the bubble but not cracking it. The last one I could tell had diminished strength, and I feared that the enzymatic effect I had induced with the shudder was wearing off.

Ea and Arla were watching me from inside the paradise. As I held onto Below's quivering body, trying to stay on my feet in the face of the aftershocks, I noticed that the Traveler looked very weak. This was my last, best chance, and it wasn't going to work. I had decided to simply kill Below and be done with him, when I noticed Arla hand the baby over to her companion, step up close to the boundary and touch it as if begging me not to give up.

The Master came awake then and began struggling with me to free himself. He had gotten some of his strength back and was able to turn and wrap his fingers around my throat. I did the same to him, and we were locked in that position. As he applied pressure, I let go with one hand and punched him in the side of the head. This slackened his grip, but not for long. I was about to deliver another blow, when to my astonishment, small geysers of flame shot from his ears and a thick smoke issued from his open mouth. What I feared most, his magic, was reclaiming some of its potency. Now I could not think of killling him, it was all I could do to simply hold on so he would not escape.

Clutching tightly on one side to his shirt collar and on the other his jacket lapel, I steeled myself against his trickery. The smoke cleared and his face melted and transformed into that of a saber-toothed cat. His hands became snakes that twined more completely around my throat. Small dark birds flew from the sleeves of his jacket, their fluttering wings blinding me for seconds at a time.

"You are already dead, Cley," he said in the deep voice of the creature he had become.

"It is all an illusion," I repeated in my mind, but I was losing the strength in my neck muscles as the twin serpents applied greater pressure. No air was passing into my lungs, and I was growing light-headed. I could feel my grip on his clothing quickly weakening.

As my hands slipped to my sides, he spun me around to face the crystal and smashed my face into it as I had done to him. He pulled me back quickly then, and I could feel his lips on my left ear.

"When this is over, I'm going to do some work on you. I think Greta Sykes could use a mate."

I was slipping in and out of consciousness, finding it hard to focus. Looking up one more time, I saw Arla in front of me, through the clear boundary. She was touching the bottom of her veil, and although I was barely alive, I knew instantly what she had in mind. I slackened every muscle in my body and dropped to my knees, so that she would be face to face with Below.

I heard the Master begin to scream, and I knew she must have lifted the green cloth. The snakes turned back to fingers, loosened, and then left my throat. For a moment, the air around us became dead calm and a strange silence pervaded the underground chamber. Then a sound like thunder was instantly everywhere, followed by a great cracking noise like a frozen river thawing all at once. The explosion blew us back across the cavern amidst a wave of crystal shards. Even when I landed, I did not stop, but rolled and bounced another few feet before coming to rest.

I looked up from where I lay and saw the Traveler walking toward me, passing through a gap in the sphere that was like a jagged doorway. Arla was behind him, carrying her son. I blacked out for a few minutes then. When I finally came to, they were standing over me.

"I forgive you, Cley," I heard her say flatly from behind the light green veil.

The Traveler leaned over and gave me his hand, helping me to my feet. "You have journeyed far," he said to me.

It took me a little while before I could see straight, but when I was thinking clearly again, I searched around the floor of the cavern for Below. Somehow he had managed to escape. Perhaps the crystal had been enough of a barrier to Arla's terrible power to save him, but it was not strong enough itself to withstand the vehemence of her gaze. She was able to break through because she had something to focus her hatred upon outside the shell. I only wondered if it was Below or myself.

On the opposite side of the sphere, we found an entrance to that network of tunnels that ran beneath the City and took to it like rats running a maze. The impossible had been accomplished, but now we had an even more difficult job—getting out of the City alive.

There, beneath the streets, we ran into a band of conspirators carrying weapons, and they told us that there was a full-fledged war being waged now above. They did not have to tell me that Below was still alive, because every now and then we felt the tremors as another piece of his miraculous creation blew apart. They said the City gates were impassable not only because of the buildup of troops but also because the rubble from the decimated Ministry of the Territory had blocked the way. We were told to head toward the eastern boundary of the City, where a large hole had been blasted through the outer wall. They could not accompany us, because they were needed to reinforce a battalion taking up positions in the waterworks.

To my surprise, many of the conspirators we met had either heard of or knew Ea. While he was being held in a cage after first arriving in the City, and while the construction of the sphere was taking place, he had spoken to the workers. They could not resist his calm demeanor and his smile. As one young woman put it, "He showed us that our own fear was the Master's greatest magic." I learned that it was through this contact that the idea of overthrowing Below had come about. Ea was the one who had given them the *O* sign and told them of Wenau. Before they pushed on toward the battle, they lined up and shook his hand.

"He told us you would return," one of them said to me. "He told us you were searching for paradise and were a changed man."

Then we were alone again in the dark underground, and as much as I tried to ignore it, the beauty was not willing to let me go so easily. I faced the prospect of withdrawal with great fear, for I knew that it would only slow us down. Arla and Ea would not leave me, though. We hid in the tunnels for two days while they tended me. The Traveler fed me sweet little berries from the pouch he wore on his belt, and they eased the pain and nausea. All the time we were down there, as I sweated out the last remnants of ignorance and fear, we heard the explosions continue. There was the distant crack of rifle fire, and the smell of burning flesh reached even below the earth.

On the third day, though I was still shaky and sometimes needed support to continue, we came up out of hiding near the eastern wall. The entire City was in ruins. It didn't appear that there was a single building left standing, just mountains and mountains of debris everywhere. The bodies of citizens, the bodies of soldiers were strewn amid the wreckage, and the smell was horrible. We made our way through the destruction and came to the hole in the wall we had been told about. Out beyond it we could see pastures and forests, and it seemed to me the world that had been always right before my eyes was a sort of paradise. I was weak and still groggy from having beaten the beauty for a second time, and I could not help but weep at the sight.

"Cley," I heard a voice say, as we moved toward freedom.

I turned around and saw the Master standing fifty yards behind us, holding a leash with Greta Sykes straining at the end of it.

"It's over, Cley. They've all either died or left," he said. "From the time as a young man when I first journeyed here across the sea and over the mountains, my mind near bursting with a sublime reality, the only thing I was unable to see was how it would end."

His face was now a death mask, gaunt as that of an unwrapped mummy. I don't know where he found the strength to hold back the werewolf.

"Let us go, Below," I said. "There's no reason to harm us any longer."

He looked absentmindedly at the ground for a moment. "I can't be bothered with you, Cley. I haven't the time. There is so much work to do. Last night, I had another dream. A magnificent vision," he said. With this, he turned and hobbled back into his City.

When we were clear of the wall and out in the meadow beyond it, Ea touched my shoulder and pointed up in the sky over the smoking ruins. There I saw what I took to be a giant bird, circling.

"A vulture?" I asked.

He shook his head. "The demon has found a home," he said.

30

Those who escaped the destruction of the City settled in a valley about fifty miles west of Latrobia where two rivers crisscross. We all refer to it as Wenau, though it is not the Earthly Paradise. People still die here, fall ill, meet with misfortune, but there is a natural beauty to the place and a kindness among its inhabitants that sometimes make it seem divine.

I am here now, writing these final words to you. I have a small place with a garden in back. Ea showed me how to hunt with a bow and how to gather berries and roots. I am far from the pompous fool I was when I first went to Anamasobia. For one thing, I no longer fear the dark and sleep most peacefully with the candles snuffed. I am, perhaps, a fool in different ways, exuberant beyond all reason at the warmth of the sun and the smell of the earth. It is not important anymore to have a title, an exalted position, though in certain ways I feel I have them in being a simple member of this village.

We have all helped one another to survive and grow. Because of the memory of Below, we have no government, so to speak, no people of power. Disputes somehow manage to get settled without bloodshed and trade takes place. We are suspicious, to a fault probably, of devices that will make our lives easier, remembering how much freedom one must forsake for their comfort. Who knows if this will continue into the future?

After we arrived here, I saw Arla every so often across the fields, working in her own garden. She and the Traveler had settled fairly close to me and raised her boy. His name is Jarek, and sometimes in the afternoon, he ran across the fields and sneaked into my room and talked to me when I was trying to write. Eventually I had to get up and go for a walk with him in the woods or go fishing down by the river.

He asked me all sorts of questions, and I did the same of him. Ea had taught him some of the ancient ways of the Beyond, and already he was well versed in the use of plants and trees to cure illness and induce visions. Ea had told him that I was a man of great learning, but I felt the most I could offer him was my silent reassurance that he was a remarkable fellow. Though my paper supply—which I purchased from the Minister of the Treasury's wife in exchange for my old topcoat—was quickly dwindling, the boy and I used it for drawing pictures of the frogs and rabbits and other denizens of the field.

Arla had nothing to do with me. I saw her passing on the path, and I said hello, but her veil did not so much as stir. It was a great effort for me to prevent these moments from crippling the pleasure of my new life, but how, in good conscience, could I have expected more? Ea stopped and chatted sometimes, and I quizzed him about paradise. He laughed and told me about the time before his long sleep. His stories about the Beyond were always designed to show me that the real Wenau was, itself, less than perfect.

One day I asked him, "Is there really a paradise on earth?"

"Oh, yes," he said.

"Where is it?" I asked. "What is it like?"

He rested his bow against the ground and put his hand

on my shoulder. "We are journeying toward it," he said. "It is everything you thought it would be."

From then on, when I saw him across the field, he called to me, "We are close, Cley. We are almost there." That went on for years and finally became our joke. Many a morning, I came out onto the steps of my home and found an animal for cooking or an armload of fruit freshly gathered from the fields, and I knew he had been there.

Then one night, very late, about three years ago, the boy came to my house. It was raining and there was thunder and lightning. He pounded on my door and called, "Cley, Cley."

When I answered the door, he was standing there drenched. He looked scared and was shaking.

"What is it?" I asked.

"My father is away hunting, and the baby wants to come out," he said. "Mother is calling for help."

We raced across the field. Inside their cottage, I found Arla lying in bed, writhing in pain. I still remembered my physiology and my anatomy from my days as a professional man. Childbirth was one of the things we studied at the academy, since it was at this point it was believed that your physiognomy was formed.

I threw the covers off Arla and looked down to see a tiny foot sticking out from between her legs. "Get me a knife," I told the boy. He brought me one immediately, one of his father's stone ones. The thing was as sharp as one of my scalpels. Holding the implement in my hand, knowing what I intended to do, filled me with great doubt. I had never believed in religion, but in that moment I truly prayed that I would not butcher her again.

She must have come around just then as I stood there holding the weapon, and she began to scream. The green veil was moving like a curtain in a windstorm. I told the boy to hold her arms down, and though he looked warily at me, he trusted me and did what I said. I walked over and shoved the blade of the knife into the fire and let it heat up for a second or two to sterilize it. As soon as it was somewhat cool, I made the incision across her stomach. From that opening, I was able to retrieve the infant—a dark-skinned girl with her father's beauty and her mother's disposition. I had to use catgut Ea had made from one of the animals he had taken to sew Arla back up.

I tell you, it was the most useful I had ever felt in my life, as if with all of the harrowing adventures I had been through, all the pain and misery I had survived, I had finally come to the moment that defined my reason for ever having been born at all. That child was called Cyn, a name her father had come up with. She was a special child, for after having given birth to her, Arla's face slowly, miraculously, began to change. By the next year, all of those mutilations I had inflicted on her had disappeared, and she no longer needed the veil to protect others. Still, she said nothing to me. When we met at the outdoor market by the river, she simply lowered her gaze and passed by.

Ea, on the other hand, often visited me with Jarek and Cyn. He let me hold the baby, and there were times when he smiled that caused me to wonder if he had not gone hunting that particular night for a reason. Whenever this notion cropped up, I quickly dismissed it as a dangerous delusion. It was during one of these visits that he told me they were leaving the next day to travel into the Beyond.

The news made me weak, and I had to hand his daughter back to him before sitting down. "Why?" was all I could say.

"We will return," he said "but it is necessary that I explain myself to my people."

"But you're a criminal there," I said. "You said so yourself."

He nodded and reached down to place his hand on my shoulder. "Things have to change, Cley," was the last thing he said to me before leaving and heading out across the field. I watched them through the open doorway with tears in my eyes. Before they were out of sight, the boy turned and waved good-bye to me.

That afternoon and evening I spent trying to alleviate the loneliness I felt by finishing off the two bottles of Rose Ear Sweet I had bartered for years back when we had first settled by the crisscrossing rivers. They did their job, and I passed out somewhere late in the night.

My troubled dreams eventually took me back to the ice floe, where I, instead of Beaton, kneeled on the frozen surface next to a dying Moissac. His branch of a hand wrapped weakly around my wrist as the wind howled, stinging my face. Through his touch, he told me to cut his chest and take the seed from it. A knife appeared in my hand. After the life left his eyes, I hacked away at the thick foliage above where his heart would have been. When I had broken a sufficient opening in him, I cried out above the fury of the storm and plunged my hand into the hedge . . . only to come fully awake in that instant to the vague echo of a door having been shut. Sunlight was shining in through the one window of my home, and I could hear the birds singing. I sat upright on my bed and brought my clenched fist into view. The nightmare had been so intense, it took great concentration to pry open my fingers, but when I did, I found within, the green veil, gathered up like a dream seed on my palm.

Coming from Avon Eos in the fall of 1999,
a new novel by Jeffrey Ford,
set in the same world as *The Physiognomy*

AVON

PRESENTS AWARD-WINNING NOVELS
FROM MASTERS OF SCIENCE FICTION

PRISONER OF CONSCIENCE
by Susan R. Matthews
78914-0/$3.99 US/$3.99 Can

HALFWAY HUMAN
by Carolyn Ives Gilman
79799-2/$5.99 US/$7.99 Can

MOONRISE
by Ben Bova
78697-4/$6.99 US/$8.99 Can

DARK WATER'S EMBRACE
by Stephen Leigh
79478-0/$3.99 US/$3.99 Can

COMMITMENT HOUR
by James Alan Gardner
79827-1/$5.99 US/$7.99 Can

THE WHITE ABACUS
by Damien Broderick
79615-5/$5.99 US/$7.99 Can